Also by Richard Dansky

Firefly Rain
Vaporware
Ghost of a Marriage
Snowbird Gothic

Praise for VAPORWARE

"*Vaporware* is life in the world of games, raw and real from a writer who did his time in the trenches - with a supernatural twist that'll make you think twice about late night log-ons and who is really lurking behind the avatar on your screen..."
James Swallow -- New York Times bestselling author

"A meticulous image of the real games industry so detailed that you'll just assume the supernatural must be part of it. So immersive it makes you want to go check on that video game your spouse is spending so much time with..."
-- Mur Lafferty, award-winning author of *Six Wakes*

"Imagine you're sitting at a bar, surrounded by videogame industry veterans. They're telling war stories about their past projects, the kind of stories you'd never see repeated in interviews or online magazines, the kind that are insider legends. Everyone's laughing out of shock or horror at some of the stuff we go through to release a game before Richard Dansky launches into his tale. That's when everyone shuts up, because Rich is telling a story, and when Rich starts talking, you know it's going to be a hell of a ride...."
--Lucien Soulban, writer, *Far Cry: Blood Dragon*

"Richard Dansky uses his background in video games to breathe realism into his characters, concepts, and environments. The result is a 21st Century techno horror story that manages the near-impossible: to be both geektastic and incredibly cool."
-- Rio Youers, author of LOLA ON FIRE

"Richard Dansky writes about passionate, complex, flawed, and completely believable people in this absorbing novel about the toll of caring so deeply about your art. Very highly recommended!

-- Jeff Strand, Stoker-Award winning author of *Demonic*

"Nobody knows the messy collision of writing and game development better than Richard Dansky. And for anyone who's ever poured heart and soul into a creative project only to watch it die, *Vaporware* is hauntingly, and almost uncomfortably, familiar."

-- Jay Posey, Writer, *Ghost Recon: Future Soldier*

Praise for FIREFLY RAIN

"Reads like Pat Conroy and Stephen King, but with Richard Dansky's distinct voice...A fascinating, harrowing exploration of the shadows known as family."

-Douglas Clegg, NYT Bestselling author

"Disturbing...Remarkable."

-Publishers Weekly

Praise for SNOWBIRD GOTHIC

"Warning: Read with caution: In *Snowbird Gothic*, Dansky displays the kind of gripping versatility of a virtuoso jazz man. His collected stories each grab you by the skull, worm their way into your head, and never, ever let you go."

-Matt Forbeck, NYT Bestselling author

A

MEETING

IN

THE

DEVIL'S

HOUSE

...AND OTHER STORIES

by RICHARD DANSKY

An imprint of Haverhill House Publishing LLC

A MEETING IN THE DEVIL'S HOUSE And Other Stories
© 2023 Richard Dansky

Cover illustration, design, and setup © Errick Nunnally

Trade Paperback ISBN: 978-1-949140-43-9

First Edition

Twisted Publishing is an imprint of:

Haverhill House Publishing LLC
643 E Broadway
Haverhill MA 01830-2420
www.haverhillhouse.com

For my sisters Marla and Becky
For their love and support
even when the stuff I was writing got icky.

Acknowledgements:

I'd like to thank the following folks, without whom this collection could not have happened. First of all, thanks to John McIlveen for taking a chance on it and putting it out into the world. Big thanks to Bridgett Nelson for her editing work and to Errick Nunnally for his spectacular cover. Thanks also to Jim Moore for the excellent foreword, and to Jeremy Bernstein, Lillian Cohen-Moore, and Laura J. Hickman for reading it and their feedback. Many thanks to Jaym Gates, James Lowder and all the editors who took a liking to stories in the collection. Appreciation to *The Cheese Gang* for their help and support, and most of all to my family for all the love and encouragement they have given me.

THE STORIES

FOREWORD

by James A. Moore

Let's be honest; there are a lot of writers out there. A lot. My to-be-read pile is probably four hundred books deep, and that's only because I've grown more selective in what I buy at this stage in my life. It could be twice that many if I let myself go. I love reading. As the old saying goes, I am a reader with a voracious appetite, but I don't have the time I used to have for reading.

So, when I find someone who makes it to the top of my must-read list, it's a rare and precious treat. There are certain authors who, when I see something new has come out, I know I'm in for a good time. It's that simple for me. I still get that old thrill whenever I see their names associated with new work. I know that whatever is coming my way will be worth the wait. Some prolific writers come out with a new book every few months. Some manage something every few years, no matter how much I might wish otherwise, but they're worth the inevitable delays.

Richard Dansky is always worth the wait. I've known Rich for years, but believe me, knowing someone doesn't guarantee I'm going to like the writing. There's a part of me that winces when a friend asks me to read their work (or even just a nice person) because, well, what if it sucks? I've had that happen a few times, and it's never easy feeling that way when you genuinely like a person. That's not a problem in Rich's case, and I'm grateful as all get out for that.

FOREWORD

His stories- seventeen in this collection- are as varied as possible, often displaying his love for his Jewish heritage, humor, and for clever horror and inventive fantasy tales. His stories are told in different voices, with different approaches, and that's rarer and more difficult than one might think.

Dansky's voice shifts and switches with his tales, sometimes a little distant and sometimes as close as an intimate whisper. That's an impressive feat. Switching from first person to third person is one thing, but to change the distance with which a story is told? That's a rare talent.

Rich keeps his stories fresh and exciting so I never feel the need to alternate with something or someone else between tales to cleanse my reading palette.

A Meeting in The Devil's House and Other Tales is lovely in its variety of tales, not fixated on one kind of story.

As I said before, I know I will enjoy myself when I read his stories. Four novels and a short story collection later, I've enjoyed and savored every word. What a delightful thing that is, and a rarity besides.

So here you are with a copy of Dansky's collection in your hands, ready to settle in and read a few tales to make your skin creep up in the most delightful way. You know what I mean. You aren't reading these stories only because they're inspirational. You are searching for a good scare and to experience a proper chill in the air. You won't be disappointed. In fact, I rather envy you if this is your first read-through.

Now, enough from me. You're here to read these seventeen tales that delight and entertain, to contemplate and savor them as you gorge on this banquet of words, and to feed the part of you that craves a good story.

You've come to the right place.

BEER AND PENNIES

It was a week after Jimmy died that I called up the Devil.

Waited for him to call himself up, truth be told. I wouldn't have known how to call up the Devil, save in the usual way: living a damn fool life and then dying. The lucky ones lived long enough to find Jesus before they grew too old for the revival to take. The unlucky wrapped themselves around trees or smeared themselves across embankments; they drowned swimming after that one beer they oughtn't have had or used the gun in a lawman's hand for suicide.

So I'd been told, anyway. The folks I'd known went more for quiet desperation and slow disintegration, and the only devils in their lives wore their own skins.

Jimmy and I had gone out to the Devil's Tramping Ground on a Monday night when it was less likely to be occupied by local kids sneaking cheap beers and huffing paint in the woods. It had a legend, the Tramping Ground did. Nothing would grow there, and anything left on that bare patch of ground in the Carolina woods overnight would get tossed out by some invisible force by morning.

The older folks, they had another part to the story. They said it was the Devil who'd clear things out of that circle of dirt and sand. That he'd show up there 'round midnight when the mood took him, and walk round and round planning mischief for mankind. That's why nothing would grow there, they said. The Devil ground it all underfoot.

Jimmy thought this was all bull crap, of course, and in those days, I followed where Jimmy led. He had some idiot idea about making a video of us doing some kind of investigation of the place, then putting it up online. What was supposed to happen next, he never got around to telling me, but he seemed pretty sure it would make us famous and then rich, though maybe not in that order.

I went along with it because I always went along with what Jimmy did. It's what you did when Jimmy was around. He came up with some pants-on-head crazy idea you spent half an hour arguing against, and the next thing you knew, you were walking backward across a train trestle at midnight 'cause Jimmy thought it might be a hoot. And you swore you were never, ever going to go along with another one of Jimmy's idiotic plans again.

At least, not until he cooked up the next one.

And the next one, and the one after that, until we stood on the edge of the clearing in the woods where the Devil's Tramping Ground lay.

It wasn't much to look at, truth be told. Just a flat sandy circle in a clearing in the woods. Burned out fire pit in the center, logs for sitting on around the edge. Nothing grew inside those logs, while outside, scrubby grass and sickly weeds spread into the woods. Empty tallboys littered the place, a sure sign of recent visitation. But of the Devil, there was no sign.

"That's it?" I asked.

Jimmy nodded. "That's it. Just a circle of dirt people been telling stories about for a hundred years."

"We came all the way out here, and it's just a *circle of dirt?*" I stalked after Jimmy, who did a fine job ignoring me as he set up his camera.

"You can leave," he finally said. "Me, I'm going to sit here tonight with some thinking juice and the best technology Sony has to offer, and I'm gonna try and see if there's more to this here "circle-of-dirt" than just dirt. You can join me if you'd like." And he sat on one of the logs and patted the log beside him, and damned if I didn't sit down, too.

"Atta boy," he said when I did. "Now, bust open the cooler and get a couple of beers. It's gonna be a long night."

And I did, and we sat and waited and drank beers in the dark until morning.

Except, of course, neither of us made it 'til morning. I dropped off around four thirty when Jimmy was already snoring like a drunk pig, and the sky hadn't fully decided to start thinking about maybe getting light. We got woken up around ten when a couple of tourists came walking up the trail, hollering about how they thought they'd found the place. Jimmy checked the camera while I kept them occupied, but the look on his face told the story.

Nothing.

"Well, we got what we came for," I said after the tourists, two fat guys who said they were writers and their skinny, bored wives, had gone back to their car. "Now we going home?"

"Just for a little bit," Jimmy said, fiddling with the camera some more. "See this? Camera stopped recording for a couple of minutes right after we dropped off."

"Maybe that was 'cause we fell asleep."

He ignored me. "I wanna go home, get a wash and a change of clothes and some more beer, then come on back and try a little something."

I could feel the hackles on the back of my neck standing up. "Jimmy, something tells me this is gonna be a real bad idea."

Grinning, he shook his head. "Ain't gonna be nothing. Safe as can be. You'll see." And he headed back down the same trail to where we'd left Jimmy's truck, and I hurried to follow him.

We were back by five that night, plenty of time to set up the camera again and start a fire in that pit. We made supper and drank a few more beers, and then Jimmy got up to show me his bright idea.

Which, it turned out, was a penny, and he tossed it to me.

"What the hell is this?" I asked.

"A penny," he said. "Ain't you never seen one?"

"I've seen one, but I don't know why you got one here. You want penny slots, you got to go all the way to Cherokee."

"Naw," he said and took the penny back. "You know the legend, right? Anything you leave in the circle overnight, the Devil tosses out. So I'm gonna leave this penny here, right near the fire, and I'm gonna leave the camera pointed at it all night. The Devil picks it up, we'll see it."

"You're an idiot," I said. "That's your big plan?"

He shrugged. "I figure a penny ain't a big thing. If the Devil does show, he won't be too put out movin' it."

I stared at him. "You serious? That's your plan? Sit here and wait for the Devil to bend down for loose change?"

"You got a better one?"

I grabbed another beer. "No. But if one comes along, I'm for it."

Jimmy laughed, put down the penny, and picked up a beer.

It wasn't a tourist waking me up the next morning, it was Jimmy, and he was cussing up a storm.

"What is it?" I asked him.

"Well," he said, looking up from the camera, "the penny's gone, but the camera's got nothing. All static from midnight on 'til about five, when a possum came in and ate what was left of your sandwich."

"Maybe the possum got the penny," I said and stood and stretched. "Or a bird picked it up 'cause it was shiny."

"Yeah, yeah." His attention went back to the camera. I was already up, so I took a stroll around the ring in hopes of nothing in particular. I could see already the penny was gone, and the only footprints I could spot belonged to Jimmy and the possum, respectively.

And then the sun busted through the clouds, and I thought I saw something gleam on one of the logs.

It was the penny. Only it wasn't on the log. It was *in* it, jammed halfway deep so that all you saw of old Abe Lincoln was his neck and shoulders. I bent down and looked at it. "Jimmy?" I said. "You might want to bring that camera over and look at this."

"Hmm?" But he saw what I was squatting down in front of and got over there in a hurry.

"Shit," he said when he got close, drawing it out to about thirty seconds long and bringing the camera in for a close-up. "You want to try and pull that sucker out of there while I record it? This ought to be good."

So I reached in and I got a good grip, and I pulled. The penny didn't go nowhere. It was jammed in there real good. I tried again, wiggling it back and forth, but no dice. It wasn't going anywhere.

"Stuck?" Jimmy asked.

"Stuck," I said. "You want to try?"

We switched places, and he gave it a shot. There was a lot of cussing and bullshit excuse-making and Jimmy yelling, "I think it's moving," but in the end, he had to give up, too. We both sat there on the ground, staring at it when we weren't staring at each other.

Finally, I said something. "Jimmy?"

"Yeah?"

"When you pulled on it..."

"Yeah?"

"Did that penny feel, I dunno, kind of warm to you?"

He looked away. "I thought that was maybe from you. Or the fire."

"Uh-uh." We sat for a minute. "Fire's been out a long time."

We sat there a while longer before he got up. "Right, I'm going home. Gonna get washed up and gonna try and figure out what the hell is wrong with the camera, and then I'm coming back. You with me?"

I stood. "I'm with you as far as going home, but that's about it. That," I said, pointing to the penny, "ain't right. That's a warning, Jimmy. We been tolerated thus far. I ain't willing to push that no further."

"C'mon," he exploded. "Right now, all we got is a penny in a log. Coulda stuck that in there ourselves with a hammer. But we come back tonight--with coffee, not beer, so we don't fall asleep again--and we keep watching, and we're gonna get something awesome, man. We're gonna get the real deal."

"I don't *want* the real deal," I said with a little heat. "I want to go home and sleep in my bed tonight and not come back here none because what you did last night got something riled up, and whatever you got planned tonight, well, I don't want to be a part of it."

"Fine," he said, and he was suddenly quiet. "Pick up the bottles. We're getting out of here. I'll come back here tonight alone."

And he did. He tried a couple more times to get me to go with him, but for once in my life, I stayed firm and told him no. Around seven, he finally gave up, cussing me out for being chickenshit, and drove off on his own. He didn't take coffee. He did take beer, the camera, and a sleeping bag.

They found him in the morning, or at least that's what the cops told me. Found him ripped to shreds and hung up in the trees. Some of the meat was missing, which had the cops thinking wild animal attack, but his head was fifteen feet up a pine tree, and you tell me what kind of wild animal does that?

In any case, they'd brought back his camera, and they asked me lots of questions about what was on it. I told them everything I knew, which wasn't much--that we'd gone out there to shoot a video, that the camera maybe acted a little funny, and that I'd given up before the third night when he wanted to keep going. I told 'em I was that third night, and who could vouch for me, and everything I could think of that Jimmy had said to me and that I'd said to him before he left. After a while, they seemed satisfied, and got ready to go. They asked me not to leave the state and told me they might have some other questions, but they didn't think I had nothing to do with it.

"Wild animal," one of the cops said. "Santers are back in this part of the state, though ain't no one gonna admit it."

I didn't disagree with him. I didn't see why I should.

And a week later, I went back out to the Tramping Ground.

Dumb-ass idea, I know. The cops would probably want to know why I was going there. Maybe a scene of the crime thing, maybe they'd think I was looking for a souvenir.

Truth was, I was looking for an answer.

I pulled up along the side of the road, where that trail back and up into the woods started. There were no other cars there, just a line of yellow police tape cut in half and whipping back and forth in the breeze. That didn't seem like it ought to stop me, so I grabbed my bag off of the front seat and went walking up the path.

I left the car unlocked. If everything went well, I wouldn't be gone long. And if it went the way I thought it might, I wouldn't be needing the car no more anyhow.

The Tramping Ground was full of footprints, that much I could see when I got there. Police footprints, paramedic footprints, sightseer footprints, you name it. They'd done a good job of cleaning up Jimmy, but here and there you could still see a little splash of blood or a scrap of fabric from something that had maybe been his.

Fifteen feet up in the trees, they said. It made me want to puke.

Instead, I reached into the bag and brought out what was in there. It was a bottle of wine, red wine, the best I could afford. I smashed the neck against a rock, and it split off, leaving a jagged top and expensive grape juice running down the sides.

"Here," I said, and poured out the wine into the circle. "Don't know if I'm doing this right. Don't know if I'm damning myself to Hell by doing this. But Devil, if you're there, this is me, inviting you. This me telling you I want some answers."

The last of the wine ran out onto the ground. I threw the bottle away into the woods. It hit a tree and smashed, and the pieces fell to the ground. Off in the distance, somebody's dog found something interesting and started barking up a storm.

Other than that, nothing.

"Well, damn," I said and shook loose a cigarette from the pack I was carrying. I struck a light and settled in to wait, and when I looked up, he was there.

He was tall, but I'd expected that. For a moment, he stood there, and I took him in. He was dressed in a shabby black suit, cuffs frayed, shoes scuffed, mud on the heels, and tie loosened past the first undone button of his sweat-stained white shirt. His face was dead-man pale, eyes bright and sharp under a shock of red hair, which itself sat beneath a worn and battered felt hat. If he had horns, I couldn't see 'em, but perhaps that's what the hat was for. At least, that was my thinking.

"Your friend was a damn fool," he said, without waiting for preamble or question. "He was a damn fool, and it killed him, and I'm hoping you're less of a damn fool than him." As he spoke, he began walking, long loping strides that took him around the perimeter of that circle of dead grass at a goodly clip.

I took a drag on my cigarette, then stubbed it out against the soggy bark of the log I was sitting on. "You're the Devil," I said. "What do I call you? Old Nick? Father of Lies? Lucifer?"

"You can call me the Devil," he said with a grunt. "I don't hold with being too familiar."

"The Devil it is," I agreed and nodded to let him know I agreed with him. He didn't acknowledge the gesture, instead choosing to stump round that place where nothing grew, brow furrowed as if by some deep thought. "So, Mister Devil, what damnfool thing did my friend do to get himself killed?"

The Devil stopped. Looked at me, looked me up and down like a dog looking at a piece of steak that's fallen onto the kitchen floor. "Three nights," he said. "Three nights of being a pain in my ass. You were there for the first two," and he pointed an accusing finger. The nail, I could see, was charcoal black. "You were there for the first two but weren't stupid enough to cross the line. You just wanted to see, and seeing was enough for you. But he wanted to feel it, feel it for himself. Feel what it's like to have the Devil his own self lay hands on you and cast you out."

I stood but cast my eyes down so they wouldn't meet his. You see things when you meet the Devil's eyes, or so Mama had always said. You see things it ain't right to see.

"So he pitched his tent in there?" I asked and pointed to a spot where the dead turf looked to be torn up a little.

The Devil shook his head. Didn't even bother to do that much. I think he figured it'd get all messed up, and he didn't want to deal with that none. He laid his sleeping bag down and climbed in. Had a couple of beers while he was waiting to fall asleep, that cheap watered down Lite crap. Can't stand it myself, and then your idiot friend had to go and make things worse by leaving his damn cans in the circle. That's not the sort of thing I stand for."

I stepped closer to the edge of the circle. Maybe two feet of green and mud separated me from that patch of deadness where the Devil waited. He stood there, watching me, arms folded across his chest. He carried himself the way a tough man carried himself. Not a bully, mind you, but a lean, hard man used to working for a living and taking care of his business when he deemed it necessary to do so.

Then again, he was the Devil, with all that implied.

"That's what you killed him for, then? Littering?"

He glared at me. "That'd have been enough. I'm the Devil, boy. I'm the evil that's walked this land since the Flood receded and the dinosaurs died. A man looks at me funny, that's enough in my book for me to work some mojo on him."

A couple more steps took me right up to the line where the grass died. I was careful not to cross it. Didn't want to transgress the circle, for whatever that was worth. Didn't want to intrude on the Devil's space.

Hell, I didn't want to give him an excuse.

"So that's it," I said cautiously.

He fixed me with a stare, his head tilted to the side, like a bird's. "I didn't say that."

"But you-"

"Don't interrupt the Devil when he's talking, son. It's a bad habit, and it'll stunt your growth."

I shut up. He watched me shutting up for a minute, making sure I wasn't going to start yammering again, and then continued. "Tell you what. You want to know about your friend so bad, I'll make you a deal. Truth for truth. You tell me why you came back for real, and I'll tell you what happened to him for real, and why. The way I look at it, you're getting the better end of the deal."

"My momma told me not to make deals with the Devil," I heard myself say. I'd have backed away, if my legs were listening to my brain, but at that moment they weren't. So I stood there, frozen, as the Devil stalked up to me. He faced me then, nose to nose, eye to eye across that line of dead grass.

"If I wanted your soul, I'd have it a hundred ways before you knew it was missing. Drinking, lying, fornicating, pride--I've got my hooks in you so deep they're meeting in the middle. But like I said, I'm offering you truth for truth. Neither of us gets anything but words from the other. Oh, and you," he said, pointing that long finger at me, "go first."

I thought about not answering, but that thought didn't stay long. I'd come back out there wanting answers, wanting to know what had happened to Jimmy, and why. Now here I was with the chance to learn the truth, the real truth, and I was hesitating.

Afraid.

Afraid like I'd been that night, scared enough to go home when Jimmy'd been brave enough to stay, brave enough to park his own self right in the middle of the Tramping Ground itself, and to wait for what came next.

"I came back to see if I could talk to you," I said. The words surprised me, but they tasted like they were true, so I kept going. "I wanted to know why you did what you did to Jimmy. I wanted to know why you did it. I wanted to know if it was really," I took a deep breath and looked into those unkind eyes, "you."

"That's most of it," he said thoughtfully, and sucked on his gums for a minute. "But you're missing something."

"Like what?"

He spun on his heel and walked six steps, into the dead center of the circle. Without turning around, he spoke. "What you really want to know is why I let you get away. After all, it wouldn't have been hard to make you stay, if I'd wanted."

The cold truth of that cut at my guts. "Maybe," I forced myself to say. "Or maybe I'd already seen what I thought I wanted to see, before you ripped Jimmy up."

He shook his head, all slow and sad. "Like I said, son, you came to see something, and to bear witness to what you'd seen. That's why you brought your cameras, and your fancy night vision gear, and all that good stuff that didn't help you none. You wanted truth, and you got a bellyful, and that was enough to let you walk away with your pride."

"But now," and he spun around, arms out like a showman's, "you're thinking maybe you missed something. That your friend dead Jimmy saw something you didn't afore he died, and you're wondering if it's worth seeing. Hell, you're wondering if it's worth dying yourself, just to see. Am I right?"

"You're right," I said, and he was. You don't lie to the Devil, no sir.

"Good," he said. "You're not stupid. Now let me give you your truth, and we can see where we stand."

He cleared his throat, and for a moment I thought he might be embarrassed by the whole thing. You know, the Devil telling the truth and all. But then he was talking again, and any thought of sympathy I might have melted away.

"In the basic, your friend's problem was that he was in my way. That's a bad place to be, son. Look around you. What do you see?"

I looked around and didn't see much. "Trees," I said. "Mud. Some trash. Grass and weeds, maybe."

He nodded. "Right. I'd call it godforsaken, but you'd think I was trying to make a joke. The point is a man comes out here to a place like this to think. To be alone, to walk to and fro in a little patch of dirt, and up and down in it, and not be disturbed. But then along comes your friend Jimmy, and he just plain pisses me off. And you know why?"

"Why?" I asked.

He looked me in the eye, and I looked away. "Because like I said, you were here to bear witness to something bigger than yourself. You wanted a mystery. Jimmy, he wanted to be the center of things. He wanted something to happen to him, so he could go home and tell the pretty girls all about his adventure. He wanted to make this the place for *his* story, if'n you know what I mean. Well, hell, that ain't right. That ain't proper. That ain't going to happen, not as long as I have power in this world. And I do have power, when I choose to raise it up in me."

The Devil's voice had been rising the whole time until it was practically a shout. His cadence was one a few preachers I'd known would have killed for, a rhythm that picked you up and carried you along until it dropped you in the silence, in the weeds of the whispers.

"I don't hold with that," he said, quiet now, his voice the sound of snake's tongue going in and out. "This is my place, and it will be until the world burns. The Jimmys of the world don't get to take that away. Not now, not ever, amen."

"Amen," I caught myself whispering, and the Devil grinned.

"Very good, boy," he said, and there was a gleam in his eye I wasn't glad to see. "Do you have what you came for?" I looked down at my feet, half to make sure my toes were outside the circle, and half to look away from him. "Yes. I understand what happened to Jimmy now. And I'll leave you be."

"Not so fast."

I looked up. He was staring at me, still smiling. "I said, do you have what you came for."

"Like I said, I know what happened to Jimmy, and that's

what I came here for. And I don't want to end up like him, so if you'll excuse me—"

"Liar."

The word hit me like a kick to the back of the knee. It's one thing when a woman calls you a liar for making up some lame-ass excuse for forgetting to call her. It's another when the one who invented lying out of whole cloth and the unformed stuff of Creation slaps it on you.

"Excuse me?"

He leaned forward, a vulture getting ready to swoop down off his perch. "I called you a liar, boy. You going to argue with me?"

I shook my head and backed away. "I think I've done enough talking with you tonight."

"Then listen." I froze. "You and I both know that's not the real thing you came here for. You came to see, just like you came the other night. Well, now you've seen, all right. You've seen *me*. And that's not something to be taken lightly."

"Fact is," he continued, and started walking toward me. I clung to the notion that it was all right, that he was inside the circle and I was outside, and never the twain should meet. "Fact is that you were maybe a little too eager to see something strange, don't you think?"

He stopped, maybe six inches from the edge of the circle, and put his hands up like he was leaning against an invisible wall.

"I don't think I know what you're talking about," I said. I found my legs could move again, if a little, and so I made them do that. One slide step back, and then another, and then I froze when I saw him noticing.

"I think you do," he said. "I think you're a little too curious for your own good. So, I'm going to give you something, something free."

"I don't want no gifts from you, sir." The 'sir 'was involuntary, and his smile got nasty when he heard it.

"It's not the sort of thing you refuse, son. The Devil wants to give you a gift, you take it. You take it and you say thank you, or he might decide to give you another one."

"I've got everything I want from you," I said.

"No, you don't," he replied, and stepped out of the circle. Grass died under his boots as he took slow steps toward me. "What, you thought there was some magic keeping me in there? You didn't draw that circle, son. Wasn't no medicine man or priest, neither. I walked that line, and I made that boundary, and I can cross it any time I please."

"Please." I echoed him. "I just want to go." My knees felt weak, felt like they were going to buckle.

The Devil shook his head, and brought his hand up in benediction. "I don't think so. You see, you gave me something tonight. It isn't often I get a chance to explain myself, and there's a certain pleasure in that. So if you gave me something, it's only right and proper that I give you something back. And if what you want is to see, well, I can give you Sight."

My legs gave out, and I dropped to my knees. "No," I said. "I don't want to see any more."

The Devil placed his hand on my forehead. "What you want is about the least important thing in the world right now. I give you Sight, so you can see what's hiding under the skin of the world. Some of it's my handiwork, some of it's the other fella's. Down these parts, you'll see a lot more that's mine. This is haunted country, son, and I give it to you in all its glory and terror. 'Cause I been working real hard, and it's about damn time someone could appreciate what I done."

Then he said something in some language I don't know and don't want to know, and his hand caught fire. And that fire, it poured down his fingers and into those sharp black nails, and from there it flowed like oily water and cheap wine into my eyes. It burned, so help me, it burned. It burned away my old way of seeing, it burned away my old eyes. I could feel it pouring in and filling every fiber, could feel it thrumming through me like a high tension wire in the wind.

And then he pulled his hand away, and I Saw.

Saw the molten hell-rock of the Tramping Ground, stamped flat with a thousand hoof prints just underneath that white dirt and sand. I saw shapes moving in the forest that weren't beasts and weren't men. I looked up and saw a line in the sky where an angel had flown by, and it was so beautiful I wanted to sit down and cry.

"One other thing," he said, and that snapped my attention right back. There were no angels here, and none coming to help me neither.

"Yessir?" I said.

He smiled. "You've laid eyes on the Devil, and you're going to walk away after you've done so. That's a rare thing, son, a rare and powerful thing. But that also means you've had the Devil's eyes upon you, and once I've seen you, up close and personal like this, I don't ever stop seeing you. I'll know where you are, boy. I'll know where to find you. You'll have the Devil looking over your shoulder any time I damn well please to cast my eye that way, and you'll be thinking 'bout that every time you kiss your mother's cheek or make love to that long-legged whore you call a lady friend. That's where the real price for your answer starts to be paid, boy. As for the rest of it? I'll think of other things. I always do."

I swallowed hard. "I don't know what I could ever do for you, sir."

"You will," he said. "Now go. I got some thinking to do." And he turned and walked away, and where he did the hell-rock bubbled up around his feet.

I waited 'til I was sure he couldn't see me, and then I turned and ran back down to the road. Nothing followed me but his laughter, but that was enough.

THE THIRTY-NINTH LABOR OF REB PALACHE

This is how Reb Palache decides, in matters of life and death.

He does not decide who lives and who dies. It is given only unto the Lord of Hosts, the Author of Life to do so, and whither He sends His faceless angel who is Death, no man may know.

Reb Palache is many things, but he is not the Lord of Hosts, nor does he know His mind. He is a trader and a teacher, a sailor and a spy, a diplomat and a pirate of bloody intent, an exile and a man who has prospered in a new land.

And right now, he is a man who sees sails across the water. They are tiny, and they are distant, but they are neither so tiny nor so distant as they were an hour ago. He raises a brass spyglass and peers through it, reflexively muttering thanks unto Adonai for the keenness of eye that he still possesses, and sees more clearly what he had known all along he would: a fat merchant ship, wallowing through the seas heavier than she was designed for. Wind bellies her sails, but it is not enough, not enough. And above those bloated white sheets flies the flag he knows, the flag he hates, the flag that says unto him that this ship is prey.

Slowly, he casts his eye lower, along the decks. The crew is working furiously, he sees. Lines are hauled, more canvas unfurled. He can almost hear the shouted orders from the frantic captain, the crack of the whip against the bare back of a sailor whose work is not fast enough.

The ship is low in the water. He sees that, too. She is weighted down, perhaps with spoils from the New World, silver and emeralds or golden idols not yet melted down.

He looks away.

His own ship runs lean, a wolfhound leaping over the waves. His men need no lashes, no frenzied exhortations. They have done this before. They see the ship before them, and they are eager to close with it. Behind him, the snap of canvas suddenly pulled taut rings out, another sail unfurled in the name of the hunter's pursuit.

He hears them calling to each other, reminding each other of duties long known. They have sailed with him long, most of this crew. He has picked them, the flotsam that Spain cast out upon the waters. Strong men, the weakness burned out of them by sun and wave and battle until they are as beaten bronze, remorseless and dutiful and united in purpose. Some he found on the docks of Lisbon, or working merchant ships out of Malaga and hiding their heritage away from the relentless eyes of the Inquisition. Some he found in the streets of Rotterdam, sons of exile and of a new land that cared less what god a man worshipped and more what he might do.

And he has shaped them, and he has taught them, and he has given them blood and gold and vengeance.

They want this, he knows. They want to pursue the vessel that runs, that stumbles away from them. If they could, they would have their ship leap out of the water and down upon it, a falcon of the waves seizing its prey in strong talons of wood and rope and steel. And failing that, they want to fall upon the men who sail that ship, who guard its treasure and tend its course, and take from them what the oceans have allowed them to possess thus far. There is no doubt among them, and no fear, and no thought that they might not be victorious. For, do they not sail with Reb Palache, the man who consults with angels every night? Do they not bear good steel made in best Damascene fashion, and have they not always triumphed before? And this is merely one ship, one lonely ship against which they will strike with a sword of wrath and fire.

This he knows. This is what he must decide.

He stares through the spyglass again. The gap between the ships has closed noticeably. There are men on deck pointing now, and urging the sailors to greater exertions. Others know it is hopeless, that the race is all but run and that only an act of the Divine can save them now. Fog, wind, rain, night – these might rescue them. Precious little else might.

And so a few men climb into the rigging with muskets and pistols, and long knives at their belts. Others struggle with the ropes, looking to find hidden speed that they might yet call upon. But the ship is low, and her prow is too square, and speed is not something her builders have blessed her with. The calculation seems simple. She is weak, she is rich, she is slow, she is poorly defended.

And yet there is something that is not right. He watches the sailors again, and then he has it. It is not that one man is too slow. It is that many of them are. These are not sailors, or at least not men who are sailors first. These men struggle too much with simple tasks, move too slowly on things that should be second nature.

They are soldiers, and this is a trap. No doubt there are more of them hidden below decks, guns primed and hearts pounding, waiting for the moment when they might leap forth and fire. Perhaps some of that weight is cannon, loaded and ready, hungry to tear the sides out of his beautiful ship. Perhaps the captain of the other ship, a wily old campaigner, looks back at

Palache through his own spyglass, and slows his vessel so that the battle might begin sooner.

It is all very clever, clever and dangerous. Palache thinks for a moment – how did he hear of this vessel? A rumor in the coffeehouses, a whisper swirling round the docks, manifests and bargains and a dozen little things, all of which put him on the trail. They mean to kill him, he knows. A plot of this scale has power behind it, has the will of the throne and the Inquisition and the long shadowy machineries of state and Church. He has stung them too many times, bled their shipping white and come upon their colonies with righteous wrath.

The wise thing to do would be to sail away, to tell his men of the trap and seek a different end to the day. They are not fools; they would understand. Eager as they are for battle, they do not wish to die unnecessarily, nor to fight merely for the sake of fighting.

But they are his men, and they are superb. And surely, knowing that this is a trap, he can prepare them. He can spy out the vessel, cast the *gematria* and know how best to attack. He can ensnare the ambushers, draw them out too soon and then bloody them, and let it be known across Iberia that no matter how they might try, they will not have his head.

He looks up at the sun. It is just past its zenith. There is plenty of time for bloody work yet before nightfall.

"Men," he says, and turns to face them, "Here is what we will do."

This is how Reb Palache prepares for battle.

He winds the phylacteries upon his arm, upon his brow, upon his chest.

He dresses himself in plain linen, and surmounts it with

leather: vest and boots and gloves.

He does not remove the skullcap that he always wears, for one's head should not be bare when one stands before the Lord of Hosts. But he is a practical man, and a man who has fought many battles, and so he wears over it a cap of toughened leather, with flaps that hang down over his ears. His beard he binds, and tucks into his shirt, that it might not be seized by an enemy and used to pull him off balance, nor may it be fouled with the blood of those who stand against him.

Over his head he drapes amulets, each inscribed with skill and care and what those who do not understand the study of the Law might call magic. There are more amulets in his right hand, clay tablets imprinted with signs and powers and hung on leather thongs. Some bear the Hand of Miriam for protection. Others, the Tetragrammaton, or numbers of significance. They are black, these amulets, painted black over red clay, and the letters and numbers and signs upon them are bright gouges like unto sunlight piercing clouds.

He moves through his men, Palache does, and he bestows the amulets upon them. Most of them are here, all but the few needed to do the ship's work. They are armed, and some are armored. There are sharpshooters here, and men bearing nothing but wicked swords, and one man who fights with a heavy hooked knife he swears came to him from the true Indies.

There is no rhyme or reason to those who receive the protections from him. He knows not himself why he chooses some and not others, save that once in a great while, there is an angel who whispers in his ear and guides him. These are potent amulets, he knows, strong enough to deflect a blow or staunch a wound. Theirs is not an obvious power, but it is enough, and more of his men are alive than would have been otherwise did he not gift them with these.

The angel whispers, and Palache drapes an amulet around the neck of a sallow, bearded man with a shaved head and a rich man's gut. What the angel has said is that he will need protection in the fight that is to come, and so Reb Palache offers what protections he might. He does not like to call upon the angel for this, prefers rather to debate with him about the nature of *Shekhinah* and the meaning of the Law, but there is no time for that now. There is merely time for the men, and a last prayer, and a fervent hope that not too many will fall.

The bald sailor nods his head and murmurs thanks. His mind is already on the battle ahead.

Overhead, men begin to shout. They are close. Soon the first shots will be exchanged, the first blood will be shed. The sailors move to their stations. The ship groans and thunders as it shoulders through the last few waves separating it from its prey. Voices – Spanish voices – cry out.

And with a sound of thunder, it begins.

This is how Reb Palache fights.

In his right hand, a sword, curved and edged on one side in the Moorish fashion. The blade is steel, but the hilt is simple brass, wrapped round with soft leather. On the blade is etched the letter vav, corresponding to the number six, which all good scholars of the Zohar know is the number corresponding to imperfection. For it is with this blade that he will mar God's creation and rend the flesh of those men who stand against him. Watch him now as he brings the blade up to parry a strike, then reverses and slashes across his opponent's throat. The man, a soldier, drops his sword and puts his hands to his neck, but he is already falling, falling, and Reb Palache has moved on, taking another man in the side as he stands over one of the Reb's crew to deliver a killing blow. The sailor--the pirate, for we must not mince words here--utters words of thanks, and then takes his fallen opponent's blade from stiffening fingers to dash off into the fray. Palache watches him for an instant, then runs to the rail and leaps the gap between his vessel and that of the accursed Spaniards. He bellows as he leaps, his voice cutting through the smoke and din of battle like the Great Teruah, the blast from the shofar.

His men hear him and roar their approval, their voices echoing his. Quickly, they clear the last of the Spaniards from the decks of their vessel and then over they go, throwing themselves at the Spanish ship and at the men who still defend her. One man misjudges his leap, his foot slipping in a slick of blood at the wrong moment, and over the side he goes. He slams against the hull of the Spanish vessel and then falls, but there is no time to think of rescue, no time for one man who might be lost.

For just as Gideon roused his tiny band, so now Reb Palache exhorts his men. In the center of the deck, he meets the Spanish captain, and their blades dance. High, low, high, dart and thrust, parry and stab, they are evenly matched, and then the press of battle closes in and they are swept apart.

In Reb Palache's belt is a pistol, primed to fire one shot and one shot only. The stock is made from cedar brought from Lebanon, and it bears many dents and marks. When he draws it, his finger does not find the trigger, nor has it ever been fired. Instead, he uses the barrel to catch the blades of his foes, and to turn them aside. The stock, he uses as a bludgeon, striking a jaw here and a skull there as needed. Men fall, stunned or wounded, he cares not so long as they are out of the fight. He is everywhere, he is nowhere, and though the angel sings in his ear he ignores its voice, for this is a matter for men.

There is a shout behind him, and the whistle of air being sliced thin by steel. He does not turn. Rather, he brings the pistol up over his head and twists, and the sword that strikes it glances harmlessly away. With his other hand, he reverses his own blade and drives it back, under his arm. It finds flesh, the meat of the man who would have killed him, and it is a killing blow. The weight of the collapsing man pulls the sword downwards, and he draws it free before it can be wrenched from his fingers. Blood drips from it, smearing his shirt and leggings and painting rough round spatters on the deck. He does not notice; his mind is on other things.

He looks around.

There is the sound of metal on wood, and metal on metal, and the Spanish musketeers are fighting for their lives as Palache's men swarm upon them. They are swinging their muskets like clubs, or reaching for daggers, for they have not had time to reload after a volley that was fired too soon, and from too far away. His own men, Palace sees, are saving their pistols for close work, and deadly.

There is a clanging in the air now, a sound he knows well: more grappling hooks thrown from vessel to vessel, more iron teeth biting deep into wood to bind the two ships together. And hot on its heels, the cacophony of running feet and men landing on the deck of a ship not their own. The battle is going his way. Were it not, it would be his ship feeling the tread of invaders ' feet, and his men calling out to fall back, and his sailors 'blood running out the scuppers into the ancient sea.

The Spaniards shout. An officer has rallied a band of them and they charge, blades out, at a knot of Palache's men who have just come aboard. The pirates hear them and turn to meet the charge, rushing forward pell-mell and hungry. These are his men, his sea-wolves, his spirits of vengeance clothed in flesh, and they shatter the Spanish charge as they meet it. There is screaming, and the thud of dead meat still warm hitting the reddened timbers, and then suddenly the Spanish officer is fighting alone. One man's thrust he parries, and then another, but a third of Palache's men has gotten behind him and brings a belaying pin down on his head with a broken-kettle crash. The Spaniard collapses, blood leaking from beneath his dented helm, and the pirates sweep onward, howling in triumph.

It is not a slaughter yet, but it will be soon.

"Enough!" he calls out, and his voice is as thunder. The angel in his ear falls silent. He is watching now, waiting to see what happens next. Perhaps the angel thinks that he is still in Canaan. Perhaps he wishes Palache were striding into battle with naught but the jawbone of an ass. But it is not his to decide what happens here, not anymore.

All around Palache, men stop. Swings end, half-completed. Fingers freeze on triggers. Sparks gutter out too close to black powder. A hush falls over the entangled vessels. Even the creaking of spars and snap of canvas is muted.

And again, Reb Palache says, "Enough."

One by one, the swords fall. They hit wood with bright clangs and dull thuds, and the odd round sound of metal rolling away. Palache's men do not strike, nor do they drop their weapons. Instead, they herd their surviving foes to the rear of the ship, and set guard upon them. Belowdecks there is more of the same, shuffling feet slowing and the moans of the wounded replacing the cries of the freshly killed.

The Spanish captain is still standing, Palache sees. He alone has not dropped his sword, and he waits before the mainmast. The deck between them clears, and once again they stand face to face.

"So," says Palache. "Do you yield?"

The captain regards him. He is a proud man, Aragonese by blood, and his features are hawk sharp. He wears leather gloves and fine clothes, and a hat with a long trailing plume. But his clothes are rent in a dozen places, and his hat has been notched, and there is dull dried blood on the silver of his blade. "You are Palache," he finally says, and raises his sword. "I have been ordered to kill you."

"I do not think you will," says Palache, softly. "You should put down your blade, and we will make terms."

The Spaniard's sword does not waver. "I think not. I do not parley with a man who consorts with devils."

"Devils?" Palache is shocked for a second." I do not consort with devils." He thinks for a moment. "I have fought a few, and a few more men who were like unto them, and I have conversed with angels. Is that enough to get you to lay down your sword?"

"I have been charged to cut out your heart, and preserve it in salt, and deliver it in a box made of cypress to my king. He will be most displeased with me if I return to him having failed." The Spaniard stares at Palache, unblinking. The tip of his sword cuts tiny circles in the air.

Beware, the angel whispers.

Palache nods, and thinks. "I do not think I can oblige your king, for he is no longer mine," he says. Then, with shocking suddenness, he drives his sword into the deck of the ship. It holds fast there, quivering. "But your king's words no longer hold sway on my vessel. For your ship is mine now, and you are a prisoner of war."

"This is not war. It is piracy, and you are but a corsair. And this is my ship, and--"

"And you are my prisoner, and a fool." There is a heaviness

to Palache's words now, and a finality. He steps back and forth, ever conscious of the sword tip following him. He is out of range, or near to it. This is a risk, a calculated one even with the angel shrieking warnings in his ear. His pistol is in his belt. His sword remains where he has left it, impaled in the deck. He has angels and amulets, and he is utterly unarmed.

The Spaniard knows this, or thinks he does. For he may be a true son of the Church, but does not believe in angels, not in those who might perch on the shoulder of a man such as the one before him now. And amulets are devil's work, and not proof against the true steel of the faithful, and in any case the hand of protection he sees around Palache's neck is a Moorish thing and of little worth.

"I offer you your life," Palache says. "Your crew as prisoners, your ship as mine by right of salvage, and its cargo payment for my men. You will be put ashore by a prize crew when it is safe; you will not be treated badly."

A sneer crosses the Spaniard's lip. "And I am to believe this from the legendary Reb Palache? The spy who converses with the devil and negotiates treaties good Christian kings must sign in blood? Who claims to study the word of God and yet sails the seas to commit bloody murder? Whose beard is shamed by his deeds, so that he dare not show it among decent and honorable men? What surety do I have, what surety can a man like you provide?"

He will try to make you kill him, the angel says. Will you?

Palache ignores its voice. "What surety would you take? An oath? Blood? None would satisfy you. Instead, I give you this-- those men who have thrown down their arms are still alive. Were I the beast you think I am, they would be."

"I do not think you are a beast," the Spaniard says, and his blade is suddenly still. "I think you are a fool."

And from the crowd a man rushes forth. He is screaming, and there is a hooked dagger in his left hand. Palache's men move to protect their captain, their teacher, but the would-be assassin is too quick. He dodges one, cuts the throat of a second, and then he is upon Palache.

Who has not moved.

And the killer swings, and the dagger comes down, and suddenly another man is there, the bald-headed Calatan who was given an amulet before the battle. His sword comes up but it is slow, too slow, and all who watch know where that dagger will end its stroke.

And Palache does not move, does not reach for his sword, does not reach for his pistol.

The dagger comes down. The tip tears at the fabric of the Catalan's shirt, cuts through it and continues, and then there is a sudden sound.

It is the sound of the blade upon the anvil, and the hammer upon the blade. It is the sound of a dagger shivering to fragments, and of clay cracking, and of a leather cord snapping. Pieces of the broken blade fall to the deck, and so does the amulet, sliced neatly in twain. And a moment later, so does the man who wielded the dagger, run through from behind by another of Palache's men.

"It's a miracle," the Catalan breathes. "Reb Palache works miracles."

"Devil," the Spanish captain says instead, but he reverses his sword and extends it to Palache. After a minute, the Reb takes it, and the killing is over.

This is how Reb Palache deals with the aftermath of the battle.

The dead are collected, and washed, and prepared for their final journey. The decks are washed clean of blood and offal. Kaddish is said for those whom wished it. With reverence, they are given to the sea.

The wounded of both sides are brought to him and to the other physicker who sails with him, for Reb Palache has studied medicine as well as Torah, and the hands that wield a sword in battle can also heal. With tinctures and amulets, scalpels and herbs and prayers, he tends to those who are suffering. The ones who will live receive all his skill and attention. Those who will not are dispatches swiftly, so that they might not suffer.

On this matter, the angel is conspicuously silent.

The prize crew for the Spanish vessel is assigned, trustworthy men and good sailors all, ones who will handle the broad-beamed craft well, and who can be relied on under any circumstance.

The prisoners have their wounds cleaned and bound. Their weapons are taken from them, and they are searched. Those who attempt to hide blades are treated roughly; those who attempt violence upon their captors are met with violence, swiftly. One or two inquire about joining Palache's crew. They rebuffed, for they are fools to ask in front of their shipmates, and weak-willed to have their alliance so easily swayed. Others, later, will show more cunning in asking, and they will be listened to, and judged.

A trusted few men descend into the hold to see what plunder might be held there. Surely there must be something to make the ship ride so low the water. The young and foolish among the crew ask about gold, or silver. The wiser wonder if there are cannon on board, their brass weighting the ship down until she wallows. But all are disappointed. The first man down below curses, and reports the bitter truth: Rocks. There is naught to be found but great heavy stones, packed into the hold to make the ship ride low. Had stormy seas come upon her, those rocks would assuredly have sent her to the bottom. Such was the gamble the Spaniards had taken, such was the risk they were willing to run to take Reb Palache. It was a compliment, after a fashion, but like most compliments, best not dwelt on. Disappointed, the men tell Palache what they have found. He thinks on it, and goes to see for himself, then issues his orders. Such men as can carry them heft stones overboard, so that the ship might ride better, and endure stronger seas. Belowdecks, the sound of the stones breaching the surface of the sea is like thunder.

A course is set: north and then east-northeast. The Reb and the man assigned to captain the Spanish ship confer, and agree. The sun is going down, and there are clouds in the distance, and night and weather may conspire to separate them. The prize crew captain knows his work, knows how to set the prisoners ashore far from any Spanish patrols, knows the name and address of Reb Palache's factor in Amsterdam. For even if the hold was filled with rocks, there are muskets and pistols and swords to sell, Spanish armor and the ship itself. Such is the way of the corsair; such is the necessity of the sea.

And finally, when all this is done, Reb Palache retires to his cabin and tends to his own wounds. He removes the garb of battle, and untucks his beard, and sees to where he has been cut, or burned, or battered. He pours himself a mug of wine, blesses it and drinks it, and thinks about food, and prayer, and about the sailor who fell to his death in the sea.

This is not yet ended, the angel says to him, and Palache nods. There is one thing left that he must do. Why the angel speaks to him, he does not know. He has studied the *Zohar* for some clue as to why, or how, or what it might mean, but there is no answer, or at least none that he has found. And in the meantime, when there is no hint of battle, he and the angel speak of *chochma*, and the number of plagues with which Egypt was smitten, and whether it might be possible to teach others among the crew to play chess.

"Send him in," Reb Palache says, just loud enough to be heard outside, and the angel goes elsewhere. He can sense its absence now as once he felt its presence, and the thought worries him. The aspect of the Divine will not be with him now; perhaps it is for good reason.

But the door opens, and there is no more time for wondering.

The Spanish captain enters. He is clean-shaven, and his cuts have been tended to, and his hands are bound before him. His eyes roam around the cabin--across the small swinging lamp of the Ner Tamid and the small ark below it, the shelves of scrolls in their watertight casings, and the physician's tools and herbs. The bed is a straw pallet, the furnishings rough save for an elegant carpet that covers the floor of near the whole cabin. There is a chair, in which Reb Palache sits, and a stool, which is empty.

"Sit," Palache says, and gestures to the stool.

The Spaniard sits. "My quarters are much finer," he says. "And my ship better. You should move across. It would be more fitting, oh pirate king."

Palache says, "I like this well enough," and pours his prisoner some wine. "Here."

"I will not drink your wine," he says, and makes no move to take up the mug. After a moment, Palache shrugs, and set it aside in easy reach.

"What am I to do with you?" Palache asks. "It would seem ignoble to kill you, yet foolish to allow such a capable enemy to go free, and to try his fortune against me again someday."

The man shrugs. "Perhaps I have learned my lesson. I might not make such a bad pirate, now that I think on it."

Palache snorts back laughter. "You wish to join my crew? I think not."

"No, no. Merely that I will not be well-received at court, even should you put me ashore safely. I might do better, and live longer, as a corsair."

"Ah. I see." A smile quirks at the corner of the rabbi's mouth. "But you will need a ship, and money to hire men, and to outfit her. Where would you find such things?"

The Spaniard leans forward. There is hunger in his voice now, and Palache thinks on the angel's warning from before. "There is treasure still on my ship. I know you did not find it. Come with me and I will show you. And you, perhaps, could leave me half, as an act of good faith, and I could swear on the holy Cross that never would we cross swords again."

Palache nods, and scratches his beard thoughtfully. "A generous offer, and you expect generosity as well." His mouth opens as if he is going to counteroffer, or agree, but there is a sudden knock on the door. "Yes? 'Palache says to the door, and "Pardon me," to the Spaniard.

A sailor pokes his head inside. "Reb, I wanted to let you know, we have done as you ordered. The rocks have been removed from the other vessel."

Palache looks at him for a moment, searching for something in his face. "All the rocks? Impressive work."

The sailor, who is young and somewhat callow and prone to

believing every tale he has heard of Reb Palache, swallows visibly. "Yes, Rebbe. Every last stone." He pauses and swallows again. "She rides high in the water now."

"I will wager she does." He waves a negligent hand. "Thank you. You are dismissed."

The sailor thanks Palache and the door closes.

"Does he know about your angel," the Spaniard asks.

"Most do, in one fashion or another. A few even believe."

"And should I?" The man's tone is mocking. "My father's priest would find it hard to believe that an angel would talk to a lowly pirate."

Palache stares at him for a moment. "I am a pirate, as you say, but not a lowly one. And I have seen many things, I think, that your father's priest would not believe." And Palache observes as he stares--the sudden nervous energy that courses through the man, the surreptitious glances toward the door.

"If we cannot speak of angels," the Spaniard says, "perhaps we can speak of emeralds. We should go now, before the sailors you have assigned to my ship find them."

"Your ship? Mine, rather, and if they find them, they will bring the emeralds to me."

"Nonetheless, we should hurry." The Spaniard stood. "We are at sea. Accidents happen. I would hate for your fortune and mine to be lost, or for the ships to become separated so that you might not find the treasure before putting me ashore."

"It has waited this long," says Palache, "it can wait a while longer. Sit. Drink your wine."

"I don't want the damn wine!" the Spaniard thunders, and kicks the stool. It spins away and crashes into the wall. "I want to go back to my ship, and--"

There is a thunderous explosion, and the ship heels sharply

to starboard. Outside there is shouting, and the clatter of pieces of wood falling to the deck. A tendril of smoke curls under the door.

"No," howls the Spaniard. "No!"

"But yes," says Palache. "An ingenious trap, I must confess. Weight the ship down so that the infernal devices rigged to it are below the water line, and thus inert. And once the unnecessary ballast in the hold is removed, the ship rises, and they dry out, and then it is just a matter of time. No wonder she ran so slow--were the bombs on the outside of the hull? I think so." The Spaniard stares at him, wordlessly. His eyes are wide and full of hate. "It was brave of you to attempt to lure me over there, I admit. Willing to sacrifice yourself, along with your crew. That is the stuff of the old aristocracy, not often seen these days."

"You." The Spaniard's jaw works against the air. Sounds occasionally emerge from it. "You knew."

"Yes."

"But your men! And yet you sit there calmly!"

Palache permits himself a smile. "My men? Why, they are my rocks, the strong bones I depend on. All were removed. You heard the man himself say such a thing."

"So you left my men to die? Bastard!" And with that, the Spaniard flings himself on Palache. But his hands are tied, and Palache has been hardened by the sea. He dodges the blow, and strikes heavily at the Spaniard's face, ribs, and gut. The man falls, wheezing on the rug. He bleeds a little from the mouth where he has been struck. The blood and drool puddle on the rug, jarring against the pattern.

"My ... my crew," he manages to wheeze. "You let them die."

"You let them die," Palache corrects him. "You were ready to sacrifice all of them as well as yourself to kill me. It does not seem fair for you to judge me for what you yourself would do."

"They were my men! Sworn to follow me, to death if necessary." He stands and staggers to the cabin door, pounding upon it with bound fists. It does not give, does not open.

"You'd do better to lead men to life," Palache says and stands. He walks to the door and taps it once. It opens.

And the Spaniard sees his ship, still sitting low in the water. Perhaps she is a bit higher than before, and perhaps it is for good reason. Near her is the wreckage of one of the ship's boats, blown to flinders. Half a powder keg floats beside it. Small chunks of charred wood are on the deck, evidence of the meticulous nature of the deception. The air smells like burned pine.

And aboard Palache's ship, he sees his men being marched to the brig. They do not resist.

"Your men deserve a better captain," Palache whispers. "Perhaps they will find one."

"Pah! What will you do with them?"

"What I have promised. You, however, will get what you desire."

The Spaniard spins, suspicious. "I do not like the sound of that."

Palache does not smile, does not blink. "No? But it is what you want, yes? Your ship back? I give her to you, with my compliments. I wish you joy of her, and her joy of her captain."

"What!" The man's eyes bulge with rage. "You cannot! You are a devil! I see that now! A devil!"

Two of Palache's sailors take the Spaniard and drag him, relentlessly, toward the edge of the deck. He is still shouting insults and curses as he goes, calling Palache a demon, a monster, a fiend. Palache merely watches him until he is safely aboard his own vessel, and his bonds are cut. Then he orders that the lines be cast off and the Spanish ship be set on its way, and that course be laid in for Rotterdam.

There is a whisper of wind that none feels but him and the angel returns. *You are cruel,* the angel says.

"Less cruel than he," Palache replies as the Spanish ship begins to diminish. "He has food, water, and good sails. If he does not deplete his stores too fast, she will not rise much in the water before she is driven upon land."

That is not what I mean, says the angel, unnamed and inscrutable. You could have perhaps made more of him. There was greatness in him, had it been nurtured.

"There was more murder and long years of damage to be undone. And I am growing old. Let him find greatness elsewhere if he survives."

There is a pause, and then the angel tries one last tack. *You could have shown more mercy.*

"Ah," says Reb Palache. "But that was all I had."

And he shuts the door, turns to his shelf, and takes down a copy of the *Arba'ah Turim* that he might study. Later, he and the angel will debate on aspects of the *Hoshen Mishpat*, but that is later. For now, the Spanish ship can still be seen, and the lone man upon it, and the great hungry ocean beyond.

WISHING
WON'T

Once upon a time--

What's that? You don't like that beginning? You should because this is a true story, and you should be glad it just happened the once.

So. Once upon a time, in a town much like this one, there was a little boy who was a lot like you. His name was Terry, and--

Why, yes, that's my name, too. Uncle Terry. Isn't that a coincidence?

Anyway, Terry--let's call him Terrence just to be a little different--was a mostly happy boy. He went to school, and he played with his toys, and he ran around in the yard of his family's house, which backed up on some woods. His mother and father often warned him not to go into the woods because they thought it was dangerous. And Terrence was a good boy and mostly did what they said.

Now the one thing that made Terrence sad was that he didn't have many friends. He was on the small side, and he could neither run nor fight well, so some of the older, bigger boys who were better at that sort of thing liked to pick on him. The meanest of the other boys was named Oscar--yes, like the character from Sesame Street--and Oscar was a bully. He would make fun of Terrence, take his milk money, and--

What's milk money? It's a thing we did when your mother

and I were your age. Our parents would give us money for milk and a snack at school every day if we behaved ourselves. I know it must seem strange to you, but you have to believe me, that's how we did things in those days.

Your mom always liked getting plain milk. I got chocolate.

In any case, Oscar and his friends, who had names like Michael and David and Chad, were always mean to Terrence. Terrence would tell his mother and father, and his father would say, "Well, son, you have to be strong. When they push you around, you have to push right back." So Terrence tried to do that, but since there were four of them and only one of Terry, he got pushed around a lot more. Sometimes, they'd even chase him home and stand outside his house and call him names. And once, they chased him into his backyard.

Now, when they did that, Terrence could do three things. He could call for his mother, which he did not want to do. It was better to get beaten up than to have other boys hear you calling for your mother.

Or, he could stand there in the backyard and get beaten up.

Or, he could run into the woods.

Terrence chose to run into the woods. And after a minute, Oscar and the boys followed him.

Now Terrence had been mostly good, which meant he'd been a little bit bad, which meant he'd explored the woods a little bit. And that let him find a trail and run quickly into the deeper woods, where he hoped he would lose the boys who were chasing him. He jumped over creeks, and he climbed over old crumbling rock walls, and he ducked around trees, and then he'd stop and listen. And every time he stopped and listened, Oscar's voice grew fainter and fainter and less and less sure until, eventually, Terrence couldn't hear him anymore.

In the dark, under the trees, Terrence stood and panted and realized he had no idea where he was. He'd only dabbled at the edges of the woods before. This time, he'd run all the way into their heart.

He looked around. The trees he saw were big and thick and old, and they went up and up and out and out. They weren't climbing trees. They were too respectable and serious for that.

And then he realized that the trees were in a circle, and in the circle was mostly dirt and leaves, but in the center was a low stone well.

Now Terrence knew very well what he was supposed to do in a situation like this, which was not, under any circumstances, go up to the well. It might have nasty snakes and spiders living in it that could bite him, or he could slip and fall in, or the ground could give way, or a million things could happen, all of which his mother had warned him about.

So naturally, Terrence did what all little boys would do. He went and took a closer look.

The well came up to Terrence's chest. He could see over the stone at the edge and look down into the well itself. When he did that, he saw nothing except a big, dark hole.

He leaned over the wall, which seemed sturdy, and shouted down into the well. "Hello!" he said. "Is anyone down there?"

The well said nothing.

Terrence shrugged and went looking for a rock. Because what good is a big hole in the ground if you can't drop something into it and hear how far it has to go before it hits bottom? He looked around, and he dug in the dirt with his fingers, and finally, he found a stone about the size of his fist. Terrence pried that stone out of the dirt, and he cleaned it off because it's important that if you're going to throw a stone in a well that it be clean, and finally, he let it go.

He never heard it hit bottom.

Instead, he heard a voice. The voice said, "PLEASE DO NOT THROW ROCKS AT ME. I AM TRYING TO SLEEP."

Terrence heard the voice, and he ran. He ran all the way home, and he didn't stop until he was safe in his room. The voice had terrified him. It was deep and low and old, and it sounded like rocks grinding away to dust over thousands of years.

Of course, Terrence didn't think of it that way. He thought it was scary.

But the next day, after school, he went back out to the well. He leaned over the edge, and he looked down, and he said, "Hello?"

The voice did not answer.

Terrence had been expecting that, so he reached into his pocket and took out a rock he'd found in his backyard. Closing his eyes, he let it fall.

"I THOUGHT I ASKED YOU TO STOP DOING THAT," the voice said.

"I'm sorry," said Terrence. "I wanted to talk to you, and you didn't answer me."

"I SEE." The voice was silent for a moment. "IF I PROMISE TO TALK TO YOU, WILL YOU STOP DROPPING ROCKS ON ME?"

Terrence thought about it for a minute. "Yes," he said. "I promise to stop dropping rocks on you if you talk to me when you come to visit."

"WELL, THAT'S SETTLED THEN," said the voice. "I WOULDN'T HAVE MINDED SO MUCH IF YOU HAD DROPPED SOMETHING I COULD EAT. BUT NOT ROCKS. I CAN'T EAT ROCKS."

"What do you eat?" asked Terrence.

"OH, ANYTHING. BUGS. SPIDERS. ANYTHING AT ALL."

Terrence looked down. He could see ants crawling on the stone of the well, doing busy ant things as they went about their day. Very carefully, he picked one up and dropped it into the well.

For an instant, Terrence heard what he thought were chewing noises. Then the voice said, "THANK YOU, LITTLE BOY. THAT WAS VERY KIND. YOU KNOW, IF YOU FEED ME, I CAN DO SOMETHING FOR YOU."

Terrence looked at the ants, and he looked at the well, and he thought for a minute. "What do you mean?"

"I CAN MAKE WISHES COME TRUE. FEED ME A LITTLE SOMETHING, AND I CAN MAKE A LITTLE WISH OF YOURS REAL."

"I don't believe you," said Terrence.

"TRY ME," said the voice, and Terrence got the sense that it was laughing. "FEED ME SOME MORE ANTS."

"OK," Terrence said, because he was curious and because at that moment he was thinking it might be nice to have a Zero bar because he was hungry because once again Oscar had taken his milk money and he hadn't gotten his afternoon snack. So he started scooping ants off the well and throwing them in, one at a time. And the ants vanished into the darkness, and the faint, strange noises kept coming from the well until finally the voice said, "THAT IS SUFFICIENT. THANK YOU. NOW LOOK INSIDE YOUR BACKPACK."

"How did you know I have a backpack?" asked Terrence.

"I KNOW LOTS OF THINGS," the voice replied. "NOW LOOK."

Terrence took off his backpack and unzipped it. Sitting there, on top of his three ring binder was a perfect Zero bar, not crunched and smooshed the way the ones at the convenience store always were.

"GO ON. TAKE A BITE."

Carefully, Terrence unwrapped the candy bar and took the tiniest, most delicate bite he could.

It did not taste like ants. It did not taste like things that lived in a well. It tasted delicious.

"I've got to go," he said suddenly and stuffed the Zero bar back into his backpack. "Goodbye," Terrence said, and ran home.

The voice did not say goodbye. It said, "I'LL SEE YOU TOMORROW."

Terrence did not come back tomorrow. He did, however, come back the next day, and he had a present for the voice in the well.

"It's a bag of crickets," he said. "I bought them at the pet shop. People use them for feeding their pet snakes and lizards and stuff." The, softer, he said, "I hope they're OK."

"I'M NOT A SNAKE. I'M NOT A LIZARD. BUT I WILL GLADLY TAKE YOUR CRICKETS. THEY SOUND DELICIOUS."

Terrence took the bag of crickets and turned it upside down over the well. One by one the crickets fell out and down and they disappeared into the darkness.

"THANK YOU," the voice said after a while. "THOSE WERE DELICIOUS, AS FAR AS THEY WENT."

"What do you mean?" asked Terrence. "Didn't you like them?"

"OH YES, VERY MUCH. IF YOU WANT TO SEE HOW MUCH, LOOK IN YOUR BACKPACK."

Terrence opened his backpack, and there was a brand new Star Wars action figure, one he'd been wanting for ages.

"You did this?" he asked the voice.

"YES. IF YOU FEED ME LITTLE THINGS, I CAN DO LITTLE THINGS FOR YOU. IF YOU FEED ME BIGGER THINGS, OR SPECIAL THINGS, I CAN DO MORE."

"What do you mean, special things?"

"I MEAN THINGS YOU CARE ABOUT. THINGS YOU LOVE. YOU DIDN'T REALLY CARE ABOUT THOSE CRICKETS, SO I ONLY HAD ENOUGH ENERGY TO DO A VERY SMALL THING FOR YOU. IF YOU'D GIVEN ME SOMETHING YOU CARED ABOUT, I COULD HAVE DONE MORE. I COULD HAVE GIVEN YOU A DOZEN ACTION FIGURES. I COULD GIVE YOU ANYTHING YOU WANT.

Terrence said "Oh," and then he went home.

The next day he went to the pet store where he'd bought the crickets and, with the money from his allowance, he bought a guinea pig. He named the guinea pig "Jimmy", and after a day or two he brought it out to the well. He leaned over the side and said, "This is my pet, Jimmy. He's a guinea pig." And he dropped Jimmy into the well.

For minute, the voice in the well said nothing. Then, it said, in a voice that was sad, "I AM DISAPPOINTED IN YOU. YOU DID NOT REALLY CARE ABOUT THIS CREATURE. IT WAS A CLEVER ATTEMPT, BUT THAT IS ALL. I THANK YOU FOR THE MEAL."

"I'm sorry," Terrence said. "I thought this would be better for you. You're supposed to care about your pets, right?"

"CARE IS SOMETHING THAT DOES NOT HAPPEN IN AN INSTANT, CHILD. IT REQUIRES PATIENCE AND TIME."

"So what do you mean, you want me to bring you something I care about."

"I MEAN SOMETHING THAT YOU TRULY LOVE. SOMEONE. IF YOU HAD A DOG OR A CAT WHOM YOU'D KNOWN AND

LOVED FOR YEARS, BUT, AH, I SEE YOU DO NOT. OR…" the voice paused. "SURELY YOU WOULD NOT DO SUCH A THING, EVEN FOR THE TREASURES I COULD GIVE YOU."

"Do what?" Terrence asked, even as he felt a tinge of cold fear climb up his back.

"YOU HAVE A MOTHER. YOU HAVE A FATHER." There was a pause. "YOU HAVE A LITTLE SISTER, WHOM YOU LOVE VERY MUCH."

"No!" said Terrence, and he ran home, laughter from the well following him as he went. When he got home, he got in trouble. The pet store had called to see if he was happy with the guinea pig, which Terrence's parents had not known he had bought. They were already mad about how he had gone into the woods, and he had to lie to them. Or maybe not lie. He told them he had gone into the woods to let Jimmy go, which was sort of kind of true. And his father scolded him for worrying his mother, and his mother told him he was a good boy but he had to use common sense, and then they sent him to his room, where he thought about the voice, and what it had promised, and how much he loved his little sister.

Are you getting sleepy? It's OK. The story's almost over. You're supposed to fall asleep.

Don't worry. You won't miss the ending.

Anyway, Terrence stayed away from the well for almost a week. That whole time, he was thinking about his little sister, and about what the voice in the well had said to him, and the sorts of things that could be his if he gave his sister to the voice. But because life is never simple, he also had to think a lot about Oscar, because Oscar and his friends still chased him after school, and since Terrence wouldn't run into the woods, they caught him and they beat him up.

After a week of this, Terrence said at dinner that he hated Oscar. His mother told him that hate was a very strong and special word, and you had to be careful how you used it. It was just like love, she said. Terrence didn't really love hamburgers, he just really liked them. And he didn't hate brussels sprouts, he just really didn't like them. It was the same thing.

That night, Terrence had an idea.

The next day, Terrence let Oscar and his friends chase him. He ran into the woods this time, but he did so slowly, so that they could follow him. And he led them along secret paths and through tangles and thickets, and one by one they dropped off and gave up, all except for Oscar.

Oscar, he led to the well. When they got there, Terrence stood with his back to the well and Oscar stood in front of him.

"Got you now, twerp," Oscar said.

"Wait," Terrence said. "Before you beat me up, there's something I want to show you."

"Oh yeah?"

"Yeah," said Terrence, and pointed at the well. "There's treasure in there. I can't get it out, and I can't tell my parents about it, because I'm not supposed to be back in here. But I was thinking maybe you and me, we could get it out together, and then you wouldn't have a reason to beat me up anymore."

Oscar sneered, and Terrence knew what he was thinking. That if there was a treasure, Oscar would take it all, and he would keep beating up Terrence no matter what.

Terrence kept his face very still.

"OK, let's see this treasure," said Oscar, and he swaggered up to the well.

"You have to look over the edge to see it. It's down at the bottom," Terrence told him. So Oscar leaned over the edge.

And Terrence pushed him.

Oscar screamed as he fell down and down and down, and then the voice in the well was screaming too, saying "WHAT HAVE YOU DONE?"

"I hate him," Terrence said quietly. "I hate him and hate is like love so I thought maybe you could eat him and that would be like me giving you something I loved."

"YOU HAVE NO IDEA—" The voice trailed off into a sound like a sick man coughing. "YOU HAVE NO IDEA WHAT YOU HAVE DONE. I DEVOUR LIGHT. I DEVOUR LIFE. I DEVOUR LOVE. I AM HATE. TO FEED UPON HIM IS TO FEED UPON MYSELF, AND YET I HAVE NO CHOICE."

"Did I do a bad thing?" Terrence asked.

"A TERRIBLE THING. GO. GO! AND NEVER COME BACK. WE ARE THROUGH, YOU AND I. FOREVER!" The voice started making sounds like a dog, choking on a chicken bone, and the stones of the well shook. First one, then a second and third and many others collapsed into the depths. Then the ground was shaking too, and Terrence ran. He ran all the way back to his house, and he never went in the woods again.

Well, that's not strictly true. He went back to where the well had been once or twice and tried to talk to the voice, but it would never answer him. As for the house, his mother and father owned it for many years, and then they gave it to his sister, since Terrence had moved far away for his job.

For my job.

Shhh. You're asleep? Good. Don't wake up. Uncle Terry's taking you for a walk to meet a friend of his. A friend with a very long memory. A friend who finally forgave him.

A friend who's hungry.

And remember. Uncle Terry loves you.

LONG
OVERDUE

"I will bet five dollars that you can get the Necronomicon through inter-library loan."

I snorted in disbelief, sending a mouthful of Coke onto the carpet by way of my sinuses. Dominic was cross-legged on the carpet, a half-eaten Hot Pocket on the plate sitting in front of him, and grinning like a bastard. I wiped my nose and glared at him. "Where did that come from? There's no way they'd let that thing go out on ILL. You can't even get into the part of the Widener where Harvard keeps theirs. I know. I've tried."

"Come on, give it a shot. It would be so cool."

I sighed, and went looking for a tissue. That was Dominic all over, a certified wuss who liked wheedling others into doing things he didn't have the balls to do. He was pale and chunky, with a goatee and a ponytail he'd spent most of freshman year cultivating, and lived in one of the single rooms in my housing unit.

I stared back over at him. "Dom, you are insane." He grinned at me idiotically, so I started ticking points off on my fingers for his benefit. "First, I'm a Lit major. Unless there's a chapter in that book on linguistically defined gender roles in tentacled thingies from beyond, I have no need for it to complete my senior thesis.

"Second, the book is insanely valuable and does not get shipped out to *any* undergraduate, even one at an upstanding liberal arts institution who thinks it would be funny to write his footnotes in Aklo. And last, you still owe me forty bucks for house beer and toilet paper, and I am not getting into any bets with you until those particular accounts are cleared up. *Capiche*?"

He looked sulky, and drew his knees up to his chin. The remnants of the Hot Pocket fell off the plate as he did so, oozing onto the floor. "I told you, I'd have the money at the end of the month. I'm doing some psych experiments and they'll pay me then." Listlessly, he prodded the unappetizing-looking lump back onto his plate. "How do you know so much about this stuff, anyway?"

"Double major for two years in medieval metaphysics. Dropped it when I decided to do the thesis--you can't part-time it with that reading list." I hoisted myself out of the unpleasantly orange chair that Physical Plant had seen fit to provide and headed for the kitchen. "Want me to take care of that plate for you?"

Dominic shook his head. "No thanks, Jase. I'm still eating." He paused. "I still think you could do it, though."

Halfway down the hall, I stopped. "Take care of the plate."

"No. Get the book."

Without thinking, I exploded. "Would you back off already? What the hell would I do with the Necronomicon if it did show up? I'd dog-ear a corner or something and they'd repossess my parents 'house to pay for the damages. Why are you so gung-ho for me to do this, anyway?" I thought about that question for a minute, then groaned as I doped out the likely answer. "Oh, Christ. Precisely which psych experiments did you sign up for?"

Dominic avoided my eyes as he answered. "Professor Staunton's," he mumbled. "But that has nothing to do with it."

"Like hell it doesn't." I stomped off in the vague direction of the sink. It was filled with plates, dishes, pots and other, less identifiable kitchen implements. "Sweet galloping Jesus, doesn't anyone in this place know what a sponge is?"

Dominic poked his head around the corner as I turned on the hot water and searched for the Palmolive. "Soap's behind the Simple Green. I think there's a sponge underneath the left-hand pile of dishes."

"Thanks." I found the dishwashing liquid, then carefully levered the teetering pile of dishes upwards until I could release the flattened green lump that passed for a scrubber from beneath it. "I think we need a new dish cleaning apparatus."

He peered at it and shrugged. "Looks all right to me."

" That's because in the five months we've lived here, Dominic, you've done the dishes precisely once. And that was when we were still eating on paper plates and you figured out that the only bread knife we had was coated in week-old peanut butter."

"Yeah, yeah." He walked into the room and sat at the university-provided table, which was round, beige, and precisely the wrong shape to be covered by any tablecloth known to man. "Anyway, the psych experiments aren't that bad; it's eight bucks an hour for thirty hours. It's just perceptual stuff."

"Perceptual stuff? The last time Staunton did one of those, they carried two students out of here on stretchers and another one tried to set the Psychology building on fire to keep the 'hungry shadows 'from eating the librarians."

"He swears that the last one was an accident. It's a reading-response thing with some visual elements, and besides, it's over two hundred bucks. That'll cover the groceries and everything."

Shaking my head in disbelief, I reached for another dish. "You're broke again? Why don't you ask your parents for the money? It's not like they're hurting."

"I just don't like doing it," he said softly. "I'd rather find the cash myself."

"Fine, fine," I said as I snagged the house's Designated Ramen Pot and commenced scrubbing vigorously. Dominic kept me company for a bit, but he quickly got bored. I glanced over my shoulder and saw him zipping up his jacket.

"Headed out?"

"I want to stop by Dr. Staunton's lab to pick up the materials for the experiment. It starts Thursday and I want to be ready."

I peered out the window. The sky was exactly the wrong shade of soft purple, and it was drizzling. Trees bent themselves at painful-looking angles in the wind, and a cold seeped into the kitchen. "In this?"

Dominic put his hand on the doorknob and shrugged. "It's Connecticut, man. It's not like the weather's going to get nicer."

"Good point." I turned back to the dishes. There were still a distressing number, and the dishtowel I was using for drying was positively moist. "Do me a favor? When you get back, let me take a look at whatever insanity Staunton is trying this time."

He smiled. "You're interested, aren't you?"

"Nope. I just want to know if I should start running."

"Fuck off," he said amiably, and went out into the brewing storm. Hands full of suds, I walked across the kitchen and shut the door behind him.

Dominic didn't get back until well after dark. By then, most of the gang had shambled back home, I'd started cooking spaghetti and meat sauce for a house dinner, and the earnest political debates in the kitchen matched the noise from the PS3 in the den. Wet, muddy sneaker prints tracked the residents' progress everywhere, and upstairs, someone fought noisily with a bathroom door. By our standards, a quiet evening.

"Yo, Dom," I called as he came in, shaking like a wet retriever. "How's campus look?"

"The same way it always looks," he muttered, trying to divest himself of a muddy Timberland while balancing on one foot. Somehow, he accomplished it and went to work on the other. "It's all mud. If they were smart they'd cover the whole thing in Astroturf."

One of the debaters at the table turned around, finger raised to warn bystanders of an incipient lecture. Raymond was a biology major, and prone to pontificating. He was well over six feet tall and close to 250 pounds, and wore nothing but flannel shirts, cowboy boots and blue jeans. Annalisa, the woman who had the room next to his, swore that he wore his boots to bed; it was the most generous explanation she could think of for the constant banging on her wall in the middle of the night.

"Actually," he chimed in, "the cost of carpeting the campus in Astroturf is prohibitive, even before you start adding in maintenance and upkeep." Raymond took a deep breath to launch himself into a cost analysis of what it would take to replace the campus 'stringy crabgrass adornment; the rest of the room took that as an opportunity to flee.

Raymond was our token wingnut. He claimed to be a

monarchist, and responded to any grand pronouncements about What Was Wrong With America with "That's why we never should have broken away from the British Empire." However, he also worked at the copy shop just off campus, and saved the lot of us a fortune in class materials fees. For that we let him slide on his recurrent political weirdness, not to mention his share of groceries.

Dominic, ever subtle, waited until Ray stopped to inhale, then elbowed him in the ribs.

"How was Staunton's?" I asked in the ensuing silence, staring intently at the bubbling sauce.

"Oh, fine. I have the papers. I'll leave them on the table for you. Who's the spaghetti sauce for?"

"Everyone. I was feeling generous. It needs about another ten minutes, though, and you'll want to keep the papers away from it. All you need is Staunton freaking out because there's a red stain on your notes that he didn't put there."

Dominic laughed. "True dat. You can read them later." He snatched the sheaf out of Raymond's hands and took a couple of steps toward the hall before stopping. He looked back over his shoulder and added tentatively, "There's one more thing. Professor Staunton said he'd help you get the book if you wanted."

"Oh, for fuck's sake." I stirred the sauce angrily and ended up catching a dollop of it in the sternum. "Jesus, that's hot."

"You OK?" Dominic's face was a mask of concern.

"Yeah, yeah, I'm fine." I dabbed at myself with cold water, and mentally wrote off the shirt as unsalvageable. "But I'm not fine with you bringing Professor freaky bastard Staunton into this, and I'm not fine with you even thinking that I want that book. I don't, OK? I don't want it, I don't need it, and I'm not even going to try to get it. Just forget about it." I turned back to the sauce. It, at least, occasionally did what I asked it to.

"I was only trying to help," Dominic whined, and oozed off in his wet socks down the hall. After a minute, a door slammed, and then there was silence.

It was Raymond who spoke first. "Funny thing, there," he said, and left it hanging.

"Yes?"

"Those papers he had. Were they from Professor Staunton?"

I nodded. "They were supposed to be. Why?"

"Well, he didn't carry them in a backpack or a folder, and it's pouring out there."

"So?" I shrugged.

"That's the point, though," replied Raymond, puzzled. "When I held them, they were dry."

I went to see Staunton the next morning. He theoretically held office hours from 10 to noon every Tuesday; I figured that I might as well make it clear to him as soon as possible that I had no intention of getting involved in his lunacy. As such, I found myself traipsing cross-campus to the Psychology Building, which looked like it had been built by subcontractors who'd done a lot of the initial work on Mordor.

The building was made of brownstone, which helped it blend into the omnipresent campus muck. It radiated the type of gloom that suggested that somewhere inside, someone was carrying on experiments on unwilling victims; for that precise reason, I generally avoided it.

Dom, for his part, said he found it "homey".

There were two ways up to the fifth floor, where Staunton's office was located: the elevator and the stairs. The elevator dated back to the building's original construction in the thirties, and was prone to stopping between floors for no good reason. The stairs, on the other hand, were narrow, steep, and gave every indication of being much taller than the building itself. Feeling the need for exercise, I took the second option.

On my way up, I thought about my personal experiences with Staunton. I'd taken the mandatory Introduction to Psychology course with him during freshman year. He'd tried to recruit me to do a Psych major on a couple of occasions, and had done so with the oily smarminess I associated with middle-aged townies who crashed campus parties to hit on women. It had not been a pleasant semester, and I was astonished and perturbed to have escaped it with an A-.

Automatically, my feet carried me to the fifth floor landing. The door out of the stairwell was half-open, and I staggered through it before it decided to shut on its own.

The door to Staunton's office was closed, and its window had been covered over with a blown-up photograph of some ancient, bearded guy smoking a pipe. Underneath the poster boy for lung cancer was a simple nameplate that read "Dr. Isaiah Staunton," white letters on black plastic. A pair of screws held it firmly onto the wooden surface of the door. Campus legend had it that a couple of years back, someone had stolen the nameplate and Staunton had gone ballistic. Apparently, he'd claimed that it was the first step in "a fatal psychic assault that could have disastrous consequences for the collective subconscious of the campus community," and that he wasn't going to stand for it, not when he had an offer on the table from Stanford. After some heated debate over whether or not letting him walk would be unfair to the Pac-12, campus administration simply screwed the next nameplate on a bit more tightly, and told Staunton not to push his luck.

Tentatively, I knocked. From within, I heard a voice say "It's not locked. Come in." Bowing to the inevitable, I did so.

Staunton was maybe forty-five years old, bald, with a long white beard. He wore an ancient yellow shirt and a wrinkled brown suit; the combination made him look like the manager for the Ozark Mountain Daredevils. His office was cramped, and every single flat surface was covered in books. The man himself sat behind his desk, a massive wooden thing that looked like it could stop a bullet. As I came in, I could see him riffling through a sheaf of papers similar to the ones Dom had brought home the night before. I approached, and he gestured vaguely at the rest of the office. "There's a chair somewhere under there," he said amiably. "Move the books if you have to, but be gentle."

"Yes, professor," I said, and did more or less that before sitting down.

He peered over the desk at me. "Mr. Jason DeLuca, is it? I've been expecting you, if you can believe that. Now, what can I do for you?"

I sat back in the chair, which was odd-smelling and creaky. "Actually, professor, I'd prefer it if you didn't do anything for me. One of my housemates told me that you'd be interested in helping me get a few books on inter-library loan, but I don't need the one he—"

Staunton held up his hand. "Stop. Let me guess: This is about Dominic Getty, right? He's a bit...overenthusiastic about some of my work, and I suspect he's been putting words into my mouth. He may, now that I think about it, have been putting words into yours as well. Yesterday, he came to me and said that you needed a book for your thesis but that the English department was being contrary about it. He asked if I'd help. I said I'd do what I can, if you came to see me to talk about it. When you showed up this morning, well, I naturally assumed..." His voice trailed off, and he shrugged. I shrugged back. It seemed the appropriate thing to do.

"Honestly, professor, I don't need any help and I don't need the book Dom was talking about. I'm sorry to have bothered you. I'll head home and straighten Dominic out." I stood from the chair, and Staunton waved negligently.

"No worries, Mr. DeLuca. I'll have a talk with him this afternoon, when he comes in to talk about the experiment he volunteered for."

"Volunteered?" One of my eyebrows went up. "I thought he was getting paid for it."

Staunton laughed. "Oh, no, not at all. I was actually all filled up, and he begged me to be a part of it for free. I would have felt bad to say no, so I let him in. It's fairly basic stuff, actually — I'm only running it now to make sure that the students in 101 get their required lab time in."

"Oh." I noticed my mouth was hanging open, thought about closing it, and decided that I had better things to ponder. Dom was lying to me, and he was apparently lying to Professor Staunton as well, all so he could get his hands on the Necronomicon for some unknown, but presumably stupid, reason. In the meantime, it sounded like my work here was done.

"Thanks, professor," I found myself saying. "I'm very sorry about wasting your time."

"Think nothing of it," he said, rising himself as I walked out. "Just leave the door open as you go, all right? I'm expecting another student shortly, and I don't want him waiting in the hallway for half an hour because he's afraid to knock."

I nodded, and walked out. A quick look at the elevator indicator panel told me that it was on the third floor and heading down, and thus wouldn't make it to the fifth for at least twenty minutes. With no desire to hang around that long, I headed for the stairs and took them two at a time all the way down, nearly trampling an assistant from one of the developmental psych labs in the process. While he was still telling me to go fuck myself, I shoved open the door to the first floor and ducked out. The elevator door pinged as I did so; reflexively, I turned left to see who was getting off.

No one was. Instead, Dominic was getting on, and my gut told me he was going to the fifth floor. Then the elevator door closed, and the grinding of pulleys in A minor indicated that it was headed up.

I cursed. With a half hour before class, I conceivably could head back upstairs and eavesdrop on whatever Professor Staunton had to say to my charming housemate. On the other hand, did I want to climb those stairs again for what could be a long-winded and very boring chewing out?

The papers, I recalled, had been bone dry. I started back up the stairs.

"So what did Staunton say?" Raymond leaned forward on the kitchen table, all quivering curiosity behind his glasses.

I put my hands behind my head. "Well, by the time the lab assistant in the stairwell finished yelling, I missed half the conversation, but what I did hear was interesting."

"Oh?"

I nodded. "Staunton spent some time yelling at Dom for 'misrepresenting 'him. Then he went off on how if Dom kept on screwing up, he'd find someone else to work with, and that other students would give their immortal souls to get this chance."

"Is that an exact quote, or a paraphrase?"

"As exact as I can get without hocking up phlegm. Which leads me to believe that something high on the fucked-up-o-meter is going on here."

Raymond stroked his attempt at a beard sagely. "So it would seem. I'd steer clear of both of them for a while, just in case."

"Seems like a good idea." I nodded, and then turned my head as I heard the front door creak open.

"Dom!" said Raymond, and I winced. "We were just talking about you!"

"Oh?" He seemed detached as he scuffed his boots on the doormat and shrugged out of his jacket. "OK."

"I, uh, talked to Staunton today," I said softly. "He said there'd been a mix-up."

Dom nodded as he wandered toward the living room. "Yeah, he told me that, too. Sorry about that, man. I'll try to do better."

"No worries, Dom," I said, but he was already gone. I turned to Raymond, who shrugged. "He seems genuinely sorry."

"I guess he does. Weird, that. I'd still stay away from Staunton. And the library, for that matter."

"You're probably right."

He nodded solemnly. "I'm always right. You just don't recognize that, yet. Let me know when you're ready to accept that rejoining the British Commonwealth is a good idea."

I fled.

It was three days later when the notification arrived in my mailbox at the campus center. I was doing my usual mid-afternoon gratuitous mail check, and there it was: a single slip of white paper with the library logo on it, nestled on top of my *SI* (which I read) and my *Utne Reader* (which I didn't, but which I was convinced would impress any woman I got back to my room that I was a Serious Thinker, and thus worth screwing).

"Oh, shit."

Raymond looked up from that week's Victoria's Secret catalog. "Hmm? Didn't get yours yet? You can have mine if you want."

"No, no." I reached into the mailbox and retrieved its contents. "Look."

"*Utne Reader*. Trash, I agree." Raymond seemed less than concerned.

"No, no, no! On top of it." I scanned the piece of paper from the library to confirm my suspicions, then thrust it at him. "What does this say to you?"

He read it and blinked. "It says that your copy of the Necronomicon, which you requested, has arrived and can be picked up. I believe 'oh, fuck 'is an appropriate rejoinder."

"Exactly," I nodded grimly.

Raymond took a single step back. "Now, I have to ask this, in order to make sure that any panicking I do is actually appropriate, but...you didn't suddenly decide to request that after all, did you?"

I shook my head. "No. And if you look closely at the paper, you'll see the request date is from February. We didn't even start talking about this until a couple of days ago."

"Hmm. On the other hand, you do get it for a whole month."

"I don't want it for a whole month. I don't want it at all. But I'll tell you what I do want: I want to know who did this in my name, and then see how far up into their throat I can kick their balls." Clutching the paper, I stormed out. Hurriedly, Raymond followed.

"So what are you going to do?" he huffed when he finally caught up with me.

"Go to the library, explain that I don't want it, and get them to send it back. If I'm really lucky, they'll tell me who signed off on the request." I set a mean pace toward the library's main entrance. "If it's who I think it is, I might even set fire to the Psych Building."

"You don't mean that, do you?" There was silence for a minute. "Well, at least let the developmental labs close up first and get the kids out of there."

I pounded up the library steps, Raymond trotting after like some demented Sancho Panza. The woman at the front desk screeched something which could have been "No Running," as I powered through the security turnstile at full speed, and headed for the inter-library loan desk.

The ILL desk was tucked in back by Documents, in the section of the first floor where frosh never dared venture. It was manned at all times by two bored-looking work-study students whose main job was to make sure there was at least one working pen behind the desk no matter what. The desk itself was some green stone that was supposed to be marble. At the left of the desk was a small bell, of the 'slam top in hopes of getting service 'type, and when I got there, neither of the two desk jockeys were anywhere to be seen.

"Crap." I slammed my hand down on the bell. It gave off a sound like a steamroller going over a bucket. I cursed, and hit it again. After a minute, a white-shirted, disheveled geek dragged himself out of the back, and when he saw that there was someone in front of the desk, he paused to put on his sunglasses.

"Yeah?"

"I got this in my mailbox." I waved the notice at him. "I didn't request this book, and I want to send it back."

"Huh. Let me see that." He leaned forward to take it from me, tried to read it, then realized that with sunglasses on he couldn't see a damn thing. "This is weird," he said when he finally deciphered the note.

"Why do you say that?" I asked through gritted teeth.

"Let me run back and check something." Without waiting for a response or handing the note back, he vanished from whence he came. I heard a muffled "Ouch," and then some thumping as large, weighty books were moved into large, weighty piles on the floor. I looked around for Raymond but he was nowhere to be seen. My fellow students drifted by in ones and twos. Finally, the work study student emerged from the depths, holding a leather-bound book that looked like it had been used to record confessions during the Spanish Inquisition.

"It looks like that book's already been picked up. This morning, as a matter of fact." He looked genuinely confused. "Which is odd, because the log back there says that it was signed for at 11:50, and we don't drop these into campus mail until noon."

"You're kidding me. What brain-dead nimrod was on duty when that happened?"

"My girlfriend."

"Ah." I waited a minute for him to offer some justification for the screw-up, and when none was forthcoming, kept going. "Who signed for it?"

"That's the odd part. According to the book, you did." He laid the ledger down on the counter and opened it. Very clearly, at 11:50 AM, there was a scribbled "Jason DeLuca."

"But I'm Jason DeLuca."

"Then you should have the book. Thanks, have a nice day." He slammed the book shut.

"No! If I had the book, would I come by here asking to rescind the loan request? And would I have this?" I snatched the notification from his hand.

"Well, that's the funny thing, isn't it?"

I reached into my jeans pocket and pulled out my wallet. Front and center was my student ID. The picture made me look like I was getting more volts than Frankenstein, but it was a pretty good likeness for me in my current state. "This is my student identification. You are not supposed to release a book on ILL without one of these. This has been in my pants all day, and I can guarantee you that neither your girlfriend nor anyone else has been in them with me."

"Hey—" he started, but I plunged forward before he could finish winding up.

"I didn't pick up this book. I want to know who did. Show me that signature." Moving slowly, he laid the sign-out book down on the desk. I flipped through the pages until I found the one I was looking for. My finger stabbed the appropriate line accusingly. "That's not my signature."

He peered at it. "But it says 'Jason DeLuca.'"

"Yes, but I didn't write it. Therefore, that is Not. My. Signature." I stared at the scribble on the page. So did he.

"You sure?"

"Of course I'm sure! My signature doesn't even look like that. It's much more…legible!"

"Oh, wow. I'm going to have to write up a report." He looked down at the signature again, at me, and then at the floor. "Hang on one more minute." He picked up the phone and dialed what sounded like a campus extension. I heard a couple of rings, then a muffled voice before Library Lad launched himself. "Sweetheart? Hi…yes, I know I'm not supposed to call you at the lab. I know. It's important. No, it can't wait. No, it's not about us. I'm perfectly happy with us….she's my study partner, for fuck's sake….no, that's not true…Oh yeah? Then how come you're spending so many late nights tutoring that guy at Chi Psi? I don't care that he's not Jewish…look, can we talk about this later? I've got a work question…yes, a work question. When you signed out that ILL book this morning, did the guy have ID? He did? OK. Thanks. Love you. Bye-bye."

He put the phone down with more force than was strictly necessary. "She says the guy who picked it up had ID. You're screwed until we get this straightened out. I'll get the complaint forms."

"Dominic," I said under my breath, and started sprinting. Behind me, I could hear my erstwhile helper shouting "You'll have to sign this or I can't file it!"

Out I went, past the desk (where Raymond was chatting up the woman on sentry duty) and down the front steps into the soup that had once been the library lawn. Dominic would have to come home sometime, and I'd be waiting for him when he did.

It wasn't until the next morning that Dom finally arrived, a suspicious-looking package from the copy shop under his arm. I'd sat up alone all night waiting for him, and irritation was writ large on my face. He met my eyes as he came through the door, and flinched.

"Hi, Dom," I said.

"Hi."

"Why did you steal the book? Were you that hard up for cash?"

He stared down at the floor. "You figured it out, huh? I thought you might."

I put my hands behind my head and smiled. "Well, it's not like you were subtle about wanting it. I figure Staunton helped you get it, and then you forged an ID so you could pick it up. Am I right?"

"Sorta." He sat at the kitchen table and thunked the package down in front of him. "I just wanted to read it so I could get in good with Professor Staunton. I need recommendations for grad school, and I figured this might help. He seemed impressed that I wanted it so badly, and promised to write me a letter if I pulled it off. He signed off on the form, and when he saw I put your name on the request he laughed. A couple of days ago I figured out that maybe this wasn't a good idea, and tried to get you to pick the book up when it arrived, but you weren't interested. I couldn't let you send it back, so I went and picked it up myself this morning. Professor Staunton told me it had come in." He paused. "I think he pulled some strings at Harvard to make it happen, but he needed an actual student to put in the request, and your old double major made you more likely to get it than me."

I grinned smugly. "I told you that Classics would get you nowhere."

"Yeah, yeah. You were right."

"And you were dumb." I waggled a finger at him accusingly. "Where did the ID come from?"

"Raymond made it for me months ago on a bet. There's a laminator down at the copy shop."

"Ah. Clever of him." I thought carefully about my next words. "Dominic, you are a whiny little prick, and I mean that in the nicest way possible."

He nodded miserably. "I know. That's why I did this." He tapped the package.

"Huh?"

"I'm real sorry, man. A couple of the pages got bent when I was reading. So I took it down to the shop and got those pages done over on parchment, and stuck them back in."

"You did what?" I blinked. "You little shit. You use my name to steal a priceless book, you lie to me about it, you damage it, and you think that taking it to the corner copy store is going to make it all right? This is not some student screenplay we're talking about here. This is a book worth more millions than I've got toes, and you damaged it. They're going to sue me, sue my parents…"

He sniveled. "I said I was sorry, man. You don't have to get so upset."

"Don't have to get upset? They're going to flay me alive for this, and you're telling me not to get upset? Oh, no. We're taking this right up to the library office right now, and you're going to tell them exactly what you did. And then, once they're through with you, I'm going to kick your ass."

"Aww, come on," Dominic protested. "Raymond did a great job. You can't hardly tell the difference." He slid the book out of the package and opened it. "See?"

I stared. The book was marvelous, terrifying, hypnotizing. Brown ink that wasn't ink marked the pages in spirals and scrawls, beckoning the reader to come closer. I could feel the little bits of Aklo I'd studied freshman year coming back to me, phrases here and there making sense. My mouth formed the words almost involuntarily, the sound scarcely more than a whisper.

Dominic slammed the book shut. "I told you. That was one of the passages that Raymond replaced. Can't tell, can you?"

Annoyed with myself, I shook my head. "I can't. An expert can. Pack it up and we're going up to campus to take care of this mess."

"Can't it wait until lunch?"

"No, it can't. Just be thankful that I'm going to let you live that long."

"So that was it?" Raymond sat on his bed, his chin in his hands. "He got off easy."

I nodded at him. "The guy from ILL said that the book was a facsimile they'd sent, not the real thing. Expensive, but not irreplaceable. His parents should be able to afford to replace it, and cover the beer-and-toilet-paper debt as well."

"That's much better than it might have been" Raymond observed. "How about Staunton?"

"I think the deans are going to nail his pelt to the wall for this."

He nodded sagely. "As well they should. Imagine using an undergrad to obtain a book like that. It's enough to make one lose faith in the tenure track system."

"Yeah, well, here's hoping." I shook my head. You did a nice job of covering up Dom's screwups, by the way."

Raymond chortled. "Thank you. It seemed like the best way out of a bad situation, and I had a suspicion that the book itself was some form of modern fake. The paper reminded me of something we had back in parchments, so I used that, and got the color printer to match the tone of the ink. Dried blood isn't that hard to match, to be honest. Imitation dried blood is easier."

"I see." I looked around his room. As always, it was immaculate, and a pair of neatly packed bags sat on the bed next to where Raymond crouched. "That's a lot of luggage for you. Going on a trip?"

"Long weekend home. I don't have any classes Friday, and I figured I'd give Annalisa a head start on her weekend … constitutionals."

I laughed. "Nice of you, especially since she's seeing that Astro TA, and they don't get a lot of evenings. Just do me a favor?"

"Sure."

"No more fake ID cards for Dominic?"

"Certainly." Raymond looked moderately mortified. "It was to win a bet. He said I couldn't do one that would fool the librarians. I wasn't going to let him cast aspersions on my work, so…" He trailed off into a shrug. "It was foolish. I recognize that.

Now, could you give me a hand with these?"

"Of course." I grabbed the bag on the left and winced at the weight of it. "Jesus, man, what do you have in here? Lead?"

"No, no. Just a book. Something I did at work recently. "

Something shifted in the bag, and I heard a loud thump. "A big book, too, from the sound of it."

"Like you wouldn't believe." He headed for the stairs, and I followed.

"How are you getting to the airport, anyway?"

"Oh, I found someone on the ride board. I think that's him now." Through the front window, I could see a black Honda pulled up to the curb. A light rain was falling, and Raymond and I hurried out to where the car awaited.

"Trunk is unlocked," called a vaguely familiar voice, and we tossed the bags in.

"Have a good weekend, Raymond. I'll see you Sunday night."

He grinned, which was uncharacteristic of him, and got into the front seat. The car roared off into the night, and I shlepped back inside. Dominic and a couple of others were sitting in the kitchen, kibbitzing, and I looked at them quizzically as I entered.

"Any of you guys know someone on campus who drives a black Honda with a vanity plate?"

"Maybe," piped up Annalisa. "What did it say?"

"PROFIAM."

Dominic snorted. "Duh. That's Professor Staunton. Why?"

I thought for a minute, considering what Raymond could possibly have photocopied at work recently and why he might be in a rush to get out of town with Professor Staunton. I thought about what that might mean and came to the conclusion that the best thing I could do right now was get very,

very drunk.

"Oh, no reason," I said quickly. "Where are we keeping the vodka these days?"

LABOR COSTS

"Tell me, Mister Upton, can you see the ghosts?"

Obediently, Peter Upton craned his neck and looked out the window. "No," he said. "Should I be able to?"

In fact, what he had seen looked moderately pleasant, in a workmanlike way. Rows of neat houses crouched down on rolling New England hillsides, shaded by trees just starting to think of shedding their leaves. Here and there a church steeple heaved itself up a little nearer to heaven than its neighbors, while the sluggish waters of the Housatonic flowed past in the distance.

"Not unless you're a prophet. But mark my words, they'll be here soon enough." Asher Perry coughed discreetly into his fist, then wheeled himself over to the window to take in the view. The hum of his chair's motors harmonized with the steady thrum of the machines on the floor below; when Asher Perry asked to see a man, it meant seeing him where he worked. And he worked in the textile mill that bore his name.

"Join me." Upton stood and walked over to stand next to the older man. Up close, he could see that Perry looked weary, the lines on his face deepened by worry and lack of sleep. "Do you know why I brought you here, Mr. Upton?"

The younger man inclined his head slightly. "I solve problems. You clearly have a problem that needs solving. All that awaits are the details."

"Hmmmph. Don't get too clever." Perry sat for a moment, then gestured broadly at the town below. "The thing you have to understand is that this is, for all intents and purposes, my town. I was born here. Grew to manhood here. Mustered into the Union army with twenty-two of my closest friends on that village green and came home with the six survivors and no legs two years later. And I built this factory up from nothing here-- here when the easy thing to do would have been to pull up stakes and set up shop in Lowell. Do you know how much of this town works in this factory, Mister Upton?"

Upton knew, of course. It was his job to know such things, to know all the pertinent things about any man who summoned him to a meeting and might have use of his particular talents. And he also knew that Asher Perry was blunt, even by the standards of New England mill owners, and had little patience for flatterers and their ilk.

"More than half," he said, and coughed gently into his hand. "Directly, that is. If you count the shopkeepers who sell to your workers, the river hands and drovers who move your goods, the men of God who tend to their souls and the ladies of the evening who tend to their other needs in a lovely house on Benefit Street, then nearly all."

Perry grunted in approval. "I love this town, and it's my mill that feeds it and pumps the blood through its veins. I put the food on the table in every house you see, and I send the doctor when any of 'em fall ill. It's my coin that buys their cradles and their coffins, and while a better businessman might think my sentiment unnecessary, I find it appropriate. This town made me, now I make it."

Perry turned his chair so that he faced Upton, staring up at him with a curious intensity. "But what happens out there if this place closes? If I'm forced to shut my doors, what happens next?"

Upton closed his eyes for a second and imagined the scene. The great looms stilled, their steamy exhalations done forever. The confused and frightened workers outside of the great doors, now chained shut. The flight of those who could afford to go, the creeping poverty and desperation of those who could not. The death of the town by inches, and the disappearance of everything Asher Perry had built.

"I can see it," he said softly. "So that is why you need me?"

Instead of answering, Perry wheeled himself back over to his desk. The chair was a solid contraption of brass, inlaid with cherry wood here and there to give it the faint appearance of not being simply utilitarian. "Here's the problem," he said and pulled two small bolts of fabric onto the desk. To Upton, they were indistinguishable. "One of these is from my works. High quality, which means I can afford to charge through the nose for it. And the other? From a mill in Burlington. Last year, they were turning out stuff that would rub a horse's backside bald. This year, they're making cloth as good as mine and five times as fast."

"I begin to see your worry."

"Hmm. Do you." Perry steepled his fingers. "I'll be straight with you, Upton. My buyers won't hold the line for long. I either have to adapt or shut down, and I can't shut down."

Upton dropped into a chair across the massive desk. "What exactly are you asking me to do, Mister Perry?"

"Steal." Perry's voice was flat and cold. "Get yourself into the Schnurr Textile Works by whatever means you have to. Find out how they're doing it, and who's doing it for them. And then bring that secret back to me so I can do the same thing here."

"How far do you want me to go to get it? Certain things…cost more."

Perry scowled. "Whatever it takes, Mister Upton. You have *carte blanche* to do whatever it takes."

He pulled open another drawer, pulling out a small bag stuffed to the gills. "Here," he said, and tossed it on the table. "Airship fare from Bridgeport to Burlington. Half your fee, as agreed. And those other things you asked for, all here."

Upton swiped the bag with an easy motion, not bothering to open it, and stood. "And from here?"

"One of my men will drive you to Bridgeport. He's already picked up your things from the boarding house and is waiting downstairs. And with that, I believe our business is concluded until you bring me what I asked for. Good day, Mister Upton, and Godspeed."

"Until I return, then." Pouch in hand, Upton headed for the door.

The sound of the machines got louder once he left Perry's office, but not oppressively so. The factory floor lay spread out before him, and of all the ones he'd seen, this was by far the most pleasant. Vast windows let in light, while massive fans and bellows kept air circulating throughout the room. Nor could he see children working the looms. It was said Perry had strict rules against it, and that he paid his people well.

Upton frowned. Sympathy was a dangerous thing to acquire in his line of work. His task was before him; best he not think of it in terms of good or evil, but merely payment. With that, he strode down the iron staircase toward the front door, and the way to Burlington.

The Burlington airship station was small, crowded, and busy. Blasts of steam and compressed air pushed platforms full of passengers skyward or let them settle towards the ground as gangs of men worked to tether incoming vessels. Everywhere, placards announced new expansions that were coming soon-- new services, new platforms, all driven by the new city that Brunswick imagined itself becoming.

As Upton's lift hit ground, he hoisted his bag and stepped off. The crowd surged around him in a hurry to disembark, but he held back until the tide had receded and the platform operator stood alone at his console.

"Excuse me, sir. Can you direct me to the Schnurr Textile works?"

The lift operator, a heavyset man in a too-tight uniform, laughed. "That way," he said, and gestured with a meaty thumb. "Just listen for the commotion."

"Commotion? Upton asked, but the platform operator was already hustling the next batch of passengers onto the platform, securing it for ascent. After a moment, Upton turned and set off in the direction the man had indicated. Vehicles whizzed past him, larger steam-driven vehicles with rumbling boilers and smaller clockwork devices like powered bicycles, zipping in and around the motorcars like flies. Horses were still in evidence here and there, but they were few and far between. *A sign of progress*, Upton told himself. Clearly, Burlington was a town that was going places in a hurry.

He rounded a corner and came across a scene of pure chaos. Perhaps a hundred yards away behind a low brick wall was a massive building labeled SCHNURR in titanic bronze letters. A dozen smokestacks belched filth, spitting black soot and thunderous cacophony skyward. No windows disrupted the grim brick exterior, but that was not what caught Upton's attention.

In front of the factory was a surly mob of hired toughs, armed with clubs and brickbats and sawed-off lengths of pipe. Giving them their orders was a fiercely mustachioed fellow standing on a platform close to the building and speaking into some type of metal cone that amplified his voice a hundredfold.

Across from the hooligans were an equally disorganized mob, only they were holding placards instead of weapons. Many of them were women, Upton noticed, and they were chanting slogans almost loud enough to drown out the yelling from the other side. Overhead, police ornithopters circled lazily, and a crowd had gathered to watch the incipient confrontation. The air was electric with tension, and the more sensitive members of the crowd were already edging away.

Upton edged forward, working his way through the crowd until he was on the edge of the throng of sign-holding laborers. He could hear now what they were saying, though the words made little sense: "Tear them up, let them go! Tear them up, let them go!" The strikebreakers, hard, unshaven men in grubby clothes and hastily pinned-on badges, were too close now, their makeshift weapons terribly real across the short gap.

Here and there, he could see workers handing out leaflets to the crowd. Most were met with hoots of derision and torn up as soon as they were distributed, but the workers kept at it doggedly. Upton worked his way over to where one, a painfully thin young woman with a long, angular face was resolutely shoving papers into the hands of anyone nearby. He tapped her on the shoulder and got as far as "Excuse me, miss," before she whirled, paper first, and nearly rammed it down his throat.

"I'm terribly sorry," she said, and lowered her hand slightly. Her voice had a slight rasp to it, one Upton instantly recognized as an early symptom of Monday Fever. All the mill girls got it sooner or later, the dust from the looms settling murderously in their lungs. The cure was fresh air and sunshine, far from the textile mills--a cure none of them could afford to take.

"Nothing to be sorry for," he said, lowering his eyes to the paper as he took it. It was the usual labor broadsheet, claiming the workers were united against unfair labor conditions and demanding humane treatment. And at the bottom, an ominous phrase, "Not even death will free us."

He looked up to see that woman was looking back at him. "You read it," she said. "Most don't."

"I try to be informed," he replied. "So is this a slowdown?"

"A strike," she said resolutely. "Schnurr Textiles is a monstrous firm. It *must* be stopped."

Puzzled, Upton turned his head. "Wait a minute. You said it's a strike. But the factory's still running. And I don't see any replacement workers—"

"Scabs," she interjected.

"Scabs going in and out. What's going on in there?"

"That's what I'm trying to tell you," she said. "You see, it's--"

And then all hell broke loose.

A brick came soaring across the line from the strikebreaker side. No one saw who had thrown in; perhaps one of Schnurr's hired thugs, or perhaps a bored and restless member of the crowd. It made no difference. The projectile caught one of the workers on the side of the head with a crunching sound and she dropped to the ground. There was a moment of stunned silence, then there were screams, and then bellows of anger as the two sides surged together. Metal and wood slammed against bone, fists slammed into faces, and from overhead, the impotent tootling of police whistles served to remind everyone that this would not be settled by law.

Upton found himself face to face with one of the strikebreakers, a squat man with an oft-broken nose and a derby crammed low over his eyes. The man roared, then swung a length of lead pipe at his head. Upton ducked underneath the swing, bringing up his bag in a vicious arc that intersected with the man's crotch. He grunted and folded, at which point Upton hammered the back of his neck with an elbow, and the man fell senseless to the ground.

Behind the unconscious man, the woman he'd been talking to stood, staring.

"You should go. You're not one of us."

"That seems to make no difference to them."

"Please, leave, before it's too late!"

But it was, or so it seemed. The line of workers wavered and then cracked, and the tide of strikebreakers poured through. They laid about themselves indiscriminately, and the resolute chants turned to panicked screams.

"Come on," the woman said, and grabbed Upton by the arm. "Let's get you out of here!"

"Get *me* out of here?" he said, even as a billy club whistled past his ear. She turned and threw a fistful of leaflets into the strikebreaker's face, then pulled Upton free from the crowd.

"This way!" she shouted, leading him down an alley to the left. He gave one last look at his target, then followed.

She led him through a maze of small streets and smaller passages, as the clamor of the riot faded in the distance. Eventually, they found themselves in a small courtyard overlooked by a crumbling tenement. "In here," she said, leading him through a door and into a cramped kitchen. A pot of soup burbled lifelessly on the stove, while clotheslines draped across the room to take advantage of the heat. "You can stay here until it dies down. They never come this far looking for us."

"I appreciate the help, miss…"

"Adelaide. Adelaide Marcus."

"Ah. Miss Marcus, I appreciate the help, but there's no need for you to stick your neck out for me. I've handled myself in worse scraps."

"You've seen nothing worse than Schnurr," she said flatly. "Did you not hear what we were calling for?"

"Tear it up, let them go," he said. "Tear up contracts? Let the workers leave?"

She laughed, a bitter, angry sound that devolved into a rasping cough. "You have no idea. Look, have you ever worked in a factory? Lived in a factory town?"

"I haven't."

"Then you don't know. Don't know they bring you in with a promise of good pay and clean clothes and a nice place to live. They don't tell you they charge for all of that, and they keep charging, and you never ever *ever* make enough working for them to pay it off because they always find new things to charge you for."

"So run."

"Try it and you'll get clapped into debtor's prison. There's no way out. Once they get a grip on you, you're theirs."

"For life?"

She turned and stared at him. "Life? What do you think happens when you die and you still owe them?

Upton ducked under a clothesline, stepped around a child's makeshift toy on the floor. "The debt gets passed along, I assume. That's the usual way of things."

Again, a bark of angry laughter. "Not anymore. They've made things more efficient, you see. Now, when you die--"

And with a crash, the door flew into the room. Shouts of "There she is!" filled the air, matched by a clamor from the front of the building. A dozen burly strikebreakers poured in, clubs in hand. One swung at Upton, who dodged as the man's arm was caught by a clothesline. He sent the man sprawling with an uppercut to the jaw, just in time to take a belt across the ribs from the next thug. Behind him, he heard a scream and a hiss as Adelaide flung the pot of hot soup at another assailant. There was the thump of another man going down, and then a gunshot, and another.

A spray of bright red across the clothes between him and Adelaide, the clang of a pot dropping to the floor and then Adelaide was screaming and more shots were being fired until she went horribly, abruptly silent. Upton tried to go to her, but a sharp blow caught him across the back of the head, and all he saw was darkness.

It was hours later when he awoke. The kitchen was empty, and he was on the floor. His cheek rested in a cold, sticky puddle, one that smelled like old copper pennies. *Blood*, he told himself as he sat up, and then *Adelaide's*. With the name came the memory of what had happened, and the sure knowledge that she was dead. Her body was gone, he saw, though the rest of the evidence of the battle remained: the dropped pot, the bloodstained clothes. Even his bag was unmolested in the corner where he'd dropped it.

All they'd wanted, it seemed, was her.

Well, Upton decided, they weren't going to get to have her. It was that simple.

LABOR COSTS

The factory was easy enough to infiltrate. The afternoon's excitement had died down and the crowds had dissipated, and under cover of darkness it was easy to get close to the building. Even at the late hour, it was still running full blast, and the thunderous clatter of the machinery within helped cover the sound of his steps. From there, it was a matter of tailing an unobservant guard on his rounds and slipping into the building behind him. When the man finally noticed someone behind him, he'd already outlasted his usefulness; Upton stashed his unconscious body in a closet, and borrowed his keys and gear before stepping onto the factory floor.

It was vast, bigger than Perry's place by far, and far more crowded. Looms and hoppers filled every available space, churning endlessly as they devoured raw materials and spat out cloth. Carts ran back and forth between the machines in corridors barely wide enough for a man, running full and empty in turn.

And nowhere were there any people.

No workers feeding fiber to the great machines. No one checking product as it came off the loom. No one adjusting feeds or tying knots or doing any of the million and one tasks that Upton knew were part and parcel of this form of operation.

In the entire juddering building, he was alone. It was just him and the machines.

Each of which, he now saw, had one thing in common, from cart to loom to carder. Every single one held a singular canister or light of some sort, a brass bracket holding a bluish glass capsule. They served no obvious purpose, and yet their omnipresence spoke to an underlying necessity. Frowning, he walked over to the nearest machine and hoisted himself up to where the canister had been inserted securely into the works. Steadying himself, he reached up and grasped it, in hopes of better understanding what it might be used for. His fingers brushed the surface of the glass, and the shock dropped him to his knees.

Not the electric current the device provided, though that was considerable. Instead, it was the shock of recognition, of understanding what was in those blue capsules.

Or rather, who.

And Adelaide, who had died earlier this day and who no doubt owed her employer a great debt, had already been put to work repaying it from beyond the grave.

At least, that was what she had told him.

Eventually, when he was able to bring himself to move once again, he removed the cylinder from the machine, and listened, gratified, as it ground to a halt. He thought about doing that for the others as well, but time was growing short, and he had no way to carry more than one with him. Instead, he contented himself with a visit to the factory's offices, making off with certain papers he found there and burning the rest, and then slipping off before anyone came to see why one of the looms had gone offline.

It was nearly dawn when he returned to Connecticut, returned to hammer on Asher Perry's factory door. After a minute, lights came on and voices sounded, and the great door creaked open to show an unkindly giant of a man in a nightshirt with a length of oak in his hand. "Go away," he said, but Upton was already pushing past him, into the factory.

"Perry? Perry!" he called. "I've got what you asked for. I've got everything you asked for, by God, and I'll not keep it a minute longer than necessary! Asher Perry, come out and take what's yours!"

A thick hand slammed onto his shoulder and spun him around. "That's enough out of you, I think," said the giant, and pushed him toward the door. "You want to see Mister Perry, you come back in the morning like a gentleman, you do."

"No, no, Hammond. It's fine. I've been expecting him." Perry's voice floated down from the top of the stairs. Both men looked up to see him there, his chair gleaming in the dim light and a look of weary anticipation on his face.

"Go on then," Hammond growled, and neatly reversed the direction he'd been pushing Upton in. "But make it quick. Mr. Perry needs his sleep."

"I have no intention of staying," Upton replied, and climbed the long iron stairwell up to where Perry sat, his footfalls echoing over the long rows of silent machines.

"Not here. In my office," Perry said when the younger man reached the top of the stairs, and so dutifully Upton followed him. "Shut the door," Perry said, and Upton did. "Hammond's no idea that there's any trouble, and I'd like to keep him innocent of such things if I can. Now, what do you have for me?"

"Everything you asked for," Upton replied, and reached into his satchel. Out came the battery, blue glass and brass, a thoroughly utilitarian design made for maximum use, not aesthetics. He put it down on the desk, though the sound of it hitting the wood was oddly muffled. Instead of a thud, it came out as almost a gasp.

Perry leaned forward and peered at the container. Deep within, a hazy form could be seen, swirling endlessly. "What is it?"

"The answer to how your competitors were able to up their

production. Take a close look and you'll see."

The older man stared for a minute, fascinated, before the blood abruptly drained from his face. "Good God," he said. "is it..."

Upton nodded. "It is. Every single one of their machines is powered by one of those. Every. Single. One."

Perry wheeled himself back from the desk, putting some distance between himself and the battery. His eyes stayed fixed on it, even as he spoke. "That...that's demonic!"

"It is. And it keeps their looms on line twenty-four hours a day. You wanted their secret, Mister Perry. Here it is." He tapped the pile of papers next to the battery. "Everything's in here. Schematics. Notes. Timetables and cost estimates. And if you're smart, you'll take it all and throw it in the fire."

"Indeed." Perry sounded distracted. Slowly, he wheeled himself back toward the desk.

"You weren't in there, Mister Perry. You didn't see the things I saw. Dead girls, Perry, dead girls with their souls wrung into glass bottles like cheap liquor, so they could keep working forever. You want no part of that here, I tell you."

Perry didn't answer. Instead, he reached out tentatively with one finger, tapping it on the glass of the battery. A faint blue spark leapt from the container to the tip of his finger, a soft keening rose up to be barely audible over the hum of the machines below. "Good God," he whispered, and reached out to cup it in both hands.

"Mister Perry, you must understand--"

"I understand perfectly, Mister Upton." He looked up from the battery, his face haggard. "The remainder of your money is downstairs, with Hammond. There's a bonus as well. Take it with my thanks for a job well done, and never darken my door again."

Upton didn't move. "You can't do this. It's hell you'd be building in here to save your little heaven. Even if it does keep the factory open, how long before they find out how you saved them? How long before they turn on you?"

Perry said nothing for a moment, turning the battery over and over in his hands as the ghost danced within. Upton waited for him to speak, then waited a while longer, then finally turned to go.

When he reached the door, Perry finally looked up. He spoke then, his voice low and his eyes straying to the window and the town beyond.

"I buy their cradles," he said. "I buy their coffins. What else would you have me do?"

MEEMAW'S
FROGS

Meemaw bought Luther a couple of frogs for his birthday, and Luther's Pa didn't like it one bit.

"Why you got to go and buy him frogs?" Pa asked. He tapped the side of the plastic cube the frogs swam in with one meaty finger, and the frogs kicked and jerked in response. "Boy his age, you should be buying him a football or something. Gonna buy him a pet, whyn't you buy him a dog?"

Meemaw, who was Pa's mother and thus used to him spouting off, shrugged and kept up working on her cross-stitch. "Luther don't want a football none," she said. "Luther don't play no sports at all. Boy just stays home and reads, is what he does."

Pa stared at the frogs for a minute. They were tiny little things, maybe an inch and a half long, all green and brown spots with bug eyes damn near popping out of their skulls. They'd come in this plastic cube mostly full of sand and water, with an ugly-ass plant in the middle and a little space for air up top. The cube was sealed, with just a hole a quarter inch across to drop food pellets into. "Damn things creep me out. How come the box is filled with water?"

"Girl at the store said they breathe water, Pa," Meemaw said patiently. "She said they didn't need nothing but food once-twice a week, and that they lived mebbe a year or so."

Pa squinted suspiciously. "Don't need to change the water?"

Meemaw kept cross-stitching, rocking back and forth on her chair nice and slow. "Nope."

"No cleaning up no frog poo?"

"Nope."

"No chance we gonna wake up one day and find a million baby frogs in there?"

"Nope," Meemaw jabbed her finger with a needle, swore a bit, and stuck it in her mouth. "Grrhh strr ssdd bbb."

"What?"

Meemaw took her finger out of her mouth and looked at it for a second to make sure it wasn't bleeding none. "I said, girl at the store--"

"What store?"

"The new one in town, the one with all them books and games and learning stuff. Luther likes it."

Pa drew in a breath to let Meemaw know, in no uncertain terms, that he didn't give one red damn what kinda store Luther liked, and that no son of his should like stores fulla books better than football, and that anyone who stayed at home all reading books and stuff on the computer when he could be outside doing chores or running through the woods or learning how to shoot was highly suspect, but Meemaw cut him off.

"I said, girl at the store where I bought them said they were both boys, and there weren't gonna be no frog babies."

"You telling me you got the boy frogs that are homosexual?"

Meemaw shook her head. "No, Pa. I got him frogs so he'd have something to take care of, and maybe keep him company." She looked over at the door to the boy's room. On the other side of it, he was no doubt sitting on his bed, reading a book. "Boy needs something to keep him company." Then she turned back to her cross-stitch, and the set of her shoulders said that there'd be no more discussion. You didn't push Meemaw at a time like that, and Pa knew it.

He grumbled under his breath that he'd rather have gotten the boy a damn dog instead.

Luther loved the frogs, and thanked both Meemaw and his Pa seven or eight times each; Meemaw for getting 'em for him, Pa for letting him keep 'em.

"S'okay," Pa had muttered. "You just take good care of 'em, you hear?"

"Yessir," Luther said and took them straightaway up to his room. He came back down half an hour later to announce that he'd set them up on the corner of his rickety old desk near the window, so they could get some sun once in a while, then ran back upstairs. An hour after that, he came down to say that he'd moved 'em to the nightstand 'cause it wasn't near as rickety. A half hour after that, he came down to say he'd decided to name 'em Dale and Cale, after Pa's favorite drivers, and after that, he didn't come downstairs no more to talk about them 'cause Pa had made a good dent on the case of Genny Cream Ale he'd bought himself for Luther's birthday, and he'd threatened to take a strap to the boy's backside if he ran down the damn stairs one more time to talk about the damn frogs.

Luther got the hint. He went back up to his room, shut the door, and, by Meemaw's estimation, spent the next hour trying to figure out how to tell which of the two frogs was Dale, and which one was Cale.

"Your son," Meemaw said, and went back to cross-stitch.

Luther was good as his word when it came to feeding the frogs. He would have walked them, too, and housebroken them as needed, but since they were frogs living in a plastic box, he had to settle for dropping four tiny brown food pellets into their tank, twice a week.

"Looks like turds," Pa grumbled to himself when he saw Luther do it, and wouldn't feed 'em himself until he heard Meemaw clearing her throat in the doorway behind him. Then he picked one pellet up, looked at it for a slow moment, and dropped it through the little hole into the tank. It sank, slowly, while Luther beamed at him and said, "See, Pa, it ain't so bad".

Pa grunted something that was pretty much just a grunt and watched the pellet fall. The two frogs hovered in the water, motionless, watching it slip past. He studied them and decided they were ugly cusses with warty little faces and fat, soft mouths. Then, all of a sudden, one- Cale or Dale, he couldn't tell which because they looked exactly the goddamn same--gave a little kick, sprang forward, and gulped that little pellet down.

"See, Pa! Isn't it amazing? He just snapped that right up!" Luther was all smiles and excitement.

"Disgusting, I mean, yeah, amazing," Pa answered him. "You sure they can't get out?"

"They couldn't get the lid off if'n they wanted to, Pa," Luther answered, all serious-like. "Can't reach it from the water line."

"Good," Pa said, and stomped out past Meemaw on his way to the teevee room.

"I think he likes you," Luther told the frogs, and dropped more pellets in the hole.

Come July, Luther got bundled up to go off to some camp or other. Meemaw'd arranged it all. She'd talked to the boy's teachers and gotten him on the list for what she told Pa was a science camp for promising but economically disadvantaged youth. Pa had asked what that meant, and Meemaw told him that it meant for four weeks, Luther was gonna get to play with the sorts of things only rich kids usually got to.

"As long as he doesn't get any ideas," Pa muttered, and gave his blessing.

Luther was overjoyed. After thanking both Meemaw and Pa for agreeing to let him go, and promising to write every day, and swearing to be a good boy who'd make 'em proud, Luther asked his Pa to do something for him.

"Feed the frogs while I'm gone, Pa? Would ya? You ain't gonna half to do it but once or twice a week." And Pa couldn't find it in his heart to say no, so he agreed to feed the damn frogs while Luther was gone.

"Thanks, Pa!" Luther said, and flung his arms around his father. "You're the best."

"Uh-huh," said Luther, and patted his boy on the back. "I guess I am."

Days passed. Pa dropped Luther off at the bus depot, where a school bus full of kids just like the boy was waiting to take them all off to wherever the heck they were going. Luther sat in the back row so he could wave to Pa out the rear window, until the bus finally pulled too far away for them to see each other.

Pa got back in his truck after that and headed back home.

He was alone in the house, Meemaw having taken her annual extended trip to go visit her sister in Branson. The quiet was nice, though Pa had to admit he missed the boy running downstairs to tell him the latest fool thing he'd done at school. He sat on the couch, turned on the teevee, and cracked open a beer.

Three weeks later and maybe three letters from Luther later, he remembered the frogs.

They were floating in their little cube when he found them. Cale was on his back, or maybe Dale was, but neither of 'em was moving. "Aww, crap," Pa said and flicked his finger against the plastic of the cube to see if either of 'em was still breathing.

Neither of 'em moved.

"Now come on, you damn...damn frogs! Git up! Move around some! Tell me you ain't dead!"

The frogs didn't move. They just drifted, lazy-like, across the top of the water.

Pa cussed a little and grabbed some of the food. He crammed it into the hole so fast half of the little turd pellets missed and bounced away. But a few made it into the water, and they either stuck on top and drifted with the frogs or sank like indecisive rocks, slowly to the bottom.

Pa cussed some more, then picked up the little plastic box and shook it. Some water sprayed out the top, and the sand and pebbles on the bottom of the case got all swirled around, but the frogs bashed against the sides and then floated away again. Plus, Pa realized as he shook it, the water inside smelled bad.

Hell, it smelled terrible.

It smelled like dead things were floating in it. Which, he was pretty sure, there were.

Pa cussed one last time, then put the case down on the windowsill. He considered calling Meemaw to ask her advice, but that seemed like a bad idea. She'd give him no end of hell about forgetting his promise to the boy and forgetting to feed the damn frogs, and what he needed right now was solid advice, not some goddamn guilt trip.

His next thought was that he'd go down to the store where Meemaw had bought them and get replacement frogs. As far as he was concerned, all of them looked just the same. And even though Luther swore he could tell Dale from Cale, he was pretty sure the boy wouldn't be able to tell the difference.

The problem being, when he called the shop where Meemaw had gotten them, the young thing on the other end of the line said they didn't carry them anymore. She said they were a seasonal item, and this apparently wasn't the season, and besides, there'd been some kind of health scare off in Oregon or Minnesota or someplace like that about how some of the frogs had come to the US sick with some kind of disease, and--

Pa hung up halfway through the explanation.

Time, he thought, for plan B. Which was to leave the frogs right where they were. Then when Luther came back and found 'em like that, he'd act all surprised and say, "Well, they were fine the last time I fed them." Which, he thought, was sorta kinda technically the truth.

But either way, Luther would get over it, and then he'd get the kid a proper pet, like a dog, or a, well, a dog.

And satisfied with his decision, he walked out of Luther's room and shut the door behind him.

When Luther came home, he hopped out of Pa's truck before it was fairly stopped moving. He ran right past Meemaw doing her cross-stitch in a rocker in the front room and went straight up the stairs without hardly saying a word. The door opened, the door closed, and Pa braced himself for the explosion. In a way, he was almost looking forward to it. He'd been practicing his "surprised" look for a week, and wanted to get some use out of it afore he forgot how.

Any second now, he told himself. Any second.

A minute passed. Then another one did. And another, and another. It was a full quarter hour before Luther came rattling back down the stairs.

"Thank you, Pa!" Luther said, grabbing Pa in a hug. "Thank you for takin 'such good care of Cale and Dale while I was gone!"

"I swear, they were fine when I--" Pa stopped and blinked. "I mean, of course, son. Gotta take responsibility for your responsibility."

"They look great, Pa. Thank you so much!" Luther gave him one last squeeze, then ran back upstairs. "I'll tell you all 'bout camp later," he yelled as he went. "We made a robot!"

Then his door slammed again, with Pa looking up the stairs after him, and Meemaw looking at Pa.

"I saw your face there, boy," she said. "Turn around and look at me."

Slowly, staring down at his shoes, Pa did. Meemaw nodded.

"Thought so. You didn't do no caretaking of them frogs. I'm guessing you thought they was dead, didn't you?"

Pa nodded, miserable-like. "They were dead. I saw 'em. Shook 'em up. Tried everything to get 'em to move. They just floated there, dead-like."

Meemaw's mouth narrowed in disapproval. "And you decided that you'd lie to your own son about that rather than take responsibility. I despair of the days I spent raising you, son, if you treat your own son that way."

"I tried to replace 'em," Pa said, by way of defending himself. "But the store said they didn't carry them no more and that some of the frogs had been all sick, and--"

She cut him off. "Well, I'm thinking it's more likely that you went up there when those little fellers were sleeping and thought they were dead. You never were too too bright." Pa opened his mouth to protest, but Meemaw shushed him. "Don't argue none, 'cause it's true. Now you just go on up there and tell your son how glad you are that his pet frogs are alive and well, and I will make sure that boy never leaves them in your care again."

Pa stared at her for a minute. Meemaw stared back, and as usual, Pa folded. "Yes'm," he said and started up the stairs.

"And don't you have one of them fits of conscience and say nothing, you hear me!" Her words chased him the rest of the way, and he went into Luther's room.

The boy was sitting next to the window when Pa came in, hunched over and talking to the plastic tank. Inside, the frogs didn't seem like they were paying no attention, swimming in lazy little circles in the cloudy water.

"Son," Pa said.

"Oh, hi, Pa," said Luther, half turned around. "Didn't hear you come in. I was telling Cale and Dale all about camp."

"I thought it was Dale and Cale," Pa said.

"Nope. Cale and Dale. That one there's Cale. You can tell on account of the way he's kind of got that little pattern of spots on his head, right there. Can you see it?"

Pa leaned in and stared at the frog Luther indicated, trying to discern any possible pattern of dots that might be visible. He saw none.

The frog--Cale, if Luther was to be believed--stopped swimming. It held there in the water, bulgy eyes staring out at Pa. It made Pa uneasy, especially cause that stare made him feel like that damn frog wasn't looking at him so much as it was looking into him, or maybe through him.

A frog ought not to do that to a man.

"Luther!" Meemaw's voice came up from the downstairs. "I need you in the kitchen, boy. Finish up what you're doin 'and git on down. Those 'taters ain't gonna peel themselves!"

"Yes, Meemaw," Luther answered. "You can stay here if you want, Pa. The frogs like you."

"They what?" Pa asked, but Luther was already gone. Windsocks would have flapped in the breeze at his departure. Pa stared after him for a minute, then turned back to the tank. Both frogs were now floating upside down, eyes closed and mouths open.

"Holy crap!" said Pa and picked the tank up. "Don't be dead, you can't be dead!" He pulled the tank close to his face, staring in at the now-motionless creatures. "You were just fine a minute ago! Don't you dare, you hear me?"

There was a moment of stillness. Then both frogs flipped over and started swimming. One bumped its snout up against the plastic on the side Pa was staring into and, with infinite deliberation, closed one froggy eye for a half second. It held Pa's gaze a minute longer, then swam away.

"Son of a bitch," Pa said. He put the tank down and backed away.

Over the course of the next week, the tank got noticeably cloudier, to the point where Meemaw suggested that it was high time that someone changed the water. Pa wanted no part of it, but lucky for him, Luther said he'd do it.

"My frogs, Pa," he said, and went off toward the kitchen.

"Why's he going to the kitchen?" Pa asked.

"He's settin 'out some water. Got to let it stand to get enough air in it for the frogs to breathe proper," Meemaw replied. "Tomorrow, he'll do the switch. Just don't go drinking out of that pitcher."

"Huh," said Pa. "Imagine that."

Pa couldn't sleep that night. Every time he closed his eyes he'd see that one frog what ought to have been dead give him that slow wink, and that would make him sit straight up, all bug-eyed and afraid.

Finally, he couldn't take it no more and swung himself out of bed. The snoring told him that Meemaw was still asleep and Luther had gone to bed hours ago. He snuck downstairs and into the kitchen. The pitcher of water the boy had left out was right where he'd left it, on the counter. Presumably, it was sucking down air, though Pa couldn't see it.

Instead, he picked up the pitcher and dumped the water down the drain. Then he set the pitcher back down on the counter and snuck right back on up the stairs to his bedroom. Those frogs weren't getting their water changed tomorrow, no sir. That meant the lid would stay on their little case for another day, and that meant there was no chance they'd get out and do whatever it is that inch-long zombie frogs do.

He had no idea, he reflected, what they might do--try and eat him, mebbe--but whatever it was, it was bound to be no good, and he'd stopped it from mebbe happening for one more night.

He closed his eyes and slept. And tiny dead frogs chased him through his dreams.

In the morning, Luther didn't say nothing about the empty pitcher. He just filled it back up again. Meemaw gave Pa the stink-eye, and the frogs 'water looked a mite worse than it had the day before, but that was the extent of things.

That night, Pa poured the water out again.

In the morning, Luther looked at him funny but didn't say nothing this time, neither. And so they went back and forth, Luther filling it up and Pa emptying it for the better part of a week and a half. Meanwhile, the water in the little tank got a little fouler every day 'til you could barely see the frogs swimming in it. Pa was just fine with that, but Luther wasn't 'cause he thought his frogs might drown in the mess. So he got up the guts to ask Pa if he was maybe sleepwalking and pouring out the water in his sleep, and Pa allowed as how that might be the case (even with Meemaw staring daggers at him while he told the bald-faced lie).

"Then I'll take the pitcher and put it in my room, and lock the door," Luther said. "That way you won't knock it over in your sleep, Pa."

"That's smart thinking, son," Pa said weekly, while he tried to figure how he could get hisself into Luther's room and dump that water without waking the boy up in the middle of the night.

Thing was, he couldn't see how. And so the next morning during breakfast, Luther announced his intention to change the water that day. Pa choked on his coffee and shot damn near half a biscuit out his nose. Meemaw thumped him on the back until he stopped coughing, at which point he allowed that it might be best if Luther did that while Pa was off at work. To give the frogs time to get used to their new home, y'see, before Pa came home.

Luther, whom Pa was beginning to suspect didn't have the good sense God gave a discarded pack of cigarettes, thought this was a good idea. And so Pa went out to the garage and Luther went off to the bathroom, on account of him not wanting to spill nasty old frog water everywhere in the kitchen.

That night, when Pa came home, Luther was waiting for him on the porch. He looked upset.

"What's wrong, son?" Pa asked as that was the fatherly thing to do.

"It's Cale and Dale, Pa," said Luther. "I was switching their water and I turned around and they disappeared!"

Pa took a step back. "Disappeared? You mean they went poof like on the teevee?"

"I mean they must've got away. I'd used Meemaw's spaghetti spoon and picked 'em up to put 'em in the fresh water while I dumped out the old stuff, and I got rid of the dirty water, and I turned around to pour the clean water in and they were gone! Must've hopped out or something!"

"Mebbe they went down the sink," Pa said, thinking it would a fine thing if they had gone down the sink, or maybe the crapper.

"They might still be in the u-bend, then. Can you look?

Please, Pa, can you look?" Luther's eyes got big as saucers, 'til Pa had to look away. He mumbled someone about getting the damn tool kid, and cursed himself for six kinds of fool when Luther ran off to get it. He didn't want to open the sink up, 'cause only bad things would happen if he did. If he was lucky, the frogs would be gone, and then Luther would bawl his eyes out. If he wasn't, the frogs would be in there, those damn dead frogs with their staring eyes and nasty slimy skin and--

"Here you go, Pa!" Luther dropped the toolbox at his feet, making one hell of a racket. Pa picked it up and headed to the bathroom, muttering under his breath as Luther tagged along. He cut the water and unscrewed the u-bend from the sink, and then handed the part to Luther. "Take a look for your frogs, son. If they ain't in there, then I don't know where they are."

And that was the problem, Pa realized. If they weren't in the U-bend, well, mebbe they had gone all the way down the drain.

Then again, mebbe they hadn't. They could have fooled Luther--Lord knew *that* wasn't hard--and hidden somewhere in the bathroom. They could wait there until night, then come out and go looking for him. He'd be in bed asleep, and he'd have bad dreams about slimy cold things on his face, and then he'd wake up and see them right there, sitting on him, staring at him, and then they'd--

"They're not in here, Pa. They're gone!" Luther sadly handed the u-bend back to Pa, who gave it a look to double-check.

"I'm sorry, son," said Pa. "Better go tell Meemaw. She got you them frogs."

"Yessir," Luther said and shuffled off down the hall. Pa watched him go, then turned back to repair the sink. He did it careful, and he did it slow. And he did it expecting any minute now, he'd be feeling little froggy feet on the back of his neck.

Instead, he got Meemaw yelling his name. And that made him straighten up, which meant hitting his head on the underside of the sink, which meant cussing, which Meemaw didn't approve of, so she yelled his name again. This time, he managed to pull himself out, and turn 'round and look at her.

"You're gonna find them frogs," she told him. "No ifs, no ands, no buts."

"Meemaw, they're gone," he said. "I took apart the sink. They weren't nowhere in there. Gotta be halfway to the water treatment plant by now."

"If they are, you'd better start a-running. Cause that boy of yours loved them frogs, loved 'em real good."

Pa sighed. "Meemaw, I gotta tell you, there was something 'bout those frogs that just wasn't right."

"Do tell."

"You know I killed 'em, right? I didn't feed 'em and I killed 'em and they was dead. And then Luther comes home, and suddenly they ain't dead, and so help me God, I caught 'em looking at me. I'm telling you, it ain't right."

Meemaw cocked her head. "And who's fault is that?" Pa opened his mouth to answer, but before he could Meemaw pointed and said, "Is that one of them there?"

"Where?" Pa tried to back away and get up and hunker down all at the same time, which meant he banged his head on the sink again. While he was lying there cussing, Meemaw smiled at him. "Nope, guess I was just seeing things. Happy hunting, son."

For the first time in his life, Pa considered moving out of the house he'd been born in.

He spent the rest of the evening looking for the frogs, Pa did, with a little help from Luther. Luther looked upstairs in his room, while Pa looked pretty much everywhere else. He looked in the kitchen. He looked in the icebox. He looked under beds and in closets and down in the cellar and up in the attic, and he looked in places no self-respecting frog had any business going.

Of the frogs, there was no sign. Luther started out hopeful, but that only lasted a couple of hours. By the end of the night he was sad and dragging, and Pa ordered him off to bed. As for Pa, he kept looking a while longer, but not too much longer. Eventually he gave up and popped open a beer, which he drank a little faster than normal. Then Pa took himself off to bed, set the alarm, and closed his eyes.

In the dark, he thought he heard croaking.

That was stupid, he told himself. Dale and Cale didn't croak. Never had when they were alive, weren't going to start now that they were dead.

He closed his eyes again. Thought about sleeping. Thought about Cale and Dale waiting for him to fall asleep. Waiting for him to be on his back with his mouth open, snoring like he did (according to Meemaw, who made a fuss about such things). Waiting for him to be defenseless. Helpless. Waiting to do something terrible.

He sat up then, and didn't close his eyes again that night.

One night turned into two turned into three, and Pa started looking like a wreck. His eyes got bloodshot and his hands got shaky. He couldn't hardly eat, he couldn't hold down beer, and twice he nearly took his truck into the ditch out where the Masonville Road crossed Route 86. At home, he kept looking for the frogs, even after Luther gave up.

"They gotta be here somewhere," he said. "Gotta be." Luther told him it was OK, and that Cale and Dale were in a better place, but that didn't stop Pa. He was convinced now, convinced the frogs wanted blood for blood and were waiting in the house for the right moment to strike.

Even Meemaw couldn't convince him to stop looking. Pa didn't go so far as to say she was in cahoots with them when she tried, but didn't say she wasn't neither. Eventually, she gave up and went back to her knitting, saying Pa must've gotten concussion on the bottom of that sink, and that only time would fix him up.

Pa heard her grumbling, and he shook his head. He didn't have concussion. He knew the frogs were out there. And he knew they were waiting for him to let his guard down--if he didn't find them first. Even if between himself and Luther, every inch of that house had been searched and no one had said they'd seen the frogs, Pa knew the truth.

It was late at night on a Sunday, a full two weeks after the frogs had vanished. Luther was in bed, reading under the covers with the help of a flashlight. Downstairs, Pa had been crashing around in the kitchen all night, shouting 'bout how Dale and Cale were hiding somewhere in Meemaw's pots. The banging had been going on for a full hour, and Luther expected it to go on for a few hours more. That was life with Pa these days, but that was all right. A fella could get used to most anything if he put his mind to it.

"Ain't that right, boys?" he said to the frogs perched on the edge of his bed. "Don't you worry none. I ain't gonna let Pa find you so he can hurt you again. Y'all can just stay here, with me, forever." He held out his hand, and one by one, Dale and Cale hopped up into it.

They sat there for a second, and then slowly, all careful-like, one of them winked.

A MEETING
IN
THE DEVIL'S
HOUSE

No roads led to the house where I was going, and you couldn't find it on any map. Built before the War of Northern Aggression, it had wrapped itself in fog and moss and vanished into history like a leading lady walking offstage before the wrinkles could begin to show. To find it, you had to know where it was, and to know where it was you had to have been there already. This kept the fools and the drifters and the tax men far from her doors, allowing her to slowly crumble, at her own pace and without any witnesses.

But I had business there, and I knew where I was going. Had been there before, on business other than mine, and so the path was familiar. Officially the place was in Mississippi, or it had been once upon a time, but when I turned onto the dirt road that led down into the mist, all the names and labels went away.

The last time the house had been painted, it had been painted white. It still held that color in most places, the ones where vines hadn't wrapped themselves around columns and up waterspouts and given the place an accent in dark green. All those columns still stood, holding up the roof over a porch that by rights should have moldered into sagging, broken wood.

It hadn't. Nor had the front door fallen from its hinges,

though the brass knocker that once adorned the heavy wood had long since been ripped out and carried away. I'd heard what had happened to the man who'd done that once, and I had no need to hear the story ever again.

The door was unlocked, as I'd known it would be. I swung it open and the floorboards sang under my feet as I stepped inside. Light punched its way in through clouds and cobwebbed windows, enough to see by but not enough to see well, but I already knew what I'd find. Old furniture under tattered drop cloths, stacks of old wood by fireplaces that would prove clean enough to use, and everywhere dust, dust, dust. Broad stairs still ran up to the second floor, with no holes or rotted out boards that I could see. Then again, I couldn't see too far. Halfway up, they vanished into the dark.

I thought about going up there, just to see what was still there to be seen. Then I came to my senses, and went back to the kitchen. Sturdy furniture was all through the house, couches and beds and overstuffed chairs, but I'd be damned if I was going to sleep on it. I knew who owned this house, and the price he extracted for favors. Instead, I made a supper of what I had in my pack, then found a place against a wall to set myself for the night. I did set a small fire, more for light than for heat, but that was the only concession to comfort I made. And night fell, and the shadows wrapped their loving arms around the house, and the crackle of the fireplace mostly drowned out the ghosts in the hall.

The next morning, the stranger came up the walk. He was middle aged, finely dressed and going bald, and he had the guilty look of a man who'd lied to his wife about where he was going. Navy suit and nice shoes, now scuffed and muddy, and the watch on his wrist was heavy and expensive looking.

He stopped, maybe twenty feet short of the front steps, and pulled a handkerchief out of his breast pocket to dab at his brow. It was hot out, a sick, sticky heat that wrapped you up and held you a little too close, and if the sun wasn't shining through the clouds it didn't skimp on warming them. Water dripped off the trees, running down the beards of moss and tap-tap-tapping onto the wet ground while the stranger stood there and looked the place up and down. It was clear he wanted no part of walking forward; just as clear he couldn't go back.

He wiped his forehead again, then tucked the wet kerchief back in his pocket and took out a phone. I could have told him it wasn't going to work--nothing like that worked in that house, where time had kicked back and taken it easy a hundred fifty years prior. But I didn't say anything; some things a man has to figure out for himself.

I watched him try a few calls, get nothing, panic, and try again. About the forth go-round, when it looked like he might do himself some harm, I stepped out and called to him.

"Hey there," I said. "You looking for someone?"

He screamed, a little boy's scream that should have been funny coming out of a big man but wasn't. The phone fell down into the mud, and he stared up at me with wide eyes.

"You ... you ..." he said, even as he knelt down to rummage for his phone. "You're ... you must be ... I'm here to ..."

I held up a hand to stop his rambling. "Peace, friend. I've got no call to hurt you."

His jaw worked for a bit before words came back out. "You ... is this your place?"

I shook my head. "Not hardly, though I know the owner.

Supposed to meet him here, or at least that's what he asked me to do."

"Ah." The man sagged, like he was being held up by invisible strings gone slack. "I'm here to meet someone, too. A business meeting." He looked around nervously. "I didn't know there'd be someone else here."

"He didn't tell me you'd be coming, neither," I said, and stepped down off the porch. He didn't move, didn't do anything but blink. I held out my hand to him. "Name's Eli."

He reached out of my hand, remembered he still had his phone, swapped hands, then realized he had mud on his fingers from the phone still. That led to a round of wiping his hands on his slacks, until he realized that they were expensive, which lead to more fumbling, until I finally couldn't take any more, and took his hand for a shake.

"Olsen, Tim Olsen," he said. "I work in, well, never mind what I work in." He looked around then, and straightened up, and cocked his head at me. "You set up inside?"

"I am," I allowed.

"Then what do you say we go in and talk. I don't like the like of that sky."

It wasn't the sky that I didn't like, but I wasn't going to tell him that. It was the sudden silence that had fallen down over the house and grounds. Somewhere, a drop of water fell off a tree branch and headed for the ground; the snare drum tat-tat it made when it hit was louder than it had any right to be. Otherwise, there was nothing.

Well, not exactly nothing. No sound, sure. But if you breathed deep and were looking for it, you'd find a faint hint of sulfur.

I shut the door behind us when we walked in, but didn't lock it. Anything that was supposed to be here, it wouldn't do no good, and nothing that was unwanted here set foot on the grounds to their own peril. Olsen let me lead him back to the kitchen, his head on a swivel as he took the place in.

"Nice," he said. "Must be expensive keeping this place up."

"I believe the owner has made certain arrangements," I replied, and kept walking. Behind me, I could hear Olsen choke for a moment.

The fire was low in the kitchen, so I built it back up while Olsen wandered around and poked his nose into the cabinets. "No food, I see."

"Nope," I replied. "But you're welcome to share what's mine."

"Thank you," he said, and nodded gravely. "I didn't realize I was going to need to accommodate myself, or I would have brought provision with. When I was told to come to this house …" He spread his arms wide and let his voice drop off. "You get invited to a man's house, you expect he's going to put food on the table."

"This is a special house," I said, keeping my voice neutral, and set about making some coffee. "Just as well not to eat or drink anything of this place. Don't want to find yourself obligated."

"Oh, I'm already--" he started, but a sound outside cut him off. It was a howl, a long, high howl that climbed in through the windows and bounced itself off the walls. It was an angry howl, a hungry howl, and it was loud.

Which meant the thing that made it was close.

"What the hell was that?" Olsen asked, his face pale.

"Not sure," I said, though I was surer than most might have been. "Nothing you want to meet face to face, though."

Olsen nodded. "The windows shut on this place? Doors locked?"

I didn't have the heart to tell him that if it wanted in, it was getting in, so I just nodded.

"Good," he said, and shuddered as the howl came again. "Would hate to miss my meeting 'cause I got eaten."

"I don't think there's any fear of that," I told him, and pulled a couple of cups out of my pack. "Coffee's ready, if you want."

"Don't mind if I do." He walked over, throwing a glance down the hall as he did. The hand that took the coffee wasn't shaking, but there was tension in the fingers. Olsen himself looked like a bundle of tangled wire now, all jangled nerves stretched taut against one another.

"What kind of meeting are you here for," I asked, and in that moment he dropped the cup. It was tin, so it didn't break when it hit, but the coffee splashed all around as it bounced and spun and rolled away.

We both watched it go, silent 'til it rolled to a stop in a corner. "Sorry," Olsen said. "Just ... nervous about the meeting, that's all."

"I don't blame you." I nodded to the cup where it sat. "Refill?"

"If you don't mind."

"I don't mind at all."

The day rolled on and we drank more coffee, and talked about things that didn't matter at all. Olsen admitted he didn't quite know when this meeting of his was likely to be, as his watch had stopped working along with his phone as soon as he'd set foot on the property.

The howls stopped after the second one, at least until the sun went down behind those moss-hung trees. Thereafter we could hear it, faint and off in the distance, along with the sound of something big crashing through the trees.

They didn't get any closer, but by the way Olsen kept looking at the door I knew the man didn't want to sleep downstairs. Sure enough, he asked if there were fireplaces in the bedrooms upstairs.

"Might've asked that when there was still light," I said, but it was easy enough to rig a torch, and Olsen himself took an armload of wood from one of those neat piles. Then it was up the stairs and into the dark, with dust choking our footsteps and rising up to fill our lungs.

"Footsteps," Olsen said, coughing and pointing.

"Mine," I told him, and it was true. He waited for me to say more, and when I didn't, he kept moving. The hallway was broad, too broad for the torch to light properly, but what could be seen mirrored the downstairs. Cloth covered mirrors and art, dust covered the rugs and everything else.

"To the left," I told Olsen. "There's a bedroom at the front of the house. Or there was, last time I was here."

"You think the owner's changed things?"

"Not hardly."

And sure enough, there the bedroom was, its four-poster clean and uncovered, and its fireplace neat and ready for use.

Olsen stopped for a moment, so I busied myself starting the

fire. After a minute, we had warmth and a fair bit of light, and he looked around the room.

There were no drop cloths on the furniture here. No covers on the mirrors, no hangings covering the portraits of men and women who'd lived and died in this house decades before. The dust stopped at the door, not a speck of it to be found.

"This isn't right," Olsen said. "This place was prepared."

"He knew you were coming, I believe," I said mildly.

Olsen shook his head. "But the dust outside. The footprints. This isn't right."

"Nothing here's right," I told him. "But here's clearly the place you were meant to be tonight."

"Oh." He looked surprised again. "In here."

I nodded. "But I reckon I'll stay too. No sense getting too spread out in a place like this. Too big for two men."

He blushed a little bit. "But there's one bed, and I--"

I cut him off. "I'll sleep against the wall. That bed's meant for you." Last comfort you'll have, I thought to myself, but didn't say. "Besides, I don't like owing a thing to the one who owns this place. Use of a bed for a night's more of a debt than I care to incur."

His mouth formed an "o." "If you think I shouldn't--" he started.

"It's for you," I said wearily. "Trust me. Now get some sleep. You've been traveling. I'll keep watch, keep an eye out for the ghosts."

"Ghosts?" He thought about it for a minute, then came to a conclusion. "All right then. If a place on God's green earth were to have ghosts, this surely would be it."

"They'll mostly stay in the hall," I told him. "I'll see to it. You get some sleep."

He sat on the bed and shucked off his shoes. "Seems strange to be trusting a man I don't know to watch over me while I sleep in this place," he said.

I didn't turn my head away from the hallways, where the shadows were starting to move. "You're here for a reason that's stranger."

"How much do you know," he asked. "About why I'm here."

"Enough. And you know I'm not here to do you harm."

"Not if you're here for the same thing I am." He snorted, then slid himself under the covers. "Night, Eli. Thank you for the watching."

"It's what I do," I told him, but he was already asleep.

Morning came wrapped in fog, with no sign of our host. I portioned out breakfast from what was in my pack, coffee and some hard cheese and bread, and Olsen and I ate in silence. When we finished, I suggested we take a walk through the trees, as staying cooped up in the house was liable to make both of us a bit tetched. Olsen declined, however, saying whatever made those howls might still be out there. If I didn't mind, he'd stay in the house.

"You do that," I said and took myself downstairs. All the dust was swept away now, I could see, and all the drop cloths had been pulled away. The house looked ready for company, though I'd neither seen nor heard anyone else during the night. 'Cept the ghosts, of course, but they had their own business to be about and didn't seem the type to do tidying.

The front door was open, which didn't surprise me, so I

walked down and out and into the trees. The fog was thick, rolling up to the edge of the porch and no further, but a dozen yards from the house it had vanished entire into the mist. Another man might have worried about getting lost; me, I wanted to stretch my legs among the cypresses.

And as I walked, I saw him there. The owner, the one whose will kept this place as it was and ruled all within it.

The Devil.

He stood in the shadow of one of the trees, back pressed up against it, slouch hat low over his eyes. And he saw me, and he saw that I saw him, and he smiled for an instant before he vanished.

I knew better than to run over to where he'd been. There'd be nothing there; there never was. Instead, I kept walking, and there he was again, up ahead on the left. A nod, a smile and he was gone again, only to reappear high up on a branch, then off in the distance, then behind me so close I could feel the heat of his breath.

"What do you want?" I finally said, with no hope of an answer.

"The last thing you think," he said, and then with brimstone stink, he wasn't there anymore. I turned to look for him, knowing I'd find nothing but feeling like I ought to do so anyway. Sure enough, he was gone. Maybe there was a streak of reddish-black in the fog where he'd been, maybe there wasn't. But I was alone out in the fog, a long way from the house, and he knew where I was.

Off in the distance and in the dark, something growled. Something big.

Maybe I wasn't as alone as I thought.

I ran. I ran for where I thought the house was, and I ran

without looking behind me. The beast in the cypresses was on the move, I could hear that much, and it was coming my way. If I stopped, if I looked back it would surely catch me, and then no power on earth could save me.

So I ran, with branches breaking behind me, and when the house loomed up out of the mist I made straight for it. Up the porch and slamming the door behind me I went, pelting up those stairs.

"Eli?" Olsen's voice came from the room where I'd left him. I didn't waste the time to answer. Instead, I ran down the hall and in, and looked out the window.

After a moment, Olsen joined me.

"There," I said and pointed down.

He looked. And he saw.

"What's that?" Olsen breathed.

"The owner? That's his dog," I said. Outside, a huge black hound scratched at the dirt with those claws the color of dried blood and old fires. Each paw was maybe nine inches across; each claw a good curved two inches. Its eyes were red, too, and too big for that wicked hound dog face they were set into. It stood there, steaming quietly in the rain while little tongues of flame licked in and out of its mouth like it was breathing. It took a couple of steps forward, and the turf where it had been standing was pushed down and burned black.

"It's huge," Olsen said after a moment's staring.

I shrugged. "The Devil likes big dogs."

"I'll bet he does."

The hound was sniffing the air now, muzzle raised and eyes narrowed.

"What's it looking for?" Olsen asked.

I thought about saying "us," but that'd be unkind. "You," I told him instead. "I'd hold still, myself. Make a noise. It's liable to hear you."

Olsen nodded, not trusting himself to speak. Instead, he backed slowly away from the window, one slow step after the other.

The hound was moving now, taking a couple of steps toward the house, then stopping to sniff the air again. I stayed where I was, watching it trot closer to the front door. Behind me, Olsen crouched down, shaking with fear. Both hands were over his mouth, the better to keep himself from making a sound.

It stopped.

Looked up.

Those dried blood red eyes met mine.

And then something made a noise off in the trees, and it was gone.

"Mother of God," Olsen said, and collapsed onto the floor.

"I wouldn't say that," I told him, and offered him a hand up. He ignored it and sat there, rocking back and forth.

"I didn't believe," he said. "I mean, I knew, but I didn't believe. Oh, God, it's real, it's real, it's all real."

"That's why you're here, isn't it?" I pulled a bottle out of my pack, then sat beside him. "You made the deal, your time ran out, and you came here to pay the piper."

Olsen nodded, miserable. "First I saw you, I thought you were him. Didn't realize you'd made a deal, too."

"My deal's different," I said. My deal was no deal, not worth explaining to a man whose last hours were running out. "But I was told to be here. Now tell me what happened."

With a shake, he pulled himself together. Behind us, the fire crackled and popped.

"I made a bargain," Olsen said. "Made a pretty good one, too. So I told myself, and for a while, I listened."

"No deal with the Devil's a good one," I told him, and passed him the bottle. He took it, took a swig without pausing, and passed it back to me.

"I had an out, you see," he said, and wiped his mouth with the back of his sleeve. "You don't get those often, I don't think.

But he gave me one."

I set the bottle down. "Damn near never," I agreed. "So what'd he give you?"

"The usual." Olsen shrugged. "Success, mostly. Success in everything I set my hand to. Business? Every venture was golden. Love? The woman I dreamed of fell into my arms. All of it, boilerplate and there for the taking."

I didn't say anything. It wasn't my place to do so.

"And he gave me a way out. Easiest one in the world."

Absently, he reached for the bottle, and I slid it closer to him. "All I had to do was get someone to take the same deal I'd taken. Same benefits, same out clause, same everything. Do that, and the lien on my soul would be free and clear." He took another sip. "That was the plan, you know. Make my pile, then pass it along before the bill came due."

"What happened?" I prompted him. "Couldn't find anyone to take the deal?"

Olsen shook his head. The shadows were longer now, creeping across the floor like a flood of black water lapping up against us. "Found too many. Greedy men, desperate men, fools--all kinds. But I realized something."

"Sending another man to hell puts a mark on a man," I said without judgment. "I can see why you'd walk away."

Olsen wagged a finger at me, a schoolteacher's gesture for a student who jumped to the easy conclusion. "Not it at all. There's plenty of men that deserve hell that I've known, and most of them would have jumped at the chance for half of what I had. No, it was something else. I looked around, you see."

"Looked around?"

"Looked around. At the success that the bargain gave me. And I realized, it didn't just happen. It had to come from somewhere. If my venture prospered, it was because a dozen hard-working men saw theirs fail. Didn't matter if they were better or smarter or more deserving. If I set my mind to something, I'd have their success and they'd be left behind."

He took a long pull on the bottle, then set it ruefully aside.

"Same thing with my wife. She'd been with a man, a good man, when I set my cap for her. And she died, and she needed comfort, and God Almighty, isn't that still a canker in my soul."

He looked up at me then, and I met his eyes. He didn't look away, not for a long minute. "You see why I didn't pass it along, then?"

I nodded. "Another man takes that bargain, might not care about the damage he did along the way. Might enjoy it, even."

Olsen's face was grim. "Yep. And that, I didn't want to carry with me, 'cause it would be a hell all its own. Better to pay the bill on my own damnation than forge another link on that chain."

I thought for a moment, then chose my words carefully. "Sounds like you outsmarted the Devil, at least a little bit. He ain't going to like that."

"He set the terms."

"Doesn't mean he'll be happy when he figures it out."

"Look," Olsen said. "For twenty-five years, I've known I was going to hell. I've been waiting for this day half my life. Now the bill's come due, and I'm ready to pay. Ready to stop worrying, ready to stop living in fear. And this is the one thing I can take with me into the dark and into the fire--that I didn't drag anyone else down with me."

I thought about saying something, but something else beat me to it. There was a splintering crash from downstairs, the sound of old wood reaching its breaking point in a moment of sudden fury.

"What the hell is that?" Olsen shouted, and then there was a howl and another crash, and we both knew.

"He sent the hound for you!" I said, and rose up. "Quick!"

Olsen was up now, too, pale and sweating but resolute. "You think we can run from that?"

"I think we'd better!"

There was another almighty crack and the sound of heavy wood hitting the floor. I grabbed Olsen by the wrist and ran.

At the top of the stairs, I looked down. The door was half gone, huge chunks of it gouged out and scattered on the floor. Through the gaps I could see the hound, its claws working at the remaining barrier in a fury.

"Before it sees us," I shouted and pulled Olsen along. He didn't resist, but he didn't help none, either. Instead, he just stumbled on, looking back toward the sound of claws scrabbling on wood.

"Why are you doing this?" he shouted. "Leave me!"

"Something's not right!" I ran down the hall, headed for the back stairs. Around one corner and then another we went, even as the thwack of wood on wood told us the hound had finished its work down below. "I saw him this morning. I talked to him, and he said—"

But then a howl rushed up from below and near bowled us over. I could hear claws on wood and the heavy thump of a body moving up the stairs; the hound was inside.

"There!" I said, and pointed to the back stairs. They were narrow, and they curved in a thin spiral too tight to take fast.

Too thin for the hound, too, I was thinking, and I shoved Olsen forward. "Down! Go!"

"What about you?"

"I'll be right behind you. Run!"

Run he did, even as a thud at the top of the stairs told me the hound had reached the second floor.

I thought about running and following Olsen. Thought about drawing the hound off and leading it on a merry chase through the house, hoping I still had enough of the Devil's favor that I might maybe survive. Thought about fighting, though I knew that was hopeless.

Behind me, Olsen's steps rang out loud against the wrought iron of the staircase. He was running for all he was worth, panting loud and hard as he ran. Ahead of me, the hound slammed into a wall at speed as it tried to take a corner. It shook its head, chuffed deep in its throat, and turned to work up more speed.

It saw me then, saw me standing there between it and its prey. Its ears went back and it growled, deep and low enough to shake a man's bones clear out of his skin. Flames twined up from its eyes, and from the corner of its mouth. Those close, those big red claws, they dug trenches into the floor with every step as it advanced.

It occurred to me that I didn't know Olsen very well. It also occurred to me that I was doing a damn fool thing and that I was about to do another.

Olsen ran. The hound advanced. And I held up one hand and said, "Sit!"

It sat. And it looked at me. And it laughed.

It laughed in the Devil's voice, of course. It laughed long and it laughed loud, and when it was done laughing, it said, "Eli, I've got a special place for fools just like you. That was the bravest damn fool thing I've seen in a thousand years."

"Best be paying more attention," I said, and cocked my head. "You going to catch him and take his soul?"

"That was the bargain." The great red tongue was hanging out now, the hound panting with the effort of making human words. "I do keep my bargains."

"Bullshit," I said. "You keep 'em as far as you want to, and if you wanted his soul you would have taken it last night, proper and legal."

The hellhound nodded. "True enough. But he didn't keep his end of things."

"What the hell does that mean?" Down below, I could hear a door slam. Brave face or not, Olsen was running, and running like he meant it.

"Come on, Eli, half the fun for me's in the waiting. A man who's counting down to the day he's got to give up his soul, he counts down to the second. He knows how long he's got, and that's what he thinks on. Drives him crazy, it does. Makes him miserable. Spreads the poison of his impending damnation all around him, which makes it good business for me."

"But Olsen didn't panic," I said.

"He was ready to go," the hound agreed. "Least he was, until he met you. 'Til you came running into the house. 'Til you listened to his story and tried to save him when the big bad doggie came clawing at the door. Now, though, now maybe he's a little less resolved. Wants to live a little more, since someone put escape into his mind."

"You used me," I said.

"That I did, 'cause that's what you're for. And now you're going to stand aside, and I'm going down those stairs so I can run Mister Olsen clear back to daylight. And he can live the rest of his natural born life wondering every moment when he's going to see me again. Wondering when it's going to end, all sudden like. And wondering, just a little bit, if maybe he did get away after all." The hound looked at me, and suddenly it wasn't a hound, it was a wolf, and it was grinning that mean-wolf grin that means you're next. "He got some hope, and now that hope's gonna burn him every day for fifty years. Good work, Eli. Couldn't have done it without you."

With that, he sprang past me, flowing down those steps with a rattle and a clatter and a howl. Somewhere, I could hear Olsen running, the beast nipping at his heels. I imagined him pelting through the trees, always one step ahead, never knowing he's supposed to be until he stumbles out onto the road and hitches a ride, and tries to go piece his life back together. But a little hope in the mix, well, that was going to be a terrible thing 'cause now he had something to lose.

If he ever saw me again, I'm sure he'd thank me. Thank me for saving him. Thank me for stalling the hound long enough for him to get away. But he ought not to, not after what I did, and deep down, he'd know it.

I sank down to the floor and waited there a while, 'til the sun was gone and the ghosts were out, and the entire place had only its normal contingent of spirits. Then I picked myself up and made ready to go. Got my pack, doused the fire, and went on out.

And the front door, whole again and sturdy, shut itself behind me.

EMPTY BOX

She didn't look like a fortune teller. She looked like a librarian, or somebody's grandma, or perhaps somebody's grandma who happened to be a retired librarian. But the neon sign in the window said PSYCHIC, and the card in the window advertised Tarot readings, and there Paul was, face to face with someone who looked like she ought to be telling teenagers to stop making out in the stacks.

"Hi," he said inauspiciously. "Are you Madame Agatha?"

She nodded. "I am. And you must be Paul, my 4:30 appointment. Come in." she turned around and led the way into her workspace. She wore tan, and had her hair done up in a severe bun, and she had thick rimmed glasses. Someone further from the stereotype of a fortune teller would have been hard to imagine, and Paul wasn't inclined to try. It was hard enough for him to believe that he was here, now, doing this thing he ordinarily would have mocked roundly.

He followed her into the sitting room, where two padded chairs sat on opposite sides of a small wooden table. The table was draped with deep red fabric, and a deck of Tarot cards sat on it next to a small pile of crystals.

Not for the first time, Paul wondered what he was doing there. But when Madame Agatha gestured for him to sit, he sat. And when she asked for his right hand, he extended it.

"Why are you here," she asked as she held his hand lightly in her own.

124

"I, uh, booked a full hour," Paul began, but Madame Agatha interrupted him. "That is what you are here for," she said, "but not why you are here. What is troubling you so much that you decided, against your better judgement, to seek out a psychic."

Paul felt himself blushing. "It's that obvious?"

"It's that usual," Madame Agatha replied. "I can tell when someone does or does not believe, and you most certainly don't. But you're lost, and you're looking for direction, and that led you here."

"And your psychic powers can't tell you why?" It sounded crass and whiny, and Paul regretted the words as soon as he'd said them. But Madame Agatha merely shook her head.

"I am privileged to see certain things. I'm not omniscient, nor am I Google. But I can help you with your problems if you are willing to let me." She cleared her throat. "But you have to be a willing partner in this. Otherwise, you're wasting your money."

Paul thought about this for a moment. "All right," he conceded. "I apologize. This is just hard for me, you know?"

"If things were easy, you wouldn't be here," said the psychic and proceeded to scrutinize his palm. "A basic palm reading is $35. A reading with the cards is $45. A full session with everything at my disposal is $70."

"Let's go with the palm reading," he said. In for a penny, in for thirty five bucks, he told himself. The worst thing that happens is some entertainment value. "Do you take credit cards."

She nodded. "Of course. But that's for later. For now, let's begin." She traced a line across his hand with one finger. "A serious break in the heart line. Is that why you're here?"

"Umm, sort of," Paul stammered. "I'm looking for some direction, some kind of general advice on things."

"Aha." Madame Agatha sounded unconvinced. "Let me see your other hand."

"What's the difference?"

"One's what God gave you, the other's what you've done with it. I've seen what you've done with it. Now let's see what's left in the tank." She let his right hand drop and took his left, *hmming* and *ahhing* over it like a comic book collector poring over a particularly rare issue. Paul held his tongue as long as he could, but finally broke in with, "What is it? What do you see?"

Madame Agatha shook her head. "Besides the fact that you stopped wearing your wedding ring very recently, not much. Your lifeline is healthy and long. The break in your heart line is even more pronounced here. You weren't fooling around, I can see that. Looks like it took you completely by surprise. "

Paul found himself nodding. "It did. I mean, one she just told me she wanted to leave, and the next thing I knew her bags were packed, and…wait a minute, where did you get that from?"

The fortune teller smiled. "Like I told you, I have the ability to see certain things. Now, what do you want from this reading? Concentrate. Think hard on the question. And when you're ready, tell me what you want."

"Like I said, I'm looking for some general direction, some guidance. I mean, she's gone, and I know she's gone, and I know she's not coming back, and I have no idea what to do or how I'm supposed to feel." He stopped, embarrassed. "Sorry, I'm babbling."

"Piffle. You're working your way toward something. Let yourself go."

"But I don't know." Paul jerked his hand back in frustration and slammed it on the table. "What do I want? I don't know what I want. I want to stop feeling like this. I want to feel like there's something good waiting for me because this, this is shit.

And you know what else? I want her to feel some of it, too. I don't want to hurt her or anything like that, but Jesus, she just walked out, cool as you please. Had the whole thing planned. Completely blindsided me and used that to get what she wanted. Hell, I'm still not sure what's going on except that she seems perfectly happy, and me, I'm miserable. So you're asking me what I want? I don't want to hurt her, but I want her to hurt. I want her to feel a little bit of what she's put me through. It doesn't even have to be a lot. But *something*, so she doesn't get to be one hundred percent entirely happy while I have to be totally miserable." He glared across the table. "So that's it. That's what I want. Are you going to find the answers to that in the palm of my hand, or should I just fuck off right now?"

Madame Agatha stared at Paul for a moment. He was dimly aware his hands were shaking, but that didn't matter. He'd said it. For the first time, he'd said it, said what he really felt, what he hadn't even admitted to himself because, hey, everything was going to be great, and they were going to be friends afterward.

Well, he didn't want to be friends. Not yet, maybe not ever. Not until the playing field was a little more level, at least. And maybe, just maybe Madame Agatha could help with that, but even if she couldn't, that was fine. He'd figure something out.

"You are very angry," she said. "Anger is a dangerous energy to give in to. Perhaps you want to tell me more about your situation. About what happened to make you feel this way."

"What's there to tell?" Paul asked bitterly. "I came home from work one day, and she told me she was leaving. Had half the house already packed up, had an apartment set up, had even bought furniture. It was a done deal without her ever talking to me. Without her ever saying she was unhappy, or that there were problems, or we should go to counseling, or anything. And

I let her do it. Let her roll right over me. Went with her preferred style of divorce, her division on the property, hell, she's still got a key to our - to my house because we were going to be great friends afterward and, hell, that's not exactly working out either because if it were, I wouldn't be here."

"Do you think she was right to leave you?"

"I have no idea." Paul's tone was flat, without affect. "I do know I wish she'd talked to me before she packed up half our life together and put it into boxes."

"All right." Madame Agatha pursed her lips for a moment. "What you want, I can't give you with a palm reading. All I can do there is see what's what and offer you advice. And you are in no mood to take advice. Now if you want, I can help you, but it's going to take considerably more effort and investment on your part. Think on it for a minute before you give me your answer."

Paul sneered reflexively. "Why would you help me?"

She answered quietly. "Because you're going to pay me to. And because someone needs to be taught a lesson. Now if you're serious, wait here a moment. I'll be right back with what you'll need to get all the revenge you ever want."

"I don't want revenge," he protested. "I just want her to feel bad, too."

"Whatever you say," said Madame Agatha and vanished into the inner recesses of her house.

Paul stood there and waited. "Idiot," he said softly. He'd said too much, let too much go, and now this crazy old woman was going to try to sell him a potion or something so he could get revenge. Revenge wasn't what he was after - it was parity. Let her suffer just a little bit, and he'd be fine, and then it could all end, and everyone could live happily ever after.

Her. He hadn't even thought of her by name. She was just...her.

"This is stupid." The words slipped out. But on reflection, he could see it was right. What was he doing, going to a fortune teller, asking for - what, a curse? A voodoo doll? - some craziness because he couldn't deal. No. It was too much, it was stupid, it was time to get out of there.

He stood. Time to go. He'd leave the money for the palm reading on the table and go and-

She returned, holding a box. "Going somewhere?" she asked, eyes sharp and bright.

"I...err...no, of course not." Paul couldn't be sure if his spine was stiffening or melting like Jell-o under her stare.

"All right then. Because if you wanted to walk out, now would be the time. Before I tell you what's in this box, and before we start talking about money."

"No, no," Paul heard himself saying. "I want this."

"Then sit back down." Agatha sat and placed the box in the middle of the table. She cocked her head, and Paul hurriedly sat. To avoid looking at Madame Agatha, he peered at the box.

It was small, maybe four inches on a side and two inches high. It had been carved, base and tight-fitting lid, from a single piece of dark wood, and a simple, hypnotic web pattern had been incised into the lid. It did not look in the slightest like a voodoo doll or a potion, and Paul found himself becoming intrigued.

"Inside this box is something that can do what you want," the psychic said. "You're going to have to be very careful about how you apply it, and where."

"What is it?" he asked. "Is the box cursed?"

"No. The box is just a box. It's what the box holds that's special."

"And that is?"

"Invisible spiders."

"Invisible…spiders?"

She sat back and crossed her arms, daring him to laugh. "Invisible spiders."

Paul thought about it for a second. "Seriously. What the fuck?"

"Language, young man."

"You have got to be kidding me. Invisible spiders? How am I supposed to believe this?"

A thin smile crossed Madame Agatha's lips. "You could open the box and find out."

Paul put his hand on top of the box. It felt cool, not that he expected anything otherwise. "Okay, what happens if I open it?"

"Then the spiders would get out, and they'd go looking for the nearest warm body that wasn't me." She paused to let that sink in. "That would be you."

"Oh." Paul smiled to humor her. "But they're not poisonous, are they?"

"Not enough to bother a human. But that's not the point, you see. Or rather, you don't see."

"Don't see what?"

"Don't see them. Don't see them crawling towards you, and they will crawl towards *you*. Don't see them scuttling up onto your shoes, on your hands, in your hair. Don't see them and then it's too late because now you can feel them, feel those feather-light footsteps as they walk ever so lightly across your skin, across your eyes, until they're everywhere, and you still don't see anything. You must be going mad, you think, and yet you feel them, feel those tiny feet as they creep into your ears and-"

"Okay, okay, I get it. Creepy crawly." Paul felt himself shuddering and silently cursed himself for letting Madame Agatha get to him that way.

"Creepy crawly," she agreed calmly, her smile fixed. "A perfect way to cause your ex-beloved some degree of discomfort without actually harming her, wouldn't you agree?"

"Well, yes, but," Paul felt himself rapidly losing control of the conversation. Invisible spiders? Come on. "How do they get back into the box?" he finally offered, weakly. "I mean, is it an invisible spider generator, or do they just live there or what?"

"Oh, you sweet dear, don't worry your head with details like that. They're predators. They can take care of themselves, and they can find their way home to me. And then they let me know, and I let them back in the box."

Paul thought about that for a second. "You can communicate with them? Like, actually talk to them?"

"We have ways of letting each other know what we want. Leave it at that. You seem like a sensitive boy. You wouldn't want to know the whys and wherefores. They'd only upset you."

Part of Paul wanted to protest, but the rest of him realized he'd be getting nowhere fast. "Fine," he said. "Let's accept for the sake of argument that this box-" he tapped the lid experimentally a few times - "is full of invisible spiders. What exactly am I supposed to do with them, how much do they cost, and do I get my money back if they don't work?"

Agatha ticked her responses off on her fingers. "One, you get the box near your ex however you can. I can only do so much for you here. Two, use of the spider box is $275, and I expect you to return the box when you're done. Not returning the box will incur an additional $50 fee, as I'll have to carve a new one. And if they don't work, you get a full refund. Don't go lying trying to get that refund, though, boy. I have ways of knowing what's been and what hasn't, and I'll know if you're trying to cheat me."

She seemed altogether serious, and to his surprise, Paul found himself considering it. He shouldn't believe in invisible spiders, but Madame Agatha seemed so sure, so matter of fact about them that it was contagious. Why not take a shot? Worst came to worst he could get his money back or, if he didn't mind looking like an idiot, go to the Better Business Bureau. And if it did work, and he could give her a night or two of the cold terrors, then he'd be all fine with that.

She hated spiders. He knew that. He wondered if Madame Agatha knew, too, and decided not to ask. He was already far enough down the rabbit hole.

He opened his mouth to haggle, and what came out instead was, "Do you take credit cards?"

Madame Agatha nodded. "Of course." She gently pushed the box over to Paul's side of the table. "First, though, there are some things you should know. One, don't agitate the box. Don't shake it, don't thump the lid again, and don't drop it. The spiders are highly sensitive, and if you irritate them, they won't come out. Two, don't open the box until it's time to use what's inside. Trying to get a sneak peek won't work, and it will just let the spiders out. Three, bring me back the box when you're done with it. And that's all you need to know." She was already reaching for her cell phone and card reader.

Paul reached for his wallet and pulled out his Visa. "I don't have to give them special instructions or anything?"

Agatha took the card, sniffed it once, and then ran it through the reader with a reassuring chirp. "The charge will appear as MA Entertainment Enterprises, in case you were wondering. And no, your intent alone should be enough. Open the box and envision them climbing all over her, and you'll get what you want easy-peasy."

"I see." Paul took his card back and tucked it away. He

picked up the box and gripped it tightly with both hands. "Anything else I should know?"

Madame Agatha shook her head. "Just do it quickly. They're hungry in there, you know."

Four hours later, Paul sat looking at the box and wondering what the hell he was going to do next. It hadn't made a peep as he brought it home. Now it sat there on his night table, waiting expectantly. And he had no idea what he was going to do with it.

The obvious solution, mail it to her as a gift, was out for the simple reason that she had seen fit not to give him her address. A move which, he admitted, had turned out to be effective even if she had no idea why.

A second thought was calling to see if she'd do coffee and giving it to her then. Of course, there was the off chance she'd open it in public, which would be awkward if there were invisible spiders in there. More likely, though, she'd refuse the gift, leaving him to awkwardly return the spiders, unused, and face Madame Agatha's thinly disguised scorn.

Assuming, of course, there were spiders in there at all. The idea there might be nothing in the box at all was a constant torment, and the temptation to sneak one little peek was ongoing. Not that it would do him any good, he reminded himself; the damn things that were supposed to be in there were supposed to be invisible.

"How the hell did I get myself into this?" he moaned to himself, knowing the answer intimately. If he'd stood up to her, if he'd stood up to Madame Agatha, if if if.

Still, there was nothing for it now but to go forward and see what happened. Worst case, after all, would be nothing.

Right?

"Stupid fucking spiders. Probably don't even exist." He rose and walked out of the bedroom. Grabbing his keys, he went out the front door and headed for the mailbox. There hadn't been anything there when he'd gotten home, but delivery ran late these days, and late arrivals weren't unusual.

That, and taking a mailbox run would get him out of the room with the damn box staring at him.

When he reached the mailbox, Paul saw he was in luck. The door was down, and various pieces of postage were sticking out. He grabbed them and looked through the pile, a nearby streetlamp providing enough light for him to do so. Most of it was junk mail, wrapped around two bills and an anomalous, hand addressed envelope.

Paul took a closer look. The address was right, but it wasn't addressed to him. It was a card of some sort, and it was for her.

It happened from time to time - a stray piece of mail intended for her wound up at his house, and they'd developed a system for dealing with it. He'd drop her an email, she'd come by, they'd chat for five minutes, and then she would take her mail and go home. He'd just do the same with this card, and-

A thought struck him. She didn't know there was only one piece of mail for her. He could easily mockup a package with the box in it and tell her both had been delivered with her name on it. She'd take the package home and then nature, or whatever it was called when you were dealing with invisible spiders, would take its course.

A car rolled by and honked its horn. Paul waved belatedly to the neighbor behind the wheel while he turned over the idea in his head. Hell, he didn't even need to be there when she picked it up - she still had a key. If he played this right, it would work out perfectly. Sure, he'd have to figure out a way to get the box back without admitting his role in the whole thing, but that had to be doable somehow.

He shut the mailbox and ambled back towards the front door, turning over alternatives in his mind. Inside, the box waited patiently.

In the end, it took a week. Three days of farting around trying to package up the box and mail it to his own address, another three days of waiting for it to arrive, and then one day working up the nerve to email her. He wrote and deleted the email a dozen times before settling on the wording, making it as simple and unadorned as possible. There was mail for her, she could come pick it up whenever, he might not be around, but since she still had a key, it was fine for her to let herself in and pick it up. When she wrote back in a couple of days to suggest a date, he told her it was fine but that he had plans that evening - she should go ahead and let herself in; the mail would be front and center.

True to his word, he placed the mail - both the actual letter that had arrived for her and the shipment containing the box of spiders - on the low table in the front hallway that she'd reluctantly left behind. Then all there was to do was wait, and constantly recheck the tape on the container of spiders to make sure there was no possible way they could get out even if the box got jostled or dropped. The date she'd specified rolled around, and he made sure to be out of the house. Part of him wanted to stay, if for no other reason than to make sure she didn't leave the box behind, but he didn't want to risk giving the game away, intentionally or otherwise.

And so Paul walked out, got in his car, and drove. He didn't stop anywhere for fear of being spotted and having his supposedly full schedule exposed as a lie. Three times he turned back towards his house, and three times he turned away, convinced that she might not have been there yet.

Finally, at midnight, he let himself head home. If she hadn't been by then, she wouldn't be coming at all, and that would be a problem for another day. But she was punctual, and she had said she was coming, and he had no reason to doubt her in this. Time to go home, luxuriate in a plan well achieved, and get some sleep.

He pulled into his driveway. There was no sign of her or her car, which bolstered his optimism. Surely she'd been and gone. Surely she'd gone home and opened the package out of curiosity, opened the box and released the flood of spiders. Surely, by now, she was covered with invisible crawling things, swarming over her-

He took a deep breath. Best not to think of it yet, he told himself. Just go inside like a regular night. Sighing, Paul opened the front door, flipped on the hallway light, and stepped inside.

And saw the empty box sitting there amidst the debris of the package he'd so carefully assembled. There was a note next to it in her perfect handwriting- "Thank you, but I couldn't possibly take your little present. You can bring the box back to Madame Agatha any time."

A cold fear gripped the back of his neck as he read it. And on his ankle, he felt the faintest of footfalls.

COIN DROP

"The new vending machine is awesome."

Geoff said this around a mouth full of chocolate bar, which was a large portion of why David ignored him. Geoff was usually talking, usually eating, and the overlap in that particular Venn diagram was large.

"Mmm-hmm?" was what David said, the bare minimum necessary to indicate that he had heard while not encouraging further conversation. *Eyes on the screen*, he told himself. *Fingers on the keyboard. Don't look. Don't look. Don't l--*

"Seriously, man. You've got to check it out." Clearly Geoff hadn't gotten the hint, or more accurately, chased it to where it had rolled under a table in the corner. David took a deep breath and swiveled his chair to face him.

"Geoff. It's a vending machine. What's the big deal?"

Geoff looked at him anxiously, then flicked his gaze left and right, as if he were guarding some great and terrible secret.

Around them, fingers mashed keys relentlessly. People got up, people sat, people drank caffeine. It was another day at another video game studio, and if someone was getting too excited over the vending machine choices, well, that was just proof that someone had been working a little too hard.

Geoff took all that in at a glance, then leaned forward. There was a smear of chocolate on his lip; dark chocolate. "It's got good food," he said, his voice a conspiratorial whisper. "I mean, *real* food."

David rolled his eyes, and nearly rolled his chair back out of earshot. "For God's sake, Geoff, it's a vending machine. Six weeks ago you were doing back flips because they got those giant Texas honeybun things you said you liked."

"No. No. No-no-no. This is different." Geoff shoved forward a handful of something crinkly and occasionally brown. Against his better judgment, David looked.

It was a candy wrapper. More than that, it was an expensive candy wrapper, from a brand of hippie-dippie fair trade chocolate that got stocked at organic supermarkets and upscale coffee houses, but not in vending machines. And definitely not in vending machines at video game companies.

" It's got to be a mistake," David said, and shrugged. "I mean, yay, nice chocolate. But there's no way they keep stocking it."

"Tell me about it," Geoff sounded sad for a moment, then brightened. "That's why I bought six. They were only charging what they used to charge for a Hershey's."

"Now I know it's a mistake," David groaned. "Okay, thanks for the heads-up. I'll check it out later. Enjoy the chocolate. And get it out of your pocket before it melts."

Geoff opened his mouth, closed it, and then trundled off, presumably to get semisolid chocolate out of his pants before it was too late. David watched him go, watched him nearly trip over a fat snake of braided cables, and then went back to work.

Two hours later, he did check it out, though not because Geoff had said he should. The most recent build was transferring to his box, he had a few minutes, and he was a little peckish, so the vending machine seemed the logical place to go.

And if he could get a good chocolate bar for the price of a not-so-good one, well, that wasn't such a bad thing.

The new machine, when he found it, was indeed new. It *looked* new, molded from some form of reflective black plastic, with odd-shaped bits of chrome and buttons that glowed, their numbers green. The front was a sheet of glass with five rows of goodies neatly lined up behind it, held in an elegant manifestation of the usual spiral dispensing arrangement. A small sign indicated that the device was, in fact, refrigerated to precisely forty-five degrees Fahrenheit, so that anything coming out of it would be chilled to that temperature, and that exact change was preferred.

David took that in, processed it, and ignored it. Instead, he looked at the selection.

There were no gourmet chocolate bars there. That did not surprise him. The particular snack Geoff had laid claim to cost about $4.50 per bar, and David had expected that as soon as word got out, the machine would have been ransacked. No wonder it was gone.

Yet there were no empty slots and no empty rows. And the stuff that was there, that filled those unbroken lines of tempting goodness, was astonishing.

There was chocolate. There were Sky Bars, a gooey, awful concoction he hadn't seen since his days playing Little League. There were Clark Bars and candy cigarettes and bags of Smarties, all the things he'd loved as a kid, now laid out for him here. And they were cheap, too.

"Damn." He fumbled in his pockets for change, and shoved a couple of quarters into the machine's slot. They went in, the *Make your selection* light went live, and he pressed a couple of buttons. There was a brief, smooth noise, one of the spirals spun, and something made a gentle *thunk* at the bottom of the case.

David reached in and pulled out the Sky Bar. It was, indeed, chilled to forty-five or so degrees, and the wrapper was that same shade of mustardy yellow he remembered. "How the hell did you get in here?" he asked it, neither expecting nor receiving an answer. He'd seen Sky Bars a few times since he was a kid--at roadside restaurants, in "retro" candy shops, and on dusty counters in tiny drugstores--but they weren't exactly the sort of thing that got stocked in vending machines, and especially not ones that also had especially good gourmet chocolate, and, well, it was a vending machine and not worth thinking about too hard. The company kept them there and subsidized the soda machine to keep people from making too many midday runs to the nearest convenience store and to prevent a plague of mini-fridges from proliferating under desks. That was all.

He took a couple of steps over to the trashcan and tore open the candy bar's wrapper. It gave easily, and inside was, in fact, a candy bar. It was milk chocolate with a faint waxy sheen, and as he held it, he could feel it start to melt ever so slightly under his fingers.

"Whatever," he said, and took a bite.

It tasted like a Sky Bar. There was the chocolate, and then beyond it was delicious, sticky marshmallow-flavored goop that looked like caulk but tasted heavenly, and then more chocolate.

It tasted, David dimly recognized, like Sky Bars had always tasted to him, back when he was an eight-year-old second baseman, wearing number fifty-four for the Conklin Beverage Sunfish t-ball team. He hadn't expected that they'd still taste that good; he'd always avoided trying one as an adult for fear of tarnishing that memory. Clearly, he'd been wrong.

He took another bite, this time into the caramel section of the candy, and headed back to his desk.

It wasn't until later that he realized something.

The quarters hadn't made any noise as they went down.

Three days later, David went back to the machine for another snack. He did not, generally, a snack by nature, but it had been a busy day, and he'd missed lunch, and besides, the Sky Bar had been exceptionally good.

Geoff was standing there, coins in hand, when he arrived. "Oh. Hi, Dave."

"Geoff.

"I see they replaced your chocolate bars. Too bad." Geoff turned, mildly incredulous. "What do you mean? They're right there."

David peered in. The machine appeared to be filled with Watchamacallits and Zagnuts, Zero Bars and Charleston Chews. Nothing gourmet was in evidence. "I bought a candy bar the other day and there weren't any more of your fancy ones to be had. They must have replaced them."

Geoff shook his head. "They're right there," he repeated, and dropped his quarters in the slot. He hammered on the buttons--five, then seven--and something dropped to the bottom of the machine with a clunk. Grinning triumphantly, he reached into the machine's dispersal slot, and pulled something out.

"See?" he said, and shoved his paw under David's nose. In it, ineluctably, was a high-end chocolate bar. It had, according to the wrapper, cocoa nibs mixed into it.

David thought for a minute, then looked back at the machine. In slot fifty-seven, there were Bit-O-Honeys. He looked down at the chocolate bar, which Geoff was still holding, awkwardly, and reached out a finger to touch it. It was there. It was real.

" Weird," he said, and stepped over to the machine. "Fifty-seven?"

Geoff nodded distractedly, already tearing the wrapper off his prize. "Yeah. Though they've got the ones with hazelnuts in fifty-nine."

"I'm cool." David fished in his pockets for a couple of coins, found them, and fed them to the machine. They disappeared down the slot and were gone, none of them bouncing down to the change return for whatever arcane reasons vending machines used to spit out perfectly good coins. And he hit first the five, and then the seven on the numbered pad.

Gears murmured. The metal spiral turned. Something fell.

And David fished out a Bit-O-Honey.

He stared at it for a minute. "Geoff?"

"Mmm?" The larger man had started to amble off, progress slowed by the delicate operation of unwrapping foil from chocolate.

"I just hit fifty-seven and got something completely different than you did." David held up his candy bar. "See?"

Geoff didn't even turn. "Musta hit the wrong button. Or there was one of yours behind one of mine. Or something. No big deal." And with that, he ambled off, his thick legs slowly kicking into gear with the infusion of sugar and milk and cocoa.

David thought about that, turning back to the machine as he did so. There still were a couple of coins in his pocket. Thoughtfully, he fed them into the machine and pressed five, then seven again.

The candy bar he pulled out wasn't Geoff's expensive chocolate. Then again, he hadn't expected it to be.

The only one in the HR rep's office was the HR rep, which was both unusual and a pleasant surprise. David had been swinging by her desk every twenty minutes to see when she'd be available, and every time he'd done so since ten a.m., there had been someone in there behind a closed door.

"Laura? You got a minute?" David stuck his head in and gave his best innocent look.

"Depends." The HR rep was behind her desk, head in her hands. "Are you going to report one of your team members for having a pair of used panties on his desk?"

"Umm, no?"

"Fine. Come on in." She sat up and waved, and David shut the door behind him.

"Used panties?" he said, once the latch had clicked.

Laura nodded, "Yeah. Said he got them out of the vending machine, and that if the company was going to put that sort of thing there, they couldn't discipline him for putting them on his desk." She shook her head, and corn-straw blonde hair went everywhere. "I told him we had three of the female employees in here screaming for his head, but it didn't make a difference. Finally, I had to send him home."

"Should you be telling me this?"

She grinned ruefully. "Probably not. But nobody's complained to me about you yet, so I'll take my chances."

David thought for a second. "Wait. Vending machine?"

Laura sighed dramatically. "That's what he said."

"They sell used panties in vending machines in Japan." David frowned. "Where did this new one come from, anyway?"

Laura pulled a brochure from a vertical file on her desk. "New company. We just switched because the rate was amazing, and because I was tired of getting bitched at about the quality of the food in the old one." She pushed the file across, and David picked it up. "But I'm pretty sure we didn't order it stocked with Japanese schoolgirl underwear."

David looked at her, and she blushed and looked away. "What? I work here. I have to know these things."

"True enough." Opening the brochure prevented him from having to say anything further. It was glossy and slick and promised what looked to be a pretty-good deal--frequent restocks, a ridiculously low pricing schedule, and numerous customization options. Switching over would have been a no-brainer.

"So what else can I do for you?"

David thought for a moment. "When do we get the machine restocked? How often?"

Laura nabbed the brochure back and flipped a couple of pages. "Here. Sensors in the machine let them know when something's running low, so they can do on-demand resupply. It's all very high-tech."

"Huh. Interesting. Thanks." He put the paperwork back down on the desk, and Laura shuffled it back to where it belonged.

"You're welcome. Any particular reason you're so curious about this thing?"

He shook his head. "Just intrigued, that's all. Everyone's really happy with the new machine, which has got to be a first. I was curious, that's all."

She nodded. "Yeah. The deal fell into our laps. I'd say too good to be true, but, hey, if I never have to see another month-old Giant Cinnamon Roll in that machine, it's worth it."

"Yeah. There is that."

"Geoff, have you ever seen the vending machine get restocked?"

Geoff looked up from his lunch, which consisted of a defeated-looking sandwich in a soggy Subway wrapper, a Diet Coke, and what looked to be a couple of examples of the vending machine's bounty. "Dude. What's with you?"

David pursed his lips. "What do you mean?"

"I mean, you're all about the damn vending machine these days. And to answer your question, no, I haven't, because I don't hang around in the break room all day wondering when Mister McSnacky is going to show up. Jesus, Dave, some of us actually have deliverables, you know."

David persisted. "So you haven't ever seen it get restocked, then?"

Geoff turned around and crossed his arms across his beefy chest. "No, I haven't, Okay? And I'm sure if you ask around, nobody else has, either, because it's a goddamn vending machine. As long as we can exchange actual money for actual snacks, we don't care if it gets restocked in the middle of the night by the goddamn Tooth Fairy, so she can drum up business. Now fuck off and let me eat my lunch."

"But--"

"I said fuck off. Okay? Thanks! Bye."

By eleven that night, everyone else had gone home. It wasn't unusual for David to be in the office that late, wasn't unusual for coworkers to be there as well, but they were a long way out from a milestone and nobody felt the need to crunch yet. And so the drifting out the door started at five, and intensified at six, and was essentially done by eight. By ten, the last hardcore grinds had gone, and the last multiplayer matches had wound down, and David was alone.

He waited another hour, just to be sure. By then the night rhythm of the building was established: HVAC clunks and starts, random elevator noises, and random beeps. But there were no human noises, no chairs scraping on the floor and no conversation, and when he was sure that would be the case going forward, David went to the machine.

As he walked, he jingled. He'd gone home at lunchtime to get his coin jar, on a hunch he didn't totally understand, and brought it back with him. The pieces of his plan hadn't been totally formed then; they still weren't perfectly clear now. But he had sixty dollars 'worth of quarters and dimes, and he had some vague suspicions about when the machine got restocked, and he had an idea.

Slot thirty-two in the machine looked to be a likely place to start. It held Chuckles, flattened gumdrops in a rainbow of flavors, and apparently, someone had liked them--or whatever they'd seen in that slot--an awful lot. There were four left and then the row would be empty. David fed in coins and pressed the appropriate buttons. A slab of sugared fruit gel fell. He did it again, three more times, and then collected his booty from the receptacle below. Above, where the candy had come from, a red light glowed softly.

One wasn't going to be enough, though. Nobody would come out to restock just one. David reached for his coin jar, and started pressing more buttons.

By midnight, the machine was a quarter empty, and David's jar was emptied of quarters. A small mountain of nostalgic candy lay on the counter in front of him, barely balanced enough to keep from spilling onto the floor. A dozen red lights made the interior of the machine seem oddly hellish, and the gaps in the candy lineup gave the whole thing a sinister, ramshackle aura.

Briefly, he'd considered following up with bills, but somehow the coins seemed like they'd done enough. And so David sat there, and occasionally ate candy, and waited.

It was nearly two when the wait ended. A beeping at the front desk indicated someone had come through the front doors, the ones supposedly key-carded to keep non-employees out. Then came the rasp of heavily laden wheels and the sound of footsteps.

David waited.

And after a minute, the re-stocker came into view.

He was short, wearing a tan uniform and cap that read Eschaton Vending on it in a dull shade of blue. He wheeled a cart in front of him, one loaded with boxes whose labels all seemed strangely blurry, and he was whistling.

"Hi there," he said as the cartwheeled to a stop. "You're here

147

late."

"It's a video game company," David replied. "There's always someone here late."

"Yeah, but not always someone buying a hundred candy bars." He jerked a thumb at David's spoils. "Any particular reason, or do you really like Zagnuts?"

"Curiosity," David said. "Trying to figure out how I'm getting Sky Bars out of a machine that's selling my buddy Escazu and someone else, used underwear. You wouldn't happen to know anything about that, would you?"

The re-stocker, who had been busy unlocking the front of the machine, stopped. He turned to look at David, and a lopsided smile played across his lips. "Actually, I kind of do.

Why do you ask? Had a bad time at the dentist?"

"No. Just curious. It's ... unusual."

There was a thoughtful silence. "It is, yeah. To you, anyway. It's also part of something bigger. Here's my advice to you: don't worry about it. It's nothing to do with you, or your friends, or your company. Nothing that matters within your lifetime. Oh, and you'll want to start flossing if you're gonna eat all that." And with that, he turned back to the vending machine and began filling empty spaces. David opened his mouth to respond, but he felt impossibly sleepy, too tired to form words.

"Shhh," was the last thing he heard, and when he woke, it was morning.

"Nice of you to buy all that candy for everyone, but it really wasn't necessary."

"Fuck off, Geoff," David replied.

"Seriously. Didn't realize buying candy was that hard, though. You going to pass out pushing a mouse next?"

"Geoff, enough. It's not funny."

A hand swung David's chair around, and he found himself face to face with his friend. "No. What's funny are the pics of you curled up on a pile of candy like you've gone full Smaug on it. All over Tumblr and Facebook already, man. You're going to be a legend."

"I don't care," David said stubbornly. "That's not what was supposed to happen."

Geoff shrugged. "Whatever. You and the vending machine work it out amongst yourselves. Me, I'm changing my desktop wallpaper." He held up his iPhone, and the background image was one of David, asleep and surrounded by candy bars in various denominations. The caption read *U CANNOT HAZ MAI NOMS!*

David regarded him stonily. "You done, Geoff?"

"Just getting started," was the reply, but Geoff walked off as he said it. David watched him go, then turned his chair back to face his monitor. Guffaws puffed up like geysers around the room as latecomers saw pictures or heard stories, but David ignored them, or tried to.

The last birthday present David's ex had gotten for him had been a toolkit, on the theory that if she left it in prominent spots around the house he might get the hint and become a little less of a useless lump without a keyboard in his hands. That, like the marriage, had failed miserably, but David had kept the toolkit on the off chance that sooner or later he might need to hit something with a hammer, or a crowbar, or maybe an Allen wrench.

It was the crowbar he brought into the office with him the next day. As crowbars went, it wasn't much--short enough to fit in the box and painted bright blue--but it looked sufficiently sturdy for what David had in mind.

The plan, when it came time to put it into action, was painfully direct. As soon as he was alone in the office, David took the crowbar and pried the front off the vending machine. It gave surprisingly easily. He'd expected cracking sounds and splintered plastic, or heroic struggles with unyielding steel, but the front panel popped off with gratifying ease. Underneath wasn't much: some electronics, a coin return slot, and the coin drop itself. The former seemed disconnected from any other system, while the latter fed into a large box, one marked with an ornate pattern of circles and lines in a shape that might have been a drunk third-grader's attempt at a tree. Frowning, he wedged the narrow end of the crowbar in behind the box, and pulled. With a groan, the crowbar bent, just the tiniest bit. David looked at it, decided not to believe what he saw, and pulled again.

The top of the box popped free with an odd, whooshing sound. David dropped the crowbar and leaned in for a look.

There were no coins in the coin box. No dollar bills, no currency whatsoever. Instead, there was something grey and oily that shifted back and forth--impossible to focus on--and it was making more of that strange noise he'd heard when the box popped free. Almost without thinking, he reached out, fingers extended and ready to dip into that strange fluid, to maybe give him a clue as to--

"I wouldn't do that if I were you."

The voice had come from behind David, as he'd hoped it would. He froze and said carefully, over his shoulder, "What happens if I do?"

"Don't know," the re-stocker said. "You might be able to get those fingers back. Or you might get pulled in all the way. Other universes are tricky." He stepped forward, gently shoving David away. "Let me deal with that before something bad happens to both of us."

"Other universes?" David asked. "Next to Zagnut bars?"

The re-stocker ignored him for a minute, instead concentrating on shoving the coin box back into place. Metal groaned. The hiss intensified. And then suddenly it was gone, and the vending machine was like new.

"Sorry," the man said, as a pair of dusty wings spread out behind him. "Had to restore the seal before it started sucking in your atmosphere. As in, all of it, and then someone upstairs would have noticed how much of the universe was suddenly gone. That would have been bad." David opened his mouth, but no sounds came out. Instead, he found himself pointing over the re-stocker's shoulder.

"The wings? Oh. Sorry. Stress. I can fold 'em up if you want." They disappeared as suddenly as they'd arrived, and a man in a coverall with a nametag was all there was standing there. "And, yeah. Still on the side of the angels, too."

"So." David worked his jaw experimentally, to see if he could make more sounds come out. "Angel. Vending machine. Other universe. That thing's ... a black hole? Filled with chocolate?"

"Kinda." The angel had the good grace to look embarrassed. "Door to one of God's starter universes, a place where physics didn't work out. Look, I told you. This doesn't affect you. It's a long-term kind of deal. So you can walk away, and I'll program this thing to give you whatever you want, whenever you want, for free--and that includes the used panties."

David shuddered. "No thanks."

The re-stocker shrugged. "Suit yourself. You really want to know, I'll tell you. But you won't like it." His voice was mild, but behind him, frost suddenly rimed the inside of the vending machine, and the number on the thermometer readout plunged down, down, down.

"This," he finally said, and smacked the freezing glass with one palm, "is going to save the universe. Or destroy it. Depends on whose side you're on."

"With Zagnuts?"

"Enough with the Zagnuts. It's your memory that's putting them in there. All I stock this thing with is ambrosia for you to imprint at the moment of purchase. Kid stuff, if you're a few billion years old. No, the thing you have to understand is that God is a cheap bastard. And I mean that with all due affection."

"He doesn't pay you?" Cautiously, David knelt down and felt for the crowbar. It was where he'd dropped it, near a suspiciously end-of-crowbar-shaped dent in the hardwood floor of the snack bar area.

"I mean with His building materials," said the angel, and traced a face in the frost with his finger. It was human, or at least it looked human, but it was beautiful and terrifying, and in the simple lines, David could see stars and galaxies and--

He tore his gaze away. The angel didn't seem to notice. "The Universe is an amazing piece of work. Brilliant. Perfectly balanced--there's *just* enough stuff in it so that about sixty-billion years from now, give or take, the whole thing's gonna start collapsing in on itself."

"And eighty-billion years after that, it'll all crunch back into itself. So?"

The angel finally turned around, and gave him a significant look. "One of us is still going to be around in a hundred and forty billion years."

He smiled. It wasn't a kind smile, and it clearly didn't mean whatever a human smile was supposed to.

"Oh," said David. "So this ..." His voice trailed off.

"Yeah. Steal just enough matter that it never crunches back down. Just keeps going forever and ever and ever. Immortality, for real, bought one penny at a time."

"Nickel," David corrected him absently, his mind racing. "It doesn't take pennies."

The alien smile was gone now, replaced by something sadder and more recognizable. "The thing is, it does. Whatever you choose to put it in, it takes it. It's that simple. Now, do me a solid." He made a complicated gesture, and the crowbar fell apart into slices as if it had seen the wrong end of a deli counter. Most of them clattered to the floor, but David found himself hanging onto a few. They were, he realized, thin enough to be mistaken for coins.

"Go on," the angel said. "Get yourself something for your trouble." He snapped his fingers, and suddenly the vending machine wasn't filled with Bit-o-Honeys and Mike and Ikes. Instead, inside there were iPads. Rolexes. Things that were entirely too shiny and expensive to be there, and yet there they were.

"Why?" David asked, and took a step forward. The metal felt heavy in his hand, and warmer than it ought to. "Why me? Why now?"

"Free will," said the angel. "You've got it. I don't. That little bit of angel brain got rewired after the big fight at the beginning, doncha know." He leaned in and whispered conspiratorially, "We can't actually rebel anymore. He fixed us that way. You guys, on the other hand, well. That's a whole other kettle of Leviathan."

"You give us the choice."

"And you rebel for us. Neat, isn't it? 'The angel was grinning now. "And like I said, it doesn't cost you anything. Nobody dies, nobody gets hurt, and you get a nice watch out of the deal. So come on. Pick something nice for yourself. You're a smart guy. You deserve it. Hell, I think the next coin that goes in there might be the one that puts us over the top. You could make history."

And then David was standing in front of the machine without having crossed the space in between, and his hand was up and a slice of crowbar was between his fingers, and it was all he could do, to hold back long enough to ask, "What happens after the Big Crunch."

The angel stared at him. The awful compulsion to drop the coin in the slot vanished. "What happens?"

David nodded. "Yeah. After everything crunches down and the cycle starts again. What happens next?"

For a moment, the angel looked thoughtful. He cocked his head skyward, frowning, and chewed on his lower lip. "Honestly," he finally said. "God alone knows, and I mean that. Could be the whole thing starts over again, exactly like this universe. Could be something entirely new. Could be, well, could be a lot of things. The possibilities, as they say, are infinite. We just know; it's not this. And that's scary."

"You don't know?"

The angel shook his head. "I don't know. Nobody does."

"So I could be preventing billions of lives from ever existing?"

"Or saving billions from ending. There's a lot of us dancing on that pinhead, you know." Briefly, the angel smiled. "One's a sure thing. One isn't. Easiest decision in the world."

"Ah," said David and dropped the rough coin on the floor. It jangled there for a second, rolling away as best it could. "Then, no thanks."

"No thanks?" The angel was incredulous. "It's a hundred fucking billion years from now. You don't know what the hell you're doing in two weeks, and you walk away from this?"

David nodded. "Not for me to decide. Maybe someone else."

"Nobody else is going to understand." The angel's voice was a low hiss now. "Nobody else is going to know, not like you do now. This is a gift, you understand. The *informed* choice. The one Adam never had."

"Then why are you surprised that I'm making it?"

"You're making it *wrong!*"

The word hung there in the air between them for a painful moment, and they stared at each other, and the universe held its breath.

And then there was laughter, bitter, pained laughter a million centuries in the making. "Oh, my," the angel said. "You actually did it. You made me into Him. Free will my ass." He dropped to the floor, still laughing, wrapped in shuddering great wings that enfolded him.

"I'm sorry," David said, but made no move to comfort the angel, or to walk away.

"Of course you are," the angel said, and looked up from

between his wings. "It's not going to do any good, you know. Someone else will do it. The fat guy, Geoff. He likes his chocolate. The ice princess over in HR. Every afternoon at three, she gets herself a package of "Petit Ècoliers," 'cause she thinks they're classier than plain old cookies. She'll come back. The guy from the IT department who's buying weed for his lunchtime toke. Someone will do it. Someone will put that last fucking coin in, and it won't matter."

David looked at the angel one last time, then started to walk away. "But that's their call. Their choice. This is mine."

"Is it?" Behind David there was light, a rising glow that filled the room with angel-shaped shadows. "Well, then. We'll see what happens tomorrow, Dave. And in a hundred billion years."

"Yeah," David said and felt an odd sense of calm spreading through him. "We will."

REB PALACHE
AND
THE DIBBUK

This is how Reb Palache responds, when he hears words that are spoken in no human tongue.

He rises from his bed, where he has not slept, though he retired just after evening prayers and it is near the dawn. On most nights, his sleep is not troubled, and his dreams are dreams of prophecy. Or, he spends the evening in discussion with the angel whose voice rides his shoulder, and finds himself as refreshed in the morning as if he had spent the whole night in dreamless slumber.

But this night, the voice of the angel has been silent, and there has been no debate or learned discourse in the rebbe's cabin. The rocking of his ship on the waves has not soothed him, nor has the familiar song of creaking rope and straining wood and muttered sailor's oath sung to him as a lullaby. He has lain awake all night, the sea air heavy on his chest and his mind full of unquiet dread.

And so when he hears the voice that calls from the prow of the ship in a language he does not know, he is already awake, already aware that something is not right, already half-dressed and half-prepared, but for what he does not know.

He is not alone on the deck, he finds, when he steps forth from his cabin. Several of the sailors have gathered at the prow. They stand in a loose semicircle, their bare feet shifting

157

uneasily on the deck as the stare at the man squatting on the rail, who is naked to the waist and howling unclean words up to the skies.

It is one of his crew, of course. There is no one else it could be —they are many days from land, and they have not sighted another ship since a day after they left port. They have not come across any wrecks, nor have they picked up castaways. And so this man, if man he still is, must be one of his.

"Let me through," he says, and the other sailors draw back to give him passage. He steps forward, over coils of rope and folded canvas, until he is perhaps three strides away from where the deck ends. He stands there, and he looks at the figure, and he waits.

The man on the railing stops his screaming. He stares at Reb Palache. His toes grip the wood of the railing, the nails thick and black. They are the claws of a beast, not a man, and they dig into the oak with a sound like the breaking of small bones. His eyes, the Rebbe can see, are wide and wild, the pupils black and staring.

There is blood on his fingers, and at the corners of his mouth.

And then the creature speaks, a series of grunts and hisses and shrieks that matches no earthy language Reb Palache has ever heard. He is a scholar, and a student of the tongues of man, and it is said that had he been at Babel he could have made peace among the nations, for he would have spoken to all. But this, this is an assault on the ear with razors and rough stone, with words that were not meant for mere humans to hear.

He sees the men beside him fall, clutching their heads. One or two stumble away, crying out softly while the others writhe on the deck. On his shoulder, the angel hisses back in the same language, its voice full of rage. *These words were never meant to be spoken in this world, the angel says. It is an affront to all Creation that they are here, and not left to echo in the empty spaces of the Sitra Achra where they were born. It is the tongue of demons the man on the prow speaks, and its memory sits on the mind as the taste of rotten flesh sits on the tongue.*

"Enough," says Reb Palache at this. "Enough," and that is all.

The man on the prow stops. He blinks and leans forward impossibly far, anchored only by those thick black claws as he spreads his arms in imitation of a bird of prey. His nails, the Rebbe sees, have gone black as well, and the flesh of his chest and belly is mottled.

"Rebbe," the man says, and smiles, and suddenly Palache knows him. This is Suleiman ibn Rashid, who has sailed with him for several years, and who has served as his factor in the markets of Tripoli for many more. They have fought together; they have shared water and salt, and each guarded the other while he slept. And now he can barely recognize the man, whose grin is the grin of a beast. "I have been waiting to speak to you for many years."

"You are not Suleiman," Reb Palache says, and makes a gesture of protection.

The creature that was his friend smiles wider, and its teeth crack and splinter as Palache watches. Behind him, he can hear the desperate scrabble of his men as they strive to place distance between themselves and this abomination. They do not go too far, though. Reb Palache is their shield, his gifts and his wisdom, and they trust in him to somehow right this wrong.

Reb Palache knows this. The beast knows it, too.

"You are very wise, Rebbe," the creature says, and it brings its hands forward in a mockery of prayer. It speaks in perfect Catalan now, sweet words with the accent of court upon them. "This flesh may be the dwelling of your friend Suleiman's spirit, but I am now master of the house, and possessor of its secrets."

There is a knife at Reb Palache's belt, a curve-bladed thing of strong, cold steel. He does not reach for it. Instead, he brings his hands forward, his fingers steepling in the familiar gesture of blessing.

"That won't work, Rebbe," says the beast. "I am a deeper power than you. I am proof against your prayers and your incantations, against the knowledge of your books and the whispered words of the thing that sings to you in the night. You cannot dislodge me, nor will you learn my name. I may come and go as I please, and there are none here who have in them the strength to stop me."

He hops down to the deck, then, and stands face to face with the Rebbe. His breath is foul, and it is cold, and it steams even in the warm summer air. "So. It is your move. Ask a question. I may answer it, if it pleases me."

"Why are you here?" asks Palache, and does not flinch.

"Ah. The obvious. Surely you know."

"I wish to hear you say it."

The thing that had been Suleiman bows mockingly. "Three things will I tell you, then. One which you wish to hear, and two which you do not."

Palache shakes his head. "I wish no additional gifts from you."

The beast waggles a finger of admonition. "These are not gifts, Rebbe. At least, none save the first, which you did ask for. And know this: I am here for you. I am here to make you suffer. I am here to make your men doubt, and to hammer upon the shield of their faith in you until it splinters. I am here to break you, and these men are the rack I will stretch you on until you are torn asunder."

There are gasps behind him, and muttered prayers. Reb Palache ignores them. "That is one," he says. "The other two?"

"Two." The beast holds up two fingers, gnarled and misshapen. "Suleiman, your friend? He stole from you in Tripoli, and he did this many times. In here," and he tapped his bulging forehead, now almost unrecognizable, "he is weeping, and he is begging forgiveness. But he would not have told you on his own."

"Go on," Palache says. His voice is ice.

"And three. You will not be rid of me. I will return, and I will wear another face, and I will clothe myself in another flesh."

"You are here now," the Rebbe says, even as the angel shrieks a warning.

"Am I?" says the beast, and throws himself overboard. He is laughing when he hits the water. Reb Palache rushes to the side of the ship. "Reef sail!" he commands. "Bring her about!"

The other men, he notices, do not move. And in the water, the thing that had been Suleiman slips beneath the waves, and does not resurface.

The men mutter. They would not be human if they did not. They speak of what they saw, and of what they heard, and if they think that the evil spirit will return.

Most think that it will try, and that Reb Palache will defeat it. And so they return to reasonably good cheer, and bend their backs to the ship's business.

Reb Palache watches them for a while, and listens, and then returns to his cabin. There, he takes down from its place a book he obtained in Milan, written on fine parchment by a man who was born blind. He opens the book, and a cool wind moves through the cabin. This he has learned to recognize; it is the breath of the angel that sits on his shoulder, and it carries with it a scent of spices and old woodsmoke.

The wind also carries with it a word, spoken by the angel and wrapped in layers of protection and will. This is why his breath has flooded the room, to surround the word and not let it escape lest it be heard by the unclean one who is listening for it, and who by hearing it might gain power.

And so it is only Reb Palache who hears the angel say *dibbuk min ha-hizonim*, naming the thing that had doomed Suleiman an evil spirit, a spirit from the Outside. In that moment, Reb Palache knew his enemy, and the pages of his book flew open to a place where the lore of such beings had been written.

A story had been written there, a tale of a man who had been cruel to his wife, and who had shamed their marriage bed with other women. This man had died, and his wife had married his brother in accordance with the Law, and their home was a much happier one. But two years after they had been married, her new husband began to speak to her of things he could not possibly have known, and to show unkindness to her, and to remind her in all ways of her husband who had died. She went to fetch the rebbe, then, who spoke to her husband and determined that he was in fact a dibbuk, the evil ghost of the man who had died. Furthermore, the dibbuk stated to the rebbe that he had come back for his wife, for he was jealous of his brother and thought that he and his wife had met in secret long before they were wed. And so, it was said, he would not leave the body of his brother until his wife was dead. If she fled, or if she lived to a ripe old age, the brother's spirit would be chained forever.

To defeat the dibbuk, the rebbe called the village together.

The women laid out the wife as if she were a corpse, and the men formed a minyan, and the rebbe lead the prayers for the dead over her. Then two strong men brought in the dibbuk, who hissed and spat and swore curses at them all, to see the body of his wife laid out as if one dead. As he stood and stared, the rebbe said Kaddish, and pronounced that the woman had left this life.

A foul wind filled the room then, and blew out the candles. The dibbuk screamed, but as the village listened the sound faded, until there was nothing but a whisper, and the man who had been a dibbuk collapsed. When they roused him, they found that the dibbuk's brother had returned, and he and his wife, who was given a new name in that the woman she had been was now dead, lived happily together for many years.

"What is the meaning of this?" the Rebbe asks the angel.

The angel tells him that all he needed to know of dibbuks was in the story, but if he wishes he can devote himself to study, and learn the ways of dibbuks, and hope that will protect his crew.

And so the Rebbe reads on, and learns that a dibbuk is in fact the spirit of one who is dead and who was evil in this life, and who seeks to perform unfinished deeds before they can rest. And these ghosts, sometimes called *dibbuk meruach ra'ah*, are distinct from other possessing demons, or from the beneficial possession of the *ibbur*, or from any of a host of other things that had been created by the hand of Adonai for purposes mysterious and unknown.

But nowhere in that book is knowledge of how one might defend against a dibbuk, or a list of which amulets might bind it, or which prayers might soothe it, or how it might be banished. Nor does the angel offer guidance, or wisdom. It sings to itself, twice, but otherwise holds in silence.

So it is for two days, though Reb Palache does not study

through every hour of day and night. He spends time on deck, acting as a captain ought, and setting the ship's course to the north and east. He hangs amulets along the rigging, climbing the rope as nimbly as the youngest among his crew. The men see this and laugh, and delight in the sight. And he paints certain symbols and certain prayers on the deck itself, and along the sides of the ship, and on the canvas of the sails, that all aboard might be protected from the dibbuk should it return.

On the third day, it does.

This is how Reb Palache knows that one of his men has been possessed: by listening for words that he knows none of them could ever speak, and sounds no man could ever make. The howling comes this time from the rigging, from high above the ship, and it echoes from bow to stern. It is a howl of madness and it is a howl of revenge, and the words that Reb Palache can distinguish in it are few and simple. "I have come for you," the dibbuk says, and "You will never be rid of me."

One of the men bursts into Reb Palache's cabin then, and tells him that someone is hurting the ship, that the rigging is being slashed by one of the crew. And the man who does this deed has been, for many years, loyal and beloved, and deep in Reb Palache's counsels.

Reb Palache rushes forth and casts his eyes up, and sees the man, who is no longer that man. He has a long, curved knife in his hand, and he saws at the ropes and tethers that are the sinews of the ship with it.

And Palache sees other sailors climbing the rigging, swarming upwards to stop this vandal who was once one of them, and he calls to them to stop but it is too late. For even as he watches, the first sailor reaches the dibbuk —for surely, it is the dibbuk who slashes and tears at and wounds the ship that carries him— and then the first sailor is falling, screaming, to the deck below. Others follow him, and the dibbuk howls triumph, and says "Send Palache! Only Palache will I contend with!"

But Reb Palache is already moving, crouching by the sides of the men who have fallen and seeing who might yet live and who will not, and for whom Palache will say Kaddish when the ship has been saved.

Then Palache rises, and bellows "Down!" to his men. They pause, and they look to him, and the dibbuk laughs as they hesitate. For now the creature is looking hungrily at them, and no longer waiting for them to rise. It slides down the ropes like a spider, and the men cry out. It is hunting them, and they cannot scramble down fast enough. One it catches, and then another, and even as it does so the Rebbe is climbing, rising past those who flee the beast.

They meet and the angel, which has been silent, sings a war song praising the Lord of Hosts, that justice might prevail. The dibbuk sings too, and it slashes at Palache with the knife, which grows curves and barbs and spikes even as it is wielded. It misses, and Palache draws his own knife, cutting at the ropes the dibbuk clings to. It sees his stratagem and scrambles away, but Palache seizes it by the heel and holds it in place. It is trapped, unable to bring its strength to bear and unable to escape. Then Palache begins to sing the song of the angel, and to offer words of praise and binding, that the dibbuk might trouble him and his crew no more.

"No!" the dibbuk bellows, and flings itself downward at its captor, its would-be destroyer. But he is ready for this as well, and lets go his grip on the rigging so that they both fall. The dibbuk's eyes, red now, with rims of deepest black, widen in surprise, and then they are falling, twisting so that Reb Palache is atop the dibbuk when they slam into the unyielding wood below. The dibbuk cries out, once, and then is silent. Aided by the fall, Reb Palache's knife has pierced it through and pinned it to the deck. Black ichor spills from beneath it as Palache wearily stands, and regards his work. At his feet, the dibbuk breathes its last.

"Wrap it in sailcloth," he says. "Weight it with rocks, and then throw it overboard." This, he knows, will do nothing, for the dibbuk is a spirit and it has already escaped the flesh which held it. It will regain its strength, and it will strike again.

The men move to do his bidding, though they perhaps do not move as swiftly as they might have, and one or two look at Palache in a way that they had never done so before. He, for his part, tends the wounded, saying prayers and offering what small medicines he might, setting broken bones and giving comfort. When there is a loud splash, he does not look up, nor does he ask for the return of his knife. There are more pressing matters at hand.

By sundown, the bodies of the dead are laid out and washed. The crew is diminished: three of their number are dead, and another taken by the dibbuk, and a handful more have hurts that might have killed them had Palache not been there to tend them. Among them there is relief, and thankfulness, and in one or two a strain of wondering: will the dibbuk come again? Will Reb Palache be able to protect them?

It is with these worries on their mind that they ask him to give them phylacteries and amulets and charms, to inscribe more seals and incantations on the ship itself so that the dibbuk might not return. It will not work, the angel tells him, but they are his men, and how can he refuse them this thing that will give them some small comfort before the blood flows again? So the signs are painted and the amulets are given, and the cold fear that grips the men's hearts is warmed slightly, for they have faith that Reb Palache will defend them.

Two days later, the dibbuk comes again. It possesses the man who stands the late-night watch, and sends him screaming to Palache's cabin with drawn sword. Two more men die stopping him before Palache intervenes and sets the dibbuk down. Three days after that, a man at the help is taken, and steers the ship toward shoals that will tear the guts out of the ship. Three men wrestle it away, but it jumps over the side clinging to them, and none resurface.

At midnight, the dibbuk (for who else would be capable of such a deed?) ties their naked corpses to the rudder, along with the bodies of all the other men slain. Sharks come, drawn by the scent of flesh in the water, and as the men watch, those who were their friends and comrades are torn asunder. The ship slows, the sails hang slack. And in the air, mocking laughter.

*

This is how Reb Palache responds when his men have lost their faith, and their hearts are ruled by fear.

They are at the door of his cabin now, knocking timidly and requesting —not demanding—entrance. That will come later, he knows. If this is delayed, if he cows them now or woos them with a promise he cannot keep, then it will be worse when they return later. And so he opens his door to invite them in, and offers them tea and wine. They are afraid, for what they have come to ask is a terrible thing. But they are hunted by a terrible thing as well, and they are like men drowning, who will cling to anything that their hands seize upon, though it might not save them, but instead drag them down.

They say, in halting words, that their love for Reb Palache

has not faded, nor are they ungrateful. But they see their friends, their brothers in arms slain, and they see Palache able to do nothing. And so, they wonder, would it not be best for all to heed the dibbuk's words? For if it will slay them all to torment Reb Palache, what are they to do save wait for the slaughter, or do the unthinkable.

Reb Palache listens, and nods sagely. Now, all things are in the balance, the angel tells him. One choice leads through the fire, all others will have you consumed, and them with you. He tells the men that he has grieved for their losses, for the men who have fallen were dear to him as well. He tells them he knows his charms and prayers have failed, and that he would see no more harm come to them on his behalf. And he would not have them have his blood on their hands, for to do so would be to mark them so that none would escape the day or its consequences.

"There is another way," he says, and they bow their heads to listen.

This is how Reb Palache banishes himself from his own ship.

The dibbuk returns in the morning, perched in the flesh of the man who led the others to Reb Palache's cabin. He squats on the roof of the cabin, calling out to the other sailors and flinging blood and dung. They ignore him; they have work to do.

By the ship's side, a small boat taken from a Spanish man-o-war bobs up and down. Two ropes hold it to Palache's vessel, and it is empty save for a small cask of water and a threadbare blanket. Its sail is furled, and its rudder is lashed. A pair of oars sit, unshipped, waiting.

It is toward this small boat that Palache walks when he

emerges from his cabin.

"What are you doing?" asks the dibbuk. It looks around uneasily.

Palache ignores him, and instead hoists a few days 'store of provisions over the side, down to the boat below. The men watch him in stony silence. They are silent as well when he strides into his cabin and takes from it a small bag, and a blanket, and a wooden box not bigger than two handspans across. These, too, he stows carefully, and then climbs down a ladder made of rope, to the craft that waits for him. He sits, careful not to rock the vessel so that it would bump up against the side of his ship, the ship he has just left.

"What are you doing?" the dibbuk asks again, its voice rising toward a shriek. Again, Reb Palache ignores him, and instead raises his right hand, in a gesture of benediction. In response, the men rush forward. They untie the hawser that holds the Rebbe's vessel close, and throw the rope coiling down. Others take long poles and push the boat away, turning it from their course so that it might find its own way. And still others leap to the work of their own ship, which had been Reb Palache's, hoisting sail and turning rudder, coaxing speed from the hull which had of late seemed so sluggish and slow.

"What are you doing?" asks the dibbuk for the third time, and throws back its head and shrieks. For even as it watches, Reb Palache and his craft grow smaller in the distance. There is war in the dibbuk's heart, whether it should stay to wreak havoc on the crew and yet let the Rebbe drift away, or whether it should abandon the ship and instead pursue Palache himself, to be certain of its revenge.

Off in the distance, Reb Palache ships the oars and, with slow, deliberate strokes, begins to row.

The words the dibbuk speaks in response are not exactly

words, in that no man could comprehend them, nor are they spoken in any language heard since the Creation of the world. Great is their power, and great is their evil. Water barrels belowdecks burst, and wine casks as well, and stacked cannonballs fling themselves about, glowing red with unholy heat. Wooden splinters fly and men throw themselves down, lest they be struck by the debris, but still the ship sails on, and still the men work at their tasks, unmoved, and still the sight of Reb Palache diminishes, a shrinking target in a vast sea.

And so the dibbuk utters one last curse, which rends the mainsail and causes the tattered edges to curl away from each other and burn. It flings itself off the deck, toward the shape on the horizon. Many yards from the ship, further than any man could leap, it strikes the water and swims furiously away.

And on board, the men stop in their labor, and watch, and when they judge it safe one or two remove the wax plugs from their ears that Reb Palache had given them before the dibbuk had returned.

Reb Palache watches the dibbuk swim towards him, a great tail of spray in its wake as if Leviathan itself were cutting through the waves. He has unfurled the sail now and freed the rudder, and the oars that he used to grant himself distance from his vessel are now unshipped and resting. The wind bears him away, but the dibbuk draws closer with each moment, and so he waits.

A wave announces the dibbuk's arrival, one that sloshes over the side of the boat, and then the beast itself is clambering on board. "You," it says. "You will not escape me."

"Nor did I try to," says Palache, and opens the box that he

had brought with him. It is carved from Lebanese cedar, cunningly made with a lock of brass. Inside are certain scrolls, and a small book. "I wished to bring you out here, where we might speak alone, and that is all."

"There is no more need to speak," the dibbuk says, and leers knowingly. "Your men have abandoned you. You are cast adrift and abandoned. I will sit here, and I will watch your slow death, and I will laugh. You have no power over me to banish me, nor could you bar me from your ship. What will you do, now that you have me?"

"I would know," Palache said slowly, "why you seek revenge on me, and why you would use others thus to do so. For any man who has quarrel with me may confront me, and find justice."

The dibbuk spits. "Justice! I had none from you. My ship you sent to the bottom, and me with it, and though I cried out for mercy you offered none!"

"I have sunk many ships," says Palache. "So this thing is possible. But none of the others whose vessels I have taken have sought vengeance in this way, nor have they been unquiet in their graves. But always have I offered mercy or justice to those who have come before me. Life, or a swift death."

"I was hidden when you scuttled her," the dibbuk replies. "I did not face you, nor did your men find me. The treasure I guarded, though, that they took, and they holed my hull, and none heard me in my hiding place as the water rose. But I heard them speak of you, and praise you, and laugh before they murdered my ship, and at your bidding, murdered me."

"These are the chances men take," Palache says gently, "though perhaps you would have done better not to have hidden. And now you have."

"And now I have," says the dibbuk, and smiles. "You may die whenever you wish."

Palache raises his hand. "A question or two first, if I may. Is it true," and he lifts from the box a small scroll, "that as has been written, you may not choose the one whom you possess, but instead must flee to the one nearest you?"

"I do not see how that matters."

"Humor me," says the rebbe, and continues, and opens the book the box contained to a certain passage marked in red. "And is it not true that once your purpose is accomplished, you will go, and trouble mankind no more?"

"It is, though you will benefit none from it, as it is your death that will satisfy me."

Palache nods at that. "And one last question. Do you know of the *ibbur*?"

"The *ibbur*?" the dibbuk asks, and then it is too late, for the angel has flown and laid its hand on the stricken man. In that moment it takes the flesh the dibbuk once possessed, welcomed in by the small voice that is all that remains of the man who once dwelt within. The angel casts the dibbuk out, as it could not do on the ship for fear that it would simply claim another. But here there is but one other body it can steal, and one other life it can defile, which frees the angel to act.

And the dibbuk, wounded and shrieking, pours itself into Reb Palache.

Who waits for it, calmly, and in the quiet spaces of his mind says "Welcome."

The dibbuk shrieks and raises its arms—Reb Palache's arms—to the heavens in supplication. And across the way the angel sits and watches, arms folded and face grim.

"You have me," Reb Palache tells the dibbuk from where his

spirit sits, inside a chamber of memories. "And you will have me forever."

"No!" snarls the dibbuk. "You will die, and I will be free of you!" And it rises, to fling itself overboard, and then the angel is there, forcing the dibbuk down.

"You will not refuse the gift of life granted by the Most High," the angel says, and its voice is the music of trumpets and drums. "I will not let you do this thing. The God of Israel neither slumbers nor sleeps, nor do I, His servant."

The dibbuk spits, black bile scorching the wood of the boat where it lands. "Then I will wait until this shell dies, and Reb Palache dies with it, and then I will be free and my labors done."

"Will you," asks the angel. "For the Lord of Hosts has brought forth manna to feed his people Israel, and will do so for Reb Palache, that he might not hunger or thirst. And great is the span of years that Adonai has granted to Reb Palache, that he might labor in the world, and for all those years thou and I will sit here, and wait."

"You cannot do such a thing," hisses the dibbuk. "It is not permitted!"

"Do not tell an angel of the Lord what is permitted and what is not," says Reb Palache. "You will enjoy conversing with the angel over the many years, I can assure you, and speaking with him of the nature of the Divine. And while you do so, the charms that I have laid on this vessel will steer it far from land and far from any other ship so that you might not be disturbed in your debate. And I will sit in the library of my memories and read and listen. Is that the vengeance you wished? For you have it, and you have it in full."

And the full terror of what it had done came upon the dibbuk, and it knew what awaited it. Vengeance it had sought, swift and bloody, and this it thought it had achieved. Not for it was the long slow trip down the years, the slow agony of patience and the knowledge that its enemy suffered not, but instead waited, and listened, and watched its every move. "You cannot do this!" it said to the angel and to Reb Palache both. "It is not permitted! It is not right!"

"Many things are not permitted," replied Palache, "and some that are permitted are unjust. But you do not want your vengeance any longer?"

"No! Not this!" And once again the dibbuk sought to throw itself from the boat, and once again the angel restrained it.

"Then perhaps there is another way."

"Yes?" asked the dibbuk, with a terrible eagerness in its voice.

For a moment, Reb Palache considered. This was the creature that had sought his death, which had murdered his men and sought to break their faith in him. It was a monster, evil and unrepentant. And yet it was also the spirit of a man who believed himself wronged, and the one did not exist without the other.

"Listen carefully," Palache finally said, "and here is what we will do."

This is how Reb Palache waits for rescue: in a small boat with a cask of water and a dead man sitting across from him. He sits with an angel whispering from his shoulder and with the sound of the waves and wind as the counterpoint to his evening prayers. He sits, and he waits, and he debates the nature of what he has done with the angel, who felt Palache too merciful. For he has offered to find the ship that he had sunk those many years ago and to say funeral rites over it for the man—who had died unknown inside it. And he had said that he would find the heirs of that man, and tell them the truth of what happened, and let them judge, which the angel had found foolish. And in return, the dibbuk would go and release its grip on this world and trouble men no more.

This, they agreed to. And now, Palache waited. For he had told his men of this plan, and he had told them to return to a certain spot a day after setting him adrift. In truth, it was an uncertain thing. Had the dibbuk not relented, then the angel would have steered them away from the meet point, never to see his ship ever more. Had his men's faith truly been broken, they would not return, and then the words he and the angel had spoken would have been put to the test indeed.

Are they coming? Asked the angel.

"They will come," said Palache, and settled in to read, and to pray, and to wait.

THE WISDOM OF NIGHTINGALES

Once upon a time, in a land far to the north and west of wherever you happen to be, there lived a princess named Amber. Now, Amber was never quite certain what she was the princess of, but since she always was referred to as Princess Amber (especially in story introductions like this one), she figured that she had the job and might as well get used to it.

The princess lived in a tower miles away from anyone else. The tower was made of ice that an evil sorcerer had conjured from the mountains to the north, and he had cast spells on it so that it would never melt. It was two hundred feet high, and its sides were as smooth and slippery as glass. There were only four windows in the tower, and they were all on the top floor where the princess lived. The tower had no doors, however, and so Amber was trapped inside. She had explored every inch of her prison, from top to bottom, and had never been able to find a way out.

Now, the evil magician (whose name was Marcos, and who had a long black beard that he used to tie into braids when he was feeling fidgety) had stolen Princess Amber from her mother when she was very small for no reason that anyone could discern. Wise old men in the village would wag their beards (which did not have braids in them) and mutter something about curses and vengeance and so forth, but generally it was agreed that one too many spells had addled Marcos' brain, and that he was just a generally unpleasant person anyway.

When he had kidnapped Princess Amber, Marcos had made sure that the tower he imprisoned her in was full of all sorts of wonderful things. It was stuffed to the seams with toys for her to play with and clothes for her to try on, with books for her to read and delicacies for her to eat. Every morning, when the princess awoke, she would wander down the ice steps to the foot of the tower where a magnificent breakfast had mysteriously appeared, full of her favorite foods. At noon, a covered tray containing a delicious lunch would materialize on her windowsill, and at suppertime, a sumptuous meal would appear wherever she happened to be. But she was never allowed to see any other children, and she was never allowed to leave.

Now, the only human beings who knew where the Tower of Ice was were the princess (who knew exactly where it was because her toes were cold most of the time) and Marcos. All around it were green hills, occasionally dotted by dandelions when the weather was warm, and by drifts of snow when it wasn't. There were no villages nearby, however, no houses or castles or even roads. On clear days the princess could look south and see a thin trail of chimney smoke twisting its way into the sky, but she never saw a human face except in the pictures in her books, and she never heard a human voice except her own. She had everything a princess could ask for, but still she was lonely.

The princess' loneliness did not go unnoticed, however. While other people could never find the Tower of Ice, there were other eyes in the world in those days, and some of the sharpest belonged to the members of the Court of Birds. It was Sir Henry Jackdaw who first noticed the tower, on his way back from plucking a snowberry from the top of the highest mountain in the northlands, and who brought the matter to the attention of the Court as a whole. When he had done so, a terrible hullabaloo broke out. Some of the birds said that they should leave well enough alone, because the princess was a human child and none of their business. Some said that they should whittle away the tower with their beaks, because surely the princess could not have done something so terrible as to deserve to be caged like that. And some just loved to argue, and so the screeching and squawking and yammering and tweeting got louder and louder until not a bird among them could hear himself think.

And suddenly, when the debate was at its loudest and most vehement, and when the estimable Sir Henry Jackdaw himself was ready to challenge the ever-cheeky Baronet Mervyn Sparrow to a duel, a quiet voice could be heard. It was the voice of Terrence, who was a nightingale and the King of the Birds' court minstrel, and he was much loved by the other birds.

"I shall go see this tower," said Terrence, "and I shall see the girl who lives within, and then we shall discuss the matter further." And since all of the other birds held Terrence in such high regard, they fell silent, and as one flew away. Only Sir Henry Jackdaw remained, and he bowed.

"Excellently spoken, Terrence old chap," he said. "Now how's this for a plan: I'll fly with you to the tower--it's a terrible long way, it is, and Heaven knows you might get lost or eaten by a hungry cloud or some such along the way - and let you make your roost there. Then in a month, I'll come back for you and bring you home. That should be plenty of time for you to make up your mind, would you say?"

Terrence nodded, and stretched his wings. "A most excellent plan, Sir Henry. Let us fly!" And away they went, with the setting sun on their left and the first shy stars of the night on their right.

It took three days and three nights for Sir Henry and Terrence to find their way back to Amber's tower. They arrived at sunset on the third day, and saw the princess leaning over the railing of her balcony. She was singing, and the wind that always swirled around the tower caught her hair and made it dance around her face.

"That's her," Sir Henry whispered (unnecessarily, as they were still a good quarter mile away from the tower, and Amber couldn't understand the language of the birds in any case). "Poor thing, to have a voice like that and to be caged."

"I'll make my own judgments," said Terrence, "Thank you, Sir Henry."

"Hmmph," said Sir Henry, and flew back home.

For the next month, Terrence observed the princess in the tower. He watched her at play and when she slept. He heard her singing, and he listened to her read stories to herself from the great library that Marcos had left for her. And sometimes, late at night, he perched on the railing of her balcony and listened to the sounds her dreams made - for nightingales can hear dreams, which is why they know the saddest and loveliest songs of all of the birds.

At the end of the month, Sir Henry returned, full of bluster and bravado. "I say, Terrence old chap, had enough of this place yet? Worms and crabapples, man, you look like you've frozen your toes off! Come back home with me and we'll get you patched up in a jiff! Tut, tut!" And then, in a much quieter voice, he added, "So, what do you think?"

Terrence shook his head. "I think something very strange."

And so it was that before the Court of the Birds, Terrence

said something that had never been said before. He told the other birds of what he had seen, and heard, and what Amber had dreamed, and then he told them that they should teach her the language of the birds, so that she wouldn't be lonely anymore.

Never before had such a clamor been heard in the Court of the Birds. Wise old owls hooted and hollered, and said they'd never heard of such a thing. The eager young robins of the King's Royal Guard, crack archers all, swore that they'd defend the princess to the death, and would fight anyone who'd deny her this gift. And such a shouting and squawking had not been heard in years.

Finally, the king of the birds, who was a great golden eagle with wings wide enough to cover the night sky, spoke. "You ask a great deal, Terrence," he said. "But for you, we are willing to set aside our ancient ways (the King of the Birds always called himself "we," and no matter how silly it sounded, no other birds would dare to argue) and teach this girl." At this there was much cheering, but the King of the Birds held up his wing for silence. Instantly, there was a hush.

"Such gifts come with a price, however. Since you request this book, Terrence, you must grant it. You are hereby charged with teaching this princess the songs of the birds, our histories, legends, customs, rites and rituals. You must teach her the proper forms of address for the lowliest thrush and the most honorable and learned heron, and you must make her swear never to reveal our secrets.

Now, for the coin's other face. This is your doom: to have your boon granted. You cannot ask such a thing and expect it to come to you without cost, as free as the spring breeze. If you choose to do this thing, you are pronounced exile, never to return to this court until the day the princess leaves her tower." Then the King of the Birds lowered his beak slightly, and said in a softer voice, "You may, of course, choose to abandon your errand and remain here instead." For the King of the Birds was truly fond of Terrence, and had no wish to banish him, but he could not bring himself to revoke the sentence he had pronounced.

"Your Majesty is very gracious," said Terrence, and bowed. The King bowed in return, an honor never granted to any other bird, and then, as the assembled hosts of the Court gasped, Terrence flew off, alone.

Princess Amber was counting the colors of the sunset when the nightingale first perched on her finger. She had gotten up to three hundred and twelve (not counting a particular shade of red she wasn't certain hadn't been caused by a passing cloud) when the bird flew up, bold as brass, and landed on her finger. She noticed that he was gentle with his claws, and that he looked her in the eye with a serious expression.

"I'm sorry, Mr. Nightingale," she said (for she had studied all the birds of the air and was quite proud that she knew what he was) "but you can't stay here. It's much too cold for you, and I don't have any birdseed. Though I am so glad you came to visit me."

"The pleasure," said Terrence, "is mine, Princess."

Now, an ordinary little girl might have fainted at hearing a bird speak. She might scream, or insist that she was hearing things, or otherwise get herself most upset for no reason at all. But Princess Amber was most certainly not an ordinary little girl. She was a Princess, for one thing, and she was very brave, for another. So she merely looked at Terrence and corrected him. "Princess Amber," she said.

"Ah. Of course. A gem among your kind." Terrence did the same hopping little bow he had performed for the king (which was a great honor, though the princess did not know it) and shifted his feet, so as not to pinch her finger. "My name is

Terrence, and I have been charged by the King of Birds with a most wondrous and terrible task, in which your assistance is dreadfully necessary."

"Oh?" said Amber. "How can I help you, Terrence?"

Terrence straightened himself up and cleared his throat. "His Most Beneficent and Rapturous Majesty has instructed me, his court minstrel, to instruct you in the language of the birds. To do so, however, I must charge you never, on pain of having all the birds of the air as your sworn enemies, to reveal what I teach you. Do you so swear?"

Amber looked down at Terrence and giggled. "Why are you talking like that?"

"Err, umm." Terrence found himself at a loss for words. "Well," he finally said, "It seemed important to sound important, and ... oh, never mind. Let me start again. My name is Terrence, and I'm here to teach you the language of the birds so you can talk to us and not be lonely. You can't tell anyone, though, or I'll get in a great deal of trouble. Now, would you like to learn?"

And Princess Amber, being careful not to displace the nightingale on her finger, did a curtsey and said, "I would be honored."

Terrence looked extremely pleased with himself. "Right. No time like the present, then. Repeat after me." And with that, he sang, and in seconds, Princess Amber was singing with him.

Word of Terrence's audacity and exile had spread like wildfire from the Court of the Birds. Every sparrow sang of it, every peacock whispered the tale and tut-tutted behind a fan of feathers. And so it was that very shortly, Princess Amber began receiving visitors on the wind. Every morning, evening and afternoon birds presented themselves to her, and she was always gracious and charming to them. They would tell her stories of the places they'd seen and the news of the wide world, and in return she would read to them from her library. Even the King of the Birds visited one day, and Terrence fussed and fretted and eventually hid, but Princess Amber was regal and charming, and eventually His Raptorous Majesty bowed to her as well.

Princess Amber became known as the Princess of the Air, and of all the birds who visited her, only her friend Terrence could sing as sweetly as she. She became friends with a great many birds. Sir Henry Jackdaw would always make a point of visiting and telling her of his latest exploits. He told her of the time he outwitted the Great Steam Dragon of Antioch by having it fly into a cloud and lose track of itself, and of the time he walked a hundred miles pretending to have a broken wing so as to lure a hungry werewolf away from a poor farmer's cottage. Other birds brought her flowers, which she wove in garlands for her hair, or gems. And these things, which her friends had brought her, she treasured more than all the things that Marcos had provided.

But there was one bird who did not love Princess Amber. The short-tempered Baronet Mervyn Sparrow was jealous. He was jealous that Sir Henry had grown more popular as a result of finding the tower, and he was jealous that Terrence was much loved in exile. So he brooded on his jealousy, and eventually he hatched a terrible plan.

Before dawn, on the second-shortest day of the year, Sir Mervyn flew south, to where he'd heard an ancient buzzard say that the sorcerer Marcos the Rambunctious dwelt. For nine nights he flew, sleeping by day, until at last the twisted ramparts of the sorcerer's castle appeared. There was but one window, and Sir Mervyn flew boldly through it.

Inside, the sorcerer's palace was dark. Mervyn could see nothing. He looked left, looked right, and then suddenly felt cold talons seize him.

"What have we here? A little morsel?" Sir Mervyn twisted to see his captor. It was a gargoyle, with a leering face and long, sharp claws. The monster hung by its toes from the window frame, and it had reached down and caught Sir Mervyn like a spider catching a slow-moving fly.

"Unhand me, sirrah," said Sir Mervyn. "I am a knight of the Court of Birds, and I am here to see your master!"

"His master," said a voice from the shadows, "is here." And with that, Marcos the Rambunctious strode into the room. He was tall and thin, and his hair made a half-circle around the back of his head. He wore black robes inscribed with sigils that danced and moved, and his fingers were never still. "What do you have to say to me, Sir Bird?"

"I have an offer," Mervyn replied, though he was frightened.

"Is he offering to become lunch, master?" asked the gargoyle.

"Hush," said Marcos. "You haven't eaten since you were turned to stone. But you, my little bird, had best make me a very interesting proposition, or I may yet allow Grigory to test his appetites."

And so it was that Sir Mervyn outlined his plan. He would teach Marcos the language of the birds (for up until this point, they had been conversing in people-speech, which all birds know but disdain as unmusical) and then fly back to the King, claiming Princess Amber had betrayed her promise. As a result Terrence would suffer some terrible fate, and Princess Amber (whom Mervyn had never visited) would lose all of her friends, and he would be regarded as a hero for having brought the treachery to light. As for Marcos, he would now know the language of the birds, and be free to converse with them as he chose.

"Very interesting," said Marcos, and pulled the shutter across his window so that Mervyn could not fly away without ...

further discussion.

A season later, Sir Mervyn returned to the Court of the Birds, his very voice all a-flutter. "Your Majesty, Your Majesty!" he called, "I have grave news! Treachery!"

The King of the Birds leaned forward. "Indeed, Sir Mervyn? Tell me of this horrible crime."

Sir Mervyn hopped onto the ceremonial Branch of Telling, and panted a bit (for it had been a long flight). "Your Majesty," he finally began.

"He said that already," whispered Sir Henry loudly, to general laughter. Sir Mervyn glared at him, and began again.

"Your Majesty, I have proof that the human girl Amber has betrayed us! I was flying far south of here, in a land of ash and metal, and I heard a human man address me in our own tongue! It was the sorcerer, Marcos the Rambunctious, and he had learned the secrets of our songs! Curious as to how he had accomplished this feat, I risked great personal danger and flew into his palace. There, I discovered the truth - the human girl had taught him! She dwells in his tower, and as thanks for all his kindnesses, she gave him our most precious gift!"

"Nonsense!" called Sir Henry.

"Vile slander!" called another bird. And once again chaos raged back and forth, until the King of the Birds called a stop to it.

"We shall see," he decreed, "the truth of this matter. We shall visit this Marcos, and we shall visit once again Princess Amber, and we shall render our judgment. And if Princess Amber has betrayed us, never more shall a bird speak to her, and Terrence shall die."

Far off in her tower, Princess Amber knew nothing of this.

She had just received some wonderful news. For a sprightly magpie of her acquaintance named Jackalyn had found a small palace far away, and in it, she had found a beautiful and wise queen who ruled her land kindly and well but who mourned a daughter who had been stolen from her long ago. And Jackalyn described the rooms of the palace, and they stirred long-buried memories that haunted Amber's dreams. So Princess Amber asked her friend to return to the palace and tell her what she saw of the woman whom the princess knew was her mother.

Thus it was that Amber's trusted friends flew back and forth, to bring Amber the latest tales of her mother. They sang to Amber the songs her mother sang, they told her about the judgments she rendered and the mercy she showed, and about the smallest details of life in the palace. But Princess Amber remembered her promise, and did not ask the birds to bring her mother a message. Instead, she was thankful for her friends' gift of stories.

The next morning, the King of the Birds and all his court flew south, to meet with Marcos. He flew over the twisted landscape and saw preparations for war. Men with swords marched to and fro, and things that were not quite men lurked in shadows, hungrily. And at the very heart of the desolation stood the castle of Marcos the Rambunctious, who wished to be known as Marcos the Conqueror.

When the King of the Birds flew into view, Marcos greeted him courteously, and spun him a gossamer net of lies. It had been Princess Amber, he said, who taught him the language of birds, on one of his many visits to the Tower. For Princess Amber, it seemed, was his daughter.

The King of the Birds listened to Marcos' tale with great

deliberation. Then, with a great rushing of wings, he flew north toward the Tower, there to pronounce his sentence. All unseen, on wings of stone Grigory the gargoyle flew behind him.

Meanwhile, Princess Amber had begun to grow sad. The tales her friends brought back of her mother's land were grimmer with each passing day. Ruffians and monsters harried the borders, driving back the soldiers of the Queen. And on the shields of the evil men who fought was the symbol of a mocking, black tower. One particularly clever magpie managed to dip her bill in ink and sketch the sign on a piece of the princess' carefully hoarded paper, and the princess gasped. There could be no doubt: the tower the bird had drawn was the mirror image of her own.

It was a day later that the King of the Birds arrived at the Tower of Ice. His face was stern, and his voice was terrible. "Terrence," he commanded, "Show thyself to thy king!"

"Yes, Your Majesty?" replied the nightingale. "This is an unexpected-"

"Silence!" the King thundered. "You shall answer our questions, and otherwise, you shall not speak. Did you, in fact, teach this human girl our language?"

"Of course, Your Majesty." Terrence was puzzled. "I did so at your command."

"You will answer only the questions that are put to you." The King's anger was terrible. "Did you not make the girl promise that she would never reveal our secrets to another human?"

"I did, Your Majesty. And she has not done so. She has not seen-"

"Another word, Terrence, and I will give you to the vultures for their sport. Do you understand me?"

At this precise moment Princess Amber emerged from her chamber and saw the King of the Birds on her balcony. She curtseyed.

The King of the Birds cocked his head at her. "Young woman, you have been accused of a terrible crime."

Princess Amber was astonished. "What crime could I have committed, Your Majesty? Surely I have been a good friend to your people."

"That remains to be seen. I have been told by your father-"

"My father?" she said, forgetting for a moment that she was interrupting a king, though truth be told, she wouldn't much have cared either way.

"Ahem. Your father, the great and noble sorcerer Marcos. He has told me that you shared with him our secret. If you have, then Terrence must pay the ultimate price for your misdeed. Now, princess, speak truly: Have you broken your vow?"

Just then there was a great commotion behind the king, and who should emerge but Sir Henry Jackdaw. In one talon was the struggling Grigory, and in the other was Sir Mervyn. "Unhand me, coward! I'll fight you!" shouted Sir Mervyn. Grigory just snarled.

"Here are your real traitors, Your Majesty," Sir Henry spat. "I caught them plotting in the distance. Sir Mervyn taught the human our speech, and this creature is his spy!"

The King of the Birds turned, and great was his anger. "Then, Sir Mervyn, as you have broken our law, you and your strange friend must die. Prepare yourselves."

"No!" All heads turned, for never before had anyone dared gainsay the King. It was Princess Amber, and she spoke in the language of the birds. "Your Majesty, I never broke my promise to you, but still the fault here is mine. Were it not for me, these poor wretches would not have conspired. I ask you to spare them, that they might repair their evil."

The King coughed with surprise. "Why are you talking like that?" he said quietly, and Princess Amber blushed. More loudly, he said, "Very well. As you have proven yourself a true friend of the Court of Birds, Princess Amber, I grant your wish. And we shall take flight against the forces of Marcos the Rambunctious, he who would be a conqueror, and rout them. None may lie to the King of the Birds and boast of the fact."

"You, little monster," he then said to Grigory, "shall stay with me, as a jester. Amuse me, and you will be treated well. Betray me, and great shall be my wrath. And as for you..." He fixed Sir Mervyn with a deadly glare, and the sparrow trembled.

"I will take charge of him if it pleases Your Majesty," said the princess.

"Very well," said the King. "I remand him to you. He is your prisoner, to do with as you will."

"Then I release him," said Princess Amber. "But I ask him to remain here, and try to learn to be my friend - and Terrence's as well."

Then another murmur swept through the crowd of birds, for they had never seen mercy before. But those birds who had witnessed the far-away queen knew that her wisdom and justice had passed to her daughter as well.

"Then all is settled," said the King, and he prepared to take flight.

"Not all," said the princess. "Your Majesty, all of this trouble was caused because Terrence didn't want me to be lonely. And now I'm not. He has been the best friend and most wonderful teacher I could imagine. But humans should not know the language of birds. See what trouble it's caused you? No, as much as I love this, it cannot continue. Not if it would cause harm to come to Terrence or any of my other friends."

"So you are asking me to take away your gift?" said the King of the Birds, amazed. "Never before has such been granted, and now you refuse it? I cannot imagine the sheer temerity!"

"Nevertheless, it is what I want - for the sake of my friends."

The King of the Birds bowed his head. "Very well, " he said, and prepared to speak the magic words which would steal the gift of tongues from the princess. Just then, however. Terrence spoke.

"Your Majesty," he said, "I think I have an idea."

The King ruffled his neck feathers, as he was unused to being interrupted. "Yes, Terrence?" he said slowly.

Terrence hopped over to the king and whispered in his ear for a moment. And then, if eagles can be said to smile, the King smiled.

"You are right, Princess Amber," he said. "A human girl should not know our language. But a gift given at king's command should not be refused, and more importantly, your friends love you as much as you love them. Therefore, I - ahem, we - have made a royal decision. Where are my magicians?"

Two portly owls waddled forth. "Here, Your Majesty," they said in unison. "What is your command?"

"This girl sings our songs. This cannot be. Therefore, she should no longer be a girl. Do you not agree?"

And at this, Princess Amber's heart leapt within her, for she wanted more than anything to be free of the Tower of Ice and to see her mother. The owls chuckled and nodded and hemmed and hawed, and finally, the shorter and fatter one said, "We can make this so, Your Majesty."

"Very good," he said. "And do you wish it also, Princess Amber?" he asked.

"Oh, I do," she said in a whisper. "Please."

The owls worked their ancient magic then, and the princess found herself shrinking and growing feathers. As she did so, she heard a kindly voice ask, "What sort of bird shall you be?"

With her last smile, she said, "A nightingale."

Now, Princess Amber's story does not end there. It is sung of by birds to this day how she flew with the King's army, and how they routed the brigands and monsters. Sir Mervyn fought bravely and well, but was slain in the last and greatest battle. His last words were a request for forgiveness, and to call Terrence a friend. Amber's mother the Queen then ruled the lands that had belong to Marcos, and under her care they bloomed once again. Marcos was driven from his castle by three shrieking ravens, who let him neither sleep nor eat until he had fled far to the south, and his tower was torn down. The Tower of Ice remained standing as a marvel of the world, but only the birds continued to visit it, for it had once housed their friend. Grigory the Gargoyle grew fond of serving the King of the Birds, who acquired the habit of sharpening his beak on his jester's nose. The King learned to laugh, and Grigory learned that Marcos' dark and evil ways were not those he would willingly choose. Jackalyn and Sir Henry found that they had much in common, and they took turns courting one another, much to their friends' amusement.

And on summer evenings, the queen of a newly healed land would sit in her garden and listen to the songs of the nightingales, who so often came to see her.

LICKING ROADKILL

Cole was licking the highway when the cops picked him up the night before Thanksgiving. Reckless endangerment, they said, and obstructing traffic, and whatever else they could come up with to get him out of the road and into a holding cell.

Later, I went past the spot where they arrested him, on my way into town to bail him out, stopping for a moment to take a look. A deer and a truck had made unfortunate contact there, and the highway was a twenty-foot-long streak of red. A couple of cars passed me going the other way. Speeding, both of them, and one didn't have its lights on. Cole had gotten lucky, I decided, even if he didn't realize it.

Bailing him out didn't take too long. We'd been through this before, the duty sergeant and me. She did the paperwork, and I handed over the money, and all the while phones rang and people shouted and cops ran out the door to deal with the usual pre-holiday drunk and disorderlies.

"You going anywhere for the holiday?" I asked the sergeant. She shook her head. "Husband's family finally came to visit this year. I get to finish this shift, then go home and cook."

"At least you'll only be dealing with one turkey at home," I ventured. It didn't get a smile. She just slid the forms across her desk. "Sign here and here. I'll have someone bring him around."

I signed. She picked up the papers. "You sure you don't want to leave him here overnight? Might teach him a lesson. Seriously, this is the third time we've picked him up this year."

"Cole's a slow learner," I said. "Besides, the wife said go get him. So I'd better bring him home."

"Guess you'd better, then." She moved off. There was some yelling in the back, and then another cop, one I didn't recognize, walked out with Cole. He had his head down, and his shaggy mess of a haircut hid his face, but I could tell it was him. There was blood on that blue work shirt of his, for one thing, and on the knees of his dungarees, too. It wasn't a good look.

"Hello, Cole," I said.

"Hey, Jerry," he said without looking up. "Sorry you had to come on out here."

"Your sister was worried about you," I said, and he flinched. Good enough; we could save any further conversation until we got in the car.

The cop - his badge said "Piscotty" - gave Cole an ungentle shove toward me. "He's all yours. Keep him out of trouble the rest of the weekend, okay? We need the room back there."

"I'll do my best." Cole turned around, but I tugged him away from the door before he could say something stupid. Instead, we walked around to my F-150 in silence. I let him in - the electronic locks had given up years ago - then walked around and climbed in myself. "Seatbelt," I said automatically, then started her up and rolled out towards home.

"Yeah, yeah," Cole muttered, but he clicked the belt anyway. "Hey, uh, thanks for getting me out of there. I didn't want to spend Thanksgiving in jail."

"I figured. And don't thank me. Like I said, it was your sister's idea." We headed down the main drag as a light rain fell.

Bars on either side of the street were spitting out customers and sucking down new ones, folks without families or looking to avoid them, prodigal sons and daughters looking to reconnect with their old classmates after returning home for the holiday and finding they'd outgrown their old familiar places.

Cole craned his head and licked his lips. "You want to stop for a drink?"

"No. Cecily said to get you straight home."

"Aw." He shrunk down into his seat, arms crossed. I took a left onto the county road and picked up speed. "You mind if I turn on the radio?"

"Don't care one way or the other." I flicked on the high beams. "Just try not to pick something that sucks."

"You think everything I like sucks," he said, petulant, but reached for the dial anyway. A little fiddling brought us past two preachers, a couple of country stations, and some talk show blowhard before he settled for a college football game between two nobody schools neither of us had ever heard of. "There. That good enough for you?"

I shrugged. "It's fine. Now you got the radio, you'll maybe want to think about what you're going to tell your sister. She's spitting tacks."

He blinked at me. "I thought you said she was worried, not mad."

"Mad is how some people show they're worried. I'm surprised you never noticed that. I picked up on it years ago."

"Yeah, and you married her anyway." Cole shuddered. "Shit. Why's she gotta be so pissed off about everything?"

We passed the town limits, a few brick houses with

crumbling sheds disappearing into the grass, and the dark. Streetlights stopped at the town line, too, so it was just two lanes of rain-slick black asphalt headed into the woods and the dark. I flicked on the high beams, watched them bounce off the mist for a few seconds and then thought better of it.

"She's pissed off because her dumbass older brother, whom she loves dearly, keeps on doing stupid shit that might get him killed or worse, and because said dumbass brother seems incapable of realizing that what he's doing is a danger to himself and others. Including, I might add, her."

Cole snarled. "Who asked you, anyway?"

"You did," I replied evenly. "Now who's winning?"

"Temple, I think," he said. "That a college? Ain't never heard of Temple before." He sniffed. "I guess if they're playing on a Wednesday night, they can't be too good."

"Probably not." Trees sped past and the rain picked up. "So, what are you going to tell Cecily?"

"Gonna tell her the truth. Tell her I was minding my own business, and the cops started hassling me for no reason. I wasn't doing nothing wrong."

I let out a long, slow breath. "I don't think that's going to fly, Cole. Not this time."

"But it's true!"

"We both know better than that. They called from the station as soon as you were brought in and told Cecily everything. She's not going to buy that act of yours, not this time."

He sat bolt upright. "But it's not an act! They did hassle me!"

"They pulled you off the road before you got turned into splat number two. And any day now, someone is going to start asking questions about why they keep having to peel you away from the fresh roadkill, and when that happens, things are going to get ugly. For you, for me, for the whole family. For Cecily."

"I don't want nothing to happen to her."

"Then you'd better get some self-control.

He grunted something that might have been assent, then turned and rolled down the window. "This OK?" he asked and didn't bother with an answer before sticking his head out into the wind.

"Oh, Cole," I muttered under my breath and kept driving.

Town disappeared in the rearview, the twinkling lights reduced to a purple glow in the cloud-scudded sky. Soon there was nothing on either side of us but darkened farmland, and it would stay that way until we reached home.

My phone buzzed. I dug it out of my pocket with one hand, checked and saw it was Cecily. "Hey babe," I said by way of a greeting. "How you doing?"

"You know damn well how I'm doing, John. You got him?" She was in one of her moods, I could tell. No small talk was going to calm her down, so it was best just to play it straight.

"Got him right here. You want to talk to him?"

"Not really, but I kind of have to now, don't I?" There was anger there, sure, but something else, too, a bone weariness that I'd rarely heard. If Cecily was feeling that way now, I didn't envy Cole none.

I nodded, then realized she couldn't see it. "I guess you'd better, yeah. Hang on, let me get him for you. Love you."

"Love you too. Now let me talk to my dumbass brother."

"Hey Cole," I said away from the phone and then punched

him in the arm when he didn't respond.

"What'd you do that for?" He sounded wounded, like I'd kicked a puppy. But he pulled his head back inside the window to glare accusingly at me.

"Phone, Cole," I said and handed him mine. "It's your sister."

He stared at it for a second, then brought it to his ear. "Hello?"

I couldn't make out any of the words Cecily used, only that there were a lot of them, and they were very loud. Cole tried to interrupt her a few times, and that went about as well as you might expect. Every so often she sounded like she was winding down, Cole'd say something else dumb, and she'd start right back up again.

That went on for the better part of ten miles before Cole handed the phone back to me. "She says she wants to talk to you now," he said, and he sounded shaken. I looked over at him, and he was pale and sweating. Whatever Cecily had said, it had put the fear of God in him.

"What can I do for you, babe?" I said as I took the phone. "Everything all right?"

"Everything is not all right, or you wouldn't be doing what you're doing." She let out a long breath. "Sorry, hon, don't mean to take it out on you."

"It's fine," I said. "You're the head of the family. You've got a lot of pressure on you."

"Don't I know it," Cecily said. "Thanks for backing me, hon. A lot of men wouldn't do that."

"You didn't marry a lot of men. You married me. Now are you sure about the rest of this? Not too late to change your mind."

"It was too late a long time ago. Love you."

"Love you too, babe," I said and hung up.

"She didn't yell at you," Cole said accusingly.

"That's because I'm not a fuckup, Cole," I said evenly. "I'm the one bailing you out of jail, not the other way around. Now what did she say to you? Maybe I can help take the sting out."

Cole shook his head. "She said she was disappointed in me. Can you believe it? Said that Ma and Pa would be disappointed in me. My own little sister telling me these things. I'm the big brother. I should be head of the family, not her."

I sighed. "Cole, we've been over this a thousand times. You and I both know you're not cut out for it, and you agreed to it. Hell, you're the one who nominated her when it came time."

"She's my little sister. There's nothing I wouldn't do for her." Now he was contrite, his moods swinging all over the place. This wasn't a good sign.

"That's why it meant so much to her for you to straighten up and fly right. How long's it been since you did meth, hmm?"

"Three weeks," he said defiantly. "Not since my last talking to. Nothing but beer since then."

"Nothing but beer." I nodded. "And if I made you pee in a cup, all that would come back would be High Life?"

"I don't drink that piss. Stag, brother."

I shook my head. "Right. Stag. That's all you'd read? No weed, no blow, no meth?"

He leered at me. "Doesn't matter. You can't make me take a pee test. You can't make me do anything. Only reason you've got a voice in the family is 'cause you married my sister."

For a moment, I wished I could have a cigarette, It would spare me the need to keep talking to Cole for a minute or two.

But Cecily had told me to quit, and so I had. It was best to do what Cecily told you to. Instead, I flicked off the radio - whoever Temple was, they were losing badly - and gunned it a little. Cecily had asked me to have this talk with Cole, too, so I was going to have it, no matter how pointless I thought it was.

"It wouldn't be me making you take the test and you know it, Cole. So come clean with me, and maybe I can make things go easier for you. When's the last time you smoked meth?"

"Three weeks ago," he repeated stubbornly.

"Uh-huh. Cole, they caught you out in the middle of the highway, licking deer meat off the asphalt." Suddenly I was tired of Cole and his bullshit. "Your sister asked one thing of you - that you kick the drugs. She offered help, she offered money, she offered a place to stay away from all your dealers and smoking buddies where you could get your head straight, and you wouldn't do it. Why is that, Cole?"

"Not wouldn't, couldn't." Now he was back to the shakes. "I would do anything for Cecily. Anything. Except that. 'Cause I can't."

Real soft, I said, "You know that's a problem, right? We can't have you getting out of control and getting the family in trouble."

"I know," he said miserably. "Maybe you should just lock me up."

"Thought about it," I said casually.

That brought his head up like a shot. "You didn't!"

"I most surely did, but Cecily shut it down. Said it wasn't right to do that to family, even fucked-up family."

"She's my sister, all right. Attagirl, Cecily! I always knew she'd have my back."

I shifted in my seat, the .45 at my hip resting there uncomfortably. "She's got the whole family to look out for," I said, but I looked away as I said it.

There was silence in the cab of the truck for a couple of miles, Cole fidgeting in his seat beside me and me just trying to keep my eyes on the road. Finally, he broke the quiet. "Where you taking me, Jerry? This is the longest ride home ever."

"Same ride as always," I told him. "Just taking it slow cause of the rain. Tires are worn down on the truck, so I don't want to skid out."

"Oh. That makes sense." He curled up in a ball, looking like a scared kid and not a grown-ass man, 42 years old, whose life had been one long litany of fuckups. "You know, I always liked you, Jerry. When Cecily first brought you round and there were some of us that weren't sure you were family material, I stood up for you, you know. I said, 'That Jerry, he's a good man, and Cecily loves him. 'Some of the others wasn't so kind."

"Thank you for that, Cole. It means a lot to hear you say that. And now here we are." *Jesus*, I thought, *why did he have to make this any harder than it had to be.*

"And now here we are," he said, echoing my tone as well as my words. Then, as I pulled the truck off to the side of the road into a dark, wooded patch, he took a look around. "Where's here? What are we stopping for?"

I took a deep breath. I knew Cole would never understand, but I owed it to him to try. "Cole. You remember when you and Cecily were growing up and you used to read her fairy tales?"

His face screwed up into a mask of puzzlement. "But I don't see what that's got to do with anything. The truck all right?"

"The truck's fine," I reassured him. "And bear with me. You

remember Snow White? When the huntsman is supposed to take the baby Snow White out into the woods and kill her so the baby couldn't come back and kill the queen some day?"

"Yeah." Cole was still hesitant. "But the huntsman let her go, and the dwarves found her, and she lived happily ever after."

I nodded. "So she did. But the queen didn't."

"Too bad for her, I say," Cole chortled. "She shoulda picked a better huntsman."

"Uh-huh," I said and drew on him.

"What the fuck, Jerry?" He scrabbled in his seat, trying to get as far away from the gun as possible. "What are you fucking around for??

"I'm not fucking around, Cole. Open the door nice and easy, then get out and stand next to the truck." I had already slipped my seat belt off and was getting ready to slide out and walk around.

But Cole had to fuck things up once again. He went to run for it, and I shot him twice in his skinny ass before he made five steps. He went down, scrabbled a bit in the dirt, and then lay still.

I walked around the truck, pistol still out, and went over to where he was sprawled on the ground. He heard me coming and raised his head off the dirt. "Why, Jerry?" he asked. "Cecily's gonna be so mad at you." He coughed and black blood came out of his mouth. That was the silver in the rounds I'd put into him, doing its work.

I knelt down beside him. "Cole, you damned fool. I tried to warn you. This was all Cecily's idea."

"My sister? My little sister? No, no, no," and then more coughing.

"You got too sloppy," I told him. "The booze and the drugs,

and you not half bothering to hide what you were from the folks down in town. Licking the highway, Cole, for fuck's sake. You were putting the whole family at risk, and Cecily made the hard call. She loves you, but she couldn't let you take us all down."

At that, Cole laughed. "Is that what she told you? Yeah, I can see why you'd believe it. You'd swallow silver for her, you got it so bad. But just you wait. She turned on me. One of these days, she's gonna turn on you."

Then he lay down for the last time and died.

"I expect she will," I said to the corpse, "But not today." I picked the dead body up and slung it into the back of the truck as gently as I could, then put a tarp over it in case I got stopped, which wasn't likely this far out. Then I pulled out my phone and called a familiar number.

"Where are you, hon?" Cecily's voice came over the line. "Is it done?"

"I'm in that wooded patch Old Man Rucker let grow up on his property, and yeah, it's done."

She let out a little sob and then said "I'm sorry you had to do that. I shouldn't have asked it of you."

"It is what it is," I said. "He's in the back of the truck, in case you want to give him a decent burial."

"I'd like that," Cecily said. "What about his court date?"

"I'll tell 'em he stole a hundred bucks out of your purse and skipped town. They won't look for him too hard."

"No, I don't expect they will." There was quiet on the line for a minute. Then, "Come home, hon. Bring my brother with you."

"Will do." I went to break the connection, but before I did, I could hear her say, "I'll be waiting."

THE UNICORN AT THE SOIREE

"The problem," the unicorn said, "is that I'm not supposed to be here." Then he shook his mane, took a sip of his sidecar, and gave a melodramatic sigh.

"Of course you're supposed to be here," I told him, and gestured to the discreetly hovering waiter that my drink needed freshening. He took the glass without a word and vanished into the crowd. Melisande's parties were *events*. They were always incredibly crowded and always impeccably staffed; to obtain an invitation for one was the surest sign that one had, to steal a phrase, arrived.

And in the meantime, they were enjoyable in their own right. I had no doubt that the tuxedoed little man would have my beverage back to me shortly. "It's just not a party without you," I said, and turned my attention back to the unicorn. He'd been brushed for the occasion, and someone had spent a great deal of time adorning his mane and beard with tiny Swarovski crystals that caught the shuddering light from the chandelier when he moved. His hooves had been shod in silver, the better to create that well-loved chiming sound of his steps to announce his initial arrival at the festivities. Only I, and a few others of his closest friends, knew that he preferred to go unshod, but that he withstood the indignity to make Melisande happy. It was her party, he'd told us earlier in the evening, and he wasn't going to do anything to spoil it.

And yet, here we were - the unicorn, me, a clingy poet called Deever who'd attached himself to our little circle a few weeks prior, and a bodyguard named Amos Plikington who doubled as the unicorn's squash partner on alternate Thursdays. How exactly he played the game was beyond me, but Plikington assured me that for a quadruped, the unicorn had a wicked backhand, and I wasn't inclined to call him a liar. And the music played, and Melisande moved through the crowd, surrounded by the beautiful people and the handsome boys who sought the impossible, and we four stood in the corner watching it all.

"That's not what I meant," said the unicorn, and snorted, pawing at the parquet floor a couple of times. "What I mean, is that I'm not supposed to be *here*. In this place. Now."

"Where are you supposed to be, then?" asked Deever, slightly tipsy. "Don't tell me you have another engagement. I mean, there's that party down in the Village that Lester's throwing, and-"

The unicorn shook his head, and the tip of his horn passed dangerously close to Deever's surgically reconfigured nose. "No, no. There is nowhere else I have to be. Nowhere else I want to be except here with Melisande, making her happy. And that is the problem."

"You know, anything you want, you just have to ask her for it. She's happy to give it to you." Plikington was drinking beer out of a brown glass bottle, and with his free hand he gave the unicorn's milk-white flank a friendly thump. "I mean, you remember that time when you wanted those thistles, and she had to have them flown in straight from Scotland for you, fresh.

Cost a fortune, but she didn't blink. She loves you that much."

"I know, I know. But that's not the point. She'd die for me. I'd die for her. Fantastic, don't you think? That we'd both be happy to end up dead for one another?" He drained the sidecar and tapped his hoof impatiently to summon the waiter to bring him another. The man glided up with his tray already loaded, the unicorn's drink (in a bucket) and mine (in a martini glass) twinned side by side. He deposited the beverages wordlessly, then slipped away before Deever could request another zinfandel spritzer.

"So if that's not the point," I said, and took a sip, "and if you're not supposed to be here, but you can't be anywhere else, then it sounds like you want to be nowhere. If I'm reading you right, that is."

"That's closer," the unicorn said moodily, but his eyes were on Melisande as the party ebbed and flowed around her. There was one fellow, a tall, handsome chap I'd seen around once or twice before, drifting closer than most for a moment or two, and then she'd spin away, laughing. "Look, how long do you think we've been together?"

"Sixteen years, nine months, and two days," said Plikington helpfully. "The date's posted kind of prominently around here."

"Uh-huh. And how long do you think unicorns usually stay with their maidens?"

"I thought they generally got captured right after they put their heads in virgin's laps. Or is that a myth?" Deever realized what he'd said, turned bright red, and shut up immediately after Plikington smacked him on the back of the head. I ignored him. The unicorn didn't.

"The horn trade's been outlawed for years, Deever. You

know that. No, what usually happens is that a virgin goes out into the woods and sings, a unicorn finds her, and they have a lovely interlude with his head in her lap. Sometimes it's a one-off, sometimes it goes on for a while, but it generally doesn't turn into a long-term relationship with real estate implications."

I cocked my head, in unconscious imitation of what he was doing. "Why not? It seems like every father's dream. No surer way to see if your little girl's a little *too* grown up than if her unicorn suddenly disappears."

He looked at me. "We've been friends a long time, so I'll let you get away with that one. And besides, you're right, even if you're being totally obnoxious while you're at it. We're not supposed to be around forever."

"You're not?" Deever sounded surprised. Plikington smacked him again.

"We're moments," the unicorn said. "Affirmations. Transcendent personifications of an ideal of purity. But we're not the goal. Not the *achievement*." The last was said with uncharacteristic bitterness, so much so that I nearly dropped my drink in surprise.

"Surely you don't think-" I started, but he interrupted.

"I don't think that moment is where you stop. Time passes. Life goes on. You grow, you change, you try new things-"

"Or you don't," I said, finally understanding. "And maybe you should."

The unicorn nodded, nearly upsetting his drink bucket. His head came up, muzzle wet, muscles corded. "It's not that I don't love her," he said. "It's that she's decided that this, whatever this is, is more important, is better than anything else she might ever have. And that's not what I'm supposed to be about."

"You want her to ..." Deever's voice trailed off, thankfully, before he could find an inappropriate verb to insert.

"I want her to live," the unicorn said. "Even though it will break my heart."

"Where is she, anyway?" Plikington suddenly said. "She's not on the floor."

We all looked; Plikington for his employer, and the unicorn for his love, and Deever in the direction that everyone else was looking.

Me, I was looking for the handsome man who'd come too close before, and I didn't see him, either.

And when I looked back at the unicorn, his eyes were bright with a terrible, terrible hope.

"The moment held is the moment lost," he said, and then there was the sound of crystal and silver, falling timelessly to the floor.

A SPLASH
OF
BLUE

He walked into the room the way a fat man would, gut first and shoulders thrown back, a slow lock-kneed shuffle that didn't promise fast action. "You the detective?" he asked?

I looked him over. He wasn't fat; the opposite, in fact. Tall and skinny, just this side of haggard, wearing what looked to be his Sunday best. Gray hair and a lined face, a tremble in the hands and a care for where each footstep landed told me he wasn't just older, he was unwell.

"I am."

He grunted and nodded, then took a few steps forward. "You the detective for the Blood?"

"I am," I said again, without getting up, though he had piqued my curiosity. I gestured to the chair on the other side of my desk, which he took as an invitation to sit down. Stiff joints meant it took him a minute to settle in; pain in his eyes meant it took another minute for him to pull himself together.

"Nice office," he grunted at me when he was finally settled. "Doing work for Blood must pay pretty good."

"Look, Mister-"

"Carson. Jubal Carson."

"Mister Carson, if you're here to talk to me, you're here to talk to me about a case, not about my office decor and not about the Blood. Now you can tell me about what you want me to do, or you can get up and walk away. Those are the only two options. Now which is it going to be?"

He stared at me for a minute with big eyes and his mouth set small and hard. "Can I get a drink of water," he asked. "Then I'll tell you about Michelle, and you can tell me what it'll cost to find her."

"That's better." I shoved my chair back from my desk and walked over to the mini fridge in the corner. There were a couple of bottles of water inside, and a couple of Diet Cokes, and a couple of beers. I grabbed two of the waters and a couple of coffee cups, and handed one of each to Carson. He grunted a thanks, then drank the water out of the bottle in one long pull.

"Now then," he said when he was finished, the empty bottle rolling around on the floor where he'd dropped it, "I want you to find someone. I want you to find Michelle."

"And she is?"

"My daughter. And she's Blood." He reached into his jacket pocket and pulled out an honest-to-God photograph, a Wal-Mart Photo Booth 4-shot strip. "Here," he said, and slid it across the table.

I picked it up. It was, to nobody's surprise, 4 pictures of a girl. She looked young, blonde and pretty in the way all 16 year old girls are pretty. Hair down past her shoulders, freckles on her face, a little too much nose and a little too much chin for anyone who wasn't in love with her to call her beautiful, but all in all she wouldn't have trouble getting someone to take her to the prom. She was wearing an NC State sweatshirt in the pictures and a pair of well-worn jeans, and she was smiling.

"My daughter. Gone two weeks now. Police say she's 18, she

can go where she wants, but she's my daughter and I say she's missing."

I studied the picture some more. "She finished high school?"

"Almost. Was gonna go to State. I wanted her to go to ECU. We fought 'bout that."

"You fight about anything else?"

He held my gaze. "Music. Curfew. Drinkin'. What she wanted to do with her life when she grew up. Pretty much everything you can fight over, when you think about it."

"Fair enough." I thought about it for a second. "Anything else you want to tell me before I decide whether or not I'm doing this?"

With slow deliberation, he leaned forward. "I can pay your rates."

"My rates are pretty standard."

"I mean the rates you charge for Blood."

I leaned forward. "What are you offering?"

"She's my daughter. Anything I got. Hope, fear, regret…"

I shook my head. "I get a lot of those. What else?"

He didn't blink. "Remorse. The genuine article." And he reached across the desk, hand open and ready.

"Remorse, you say?"

Carson gave me a dry, humorless grin. "More'n you'll ever know, and truer than the Bible. You get that, plus your regular rates, plus the same again if you bring her home."

I thought about it for a moment. "You sure?"

"I'm here, ain't I?"

"Fair enough." And I took his hand in mine, and I closed my eyes, casting out for the true feeling he was offering me.

There it was, just below the surface. It was strong, and it was genuine. I reached out for it and it came easily, flowing like spring meltwater into me.

I opened my eyes. Carson had pulled his hand back, and in mine, I could see what he'd given me. Remorse, glowing ice blue and cold to the touch. Carefully, I got a couple of old cloth napkins that I kept for this type of thing out of my desk and tied the stuff up. It sat there on my desk, quietly glowing and waiting.

"Good enough?" Carson asked.

"Good enough," I told him. "But I still get my fee, even if she's fine and she doesn't want to come back."

"Just knowing where she is'll be enough."

The Remorse tugged at me. Distracted, I pushed it away. Something about this wasn't sitting right, but I needed the work and I wanted what he was offering. Genuine Remorse doesn't come down the pike that often.

Besides, there was the girl. Probably shacked up with a boyfriend somewhere to get away from an old man she didn't get along with, easy to find and easy to collect. But just in case she wasn't...

"I'll take it," I said. "But I'm going to have to need to see her room."

They say the Blood comes to us from the Otherworld, from the places off the edge of the map where the Fair Folk and their cousins dwell, and where every so often a mortal takes a demon lover. The child of that union - and there is always a child, or so the legend goes - brings the Blood back into the world, and passes it down through the generations of their descendants. It can get thinned, it can get watered down, but it never quite goes all the way away.

And those with the Blood, well, we can do marvelous things. No rhyme or reason to them - one Blood might be able to understand the talk of the birds, another one to turn his fingers to knives. Most folk could just do little things, party tricks and cantrips and little illusions. But sometimes Blood meets Blood between the sheets, and strange combinations happen, and strange powers arise.

Me, I could taste emotions, among other things. Feed on 'em for strength, if freely offered. Useful in my line of work, awkward at other times. It was my Gift, and I made it work for me. But all of us, with Gifts great and small, knew one another by Blood. We understood each other. Watched out for each other. And did things for each other that we maybe wouldn't do for normal folk.

Like take this job.

The house, if you wanted to call it that, was up Butner way. It was a ramshackle thing with a wraparound porch and a sagging barn, and most of the fields around it had gone to seed. Squint, and you'd think the landscape was moving in on the house and waiting for a sign of weakness before devouring it.

Inside, the place was under siege. The kitchen was neat, and so were a couple of chunks of common area. The rest was given over to dust and clutter, like Carson had given up on keeping the place tidy and was fighting a holding action to protect the bits he used. Everything I saw in the place spoke of him - no sign of a woman's touch anywhere in the decor. I could see why a girl would want to get away from this place.

But he'd said she was going to school in the fall. Escape hadn't been so far away.

I cleared my throat to ask Carson a question but he was already plunging down a hallway toward what I guessed was Michelle's room. "Sorry, bulb's out," he offered, then opened the door.

It was a revelation.

Every square inch of wall space was covered, half in posters of faraway and imaginary places. The other half was hand drawn or painted, clearly the work of the girl who lived here. They were passable, I suppose - landscapes and castles and misty mountains far away, executed with energy but not a whole lot of skill.

Naturally, I lied about them. "These are some nice pieces. Your daughter has some skill."

"They're crap," Carson said, stomping into the room. "They're crap, I told her they were crap, and her teacher told her they were crap, and she kept on saying she was going to be an artist anyhow 'cause she had vision. I wanted her to go to ECU, get a degree in something useful, but she was having none of it." He stopped unexpectedly and stared down at the floor. "That was our last fight," he said sadly, and sat abruptly on the white-sheeted bed.

"What did her mother say?"

He looked up at me. "Her momma's gone. Been that was since she was a little girl. Been just us for fifteen-odd years. And now she's gone, and I'm goin'…" He coughed a couple of times, which made me not want to ask about his health.

"What did her mother die of," I asked instead, looking for something useful and safe.

If we'd been outside, he would have spat. "Never said she

was dead. Just that she was gone. Don't know where she went, wouldn't tell you if I did."

"If your daughter had communication with her, maybe she..."

"My daughter knows her momma left her. She wanted no part of that if it came back into her life. You find her, you ask her and she'll tell you it's true."

I thought about saying something, but thinking was about as far as that idea got. "You got a name for that teacher you said thought her art wasn't good enough?"

"Why you want to talk to her for?" Carson grumbled.

"If she really did say that Michelle's stuff wasn't any good, that might have sent her off in a different direction - or it might have made her try harder. Either way, I'll just be asking a few questions."

"Fine. I'll go get the name." Carson stumped off. I took advantage of the opportunity to case the room.

There wasn't much to see, apart from the art on the walls. Clothes were neatly folded, and I had a hard time seeing what she might have taken with her. No computer on her desk, no diary in her desk drawer, and all the sheets and window shades were white. The kid couldn't have had less personality in her room if she tried. I checked the lone closet and it was full, too - dresses and jeans and suchlike, and if she'd taken anything from there, I couldn't tell you what it was.

I stepped back out and closed the door, and Carson handed me a sheet of paper. "Her last report card," he said. "Make of it what you will.

The school she went to was in Oxford, and the teacher I wanted to talk to was out sick. I bullied her home number out of the receptionist, then dialed what she gave me.

On the third ring, someone picked up. "Hello?"

"Jean Nimitz?"

The answer was cautious, defensive. "Speaking. Do I know you?"

"No ma'am, you don't, but I promise you, I'm not asking for money. I'm calling on behalf of a parent whose daughter has gone missing, and-"

"Jubal Carson can go to hell, if that's what this is about." The venom in her voice took me aback.

"Ma'am, I can assure you that while I may be working for Mister Carson, I in no way share his views. Whatever they might be."

There was a pause, and then a chuckle. "All right, then. I'll tell you this: Michelle had the eye of an artist. Not the control, not the means to make her visions real. Which was fine. She wanted to study art so she could go into advertising. Pick the pictures that would convey the message, instead of trying to make them herself. Her father never understood that, and thought she was signing up for a life of disappointment, just like her mother."

"Do you know what happened to her mother?"

The response was distinctly flat. "They say she ran off. Funny thing is nobody can seem to agree on who she ran off with. You can make of that what you will."

"Popular lady?" I ventured, which got me another laugh. "Thank you for your time and help with this. I just have one more question. I don't expect her father to know this one, and I won't be bringing the answer back to him, but did she have any friends she hung out with whom she might have told her plans to? Any place she liked to go."

Nimitz harrumphed a bit before finally deigning to answer. "She didn't really have friends at the school. Too dreamy. Too...fey, I guess you'd call it. So I encouraged her to find other people who might be more understanding. There's a lot of artists in Durham, painters and sculptors mostly, and she started hanging around with them. And the more she did that, the madder her dad got, or at least that's what she told me."

"That's extremely helpful," I said. "Thanks for your time."

"Listen to me: that girl went away two weeks before graduation. There was a whole world waiting for her. A whole wide world. You find her, all right? You make sure she's OK."

"I'll do my best," I said, and cut the connection.

Every small city's First Friday is the same. Every third floor walkup in the downtown district suddenly turns into a gallery, every piece of art hung on a wall is a showing, every plate of store brand crackers and cheese is a reception. 90% of the foot traffic is just the artists drifting from neighbor to neighbor, nobody selling nothing because the only ones there to sell to are exactly like them.

Which is to say, broke. And broke and dreamy put together sometimes makes for a bad luck combo, which is why I went downtown when the doors got propped open, and the lights went on. Nimitz had emailed me about half an hour after we'd hung up, given me a list of names she'd suggested Michelle go looking for.

I'd checked those names out. Found a couple that matched up with local artist types, the sorts who'd call it a big deal if they got their stuff hung on the wall of a local pizza joint. And I went looking for them.

The first name on the list was Jason Hernan. His place was unusual, in that it was ground floor and he'd put out grape bug juice to go with a plate of chocolate chip cookies. "Don't drink wine," he said apologetically when I caught his eye, "but help yourself." Then he turned back to someone who'd had a momentary inclination to buy, and I was forgotten.

I looked around. He had a couple of rooms 'worth of art hanging on the walls, all of it jagged, irregular shapes and unrecognizable portraits. Everything was grey and red and black, sharp lines and bold slashes. A few people, some of them looking like they weren't members of his immediate family, circled around the space and sipped their juice. Occasionally one would say something like "primal ferocity," and someone else would nod, and I'd pretend I'd heard nothing.

Instead, I studied one particular piece that struck me as better than the rest put together. It was a portrait, full length, but done up in the kid's style so it was all sharp angles and bloody grey lines. There was no face, but somehow the impression of the model's personality came through: strong, defiant, bloodied but unbowed.

"You like it?" he said, bumping up against my elbow. I managed to avoid spilling my drink.

"It's striking," I said, and turned to look at him. He was young, maybe 25 at the outside. Sharp features, an axe of a nose, and short black hair cut close to the scalp. He was maybe 5'8", wide-eyed and eager, and he didn't look like he could take a decent sized kitten in a fair fight. "You really got her essence."

He nodded. "So much of this comes from the subject matter. You get a good model, it inspires you so much. Other times," and he shrugged, "you might as well be painting potatoes."

"You got lucky with this one," I said. "How much?"

He thought for a minute, pride in the piece warring with fear of scaring me off. "$500."

I gave a low whistle. "That's a lot. You got any other pieces with the same model? Maybe smaller?"

His shoulders slumped. "No, that was the only time she sat for me. I told her I wanted her back for another session and she just sort of laughed. Said she'd seen how I saw her, and now she wanted to see how someone else did."

"You know who else she modeled for?"

He nodded. "Upstairs. Kelton, in 31. I saw her going up the stairs. Asked her to come back and pose again, and she said it wasn't what she was looking for."

I looked at those savage lines, those harsh reds and dirty greys, and I thought about what they must have said to her. "Never can tell," I said instead. "Tell you what. $300, and I'll take this. $350, I'll take it if you tell me the model's name."

Hernan thought about it for a minute, and rubbed his scalp for about as long as he was thinking. "$450 and I give you her name?"

"$400," I replied. The actual price didn't matter to me, but I needed to make the kid feel like he was getting one over on me.

"$425?"

"Deal." I put out my hand to shake. After a second's hesitation, he took it. "All right. Let me put a "sold" sticker on it and I'll ..."

"You can keep displaying it," I said. "Piece like that ought to be seen. I'll come back for it in a few days. But right now, I need that name."

He blinked. "Shelly Carson," he said. "She said her name was Shelly Carson."

Shelly. Michelle. And the man who'd come to see me was a Carson.

"Thanks," I told him, and handed him a piece of plastic to ring up the sale with. He popped it through his iPhone, had me scribble a few loops with my finger, and said we were done.

"Don't sell it again," I told him. "That picture's mine now."

"Oh, no, no no." The kid was white as a sheet. "Whenever you want. Come back. Whenever."

But I was already out the door and climbing the stairs toward 31.

The story in 31 was the story I'd get all night. There was one painting there that stood apart. It featured a female figure, this time leaning up against a wall in the near distance but staring out at the viewer with frightening intensity. Only her eyes had been filled in; the rest of her face was a blank.

Amie Kelton, who was the artist in residence at this apartment, cheerfully talked about her model. Said she'd been in for one sitting, then moved on. Said that pretty much everyone in the building had worked with her, that she'd only done one sitting. That they'd all love to work with her again because she was so damn good.

I thanked her and went out into the hall. This time, I didn't feel the need to buy the painting.

A SPLASH OF BLUE

✦

The last door on the floor opened up into a room that was a little livelier than I was used to. Music was playing, some European whump-whump thing popping out of impossibly tiny speakers. The room was mostly full, the walls hung with pieces that ranged from "had potential" to "actually good". I spotted the artist immediately, as she was holding court in the center of the room. Johnette Lee, maybe five foot four, mixed Asian-white ancestry, solid build and dried paint under her fingernails. She was laughing and the rest of the group was laughing with her, so I decided not to interrupt, and instead went looking for the one picture I was looking for.

I found it soon enough, hanging on the back wall. It was a small thing, maybe nine inches by twelve, done up in warm yellows and deep brown and accents of green. No way it should have worked, but it did, with a splash of blue for the dress of the female figure who danced in front of a ramshackle house with light in its windows. A look around told me the girl - Shelly or Michelle or Mickey or any of the other names she'd given the artists and would-be artists who'd paths she'd crossed wasn't in any of the other paintings. The house was, though, and the hills and fields beyond it. They were landscapes of a place that never was, a panorama of an imagined world that went on and on. All of them, it seemed, peeked in on this other place and made it seem warm and inviting.

But it was the girl in the blue dress I was after.

Eventually Lee's admirers drifted away, and I was able to drift closer. She saw me coming, sized me up as someone who probably didn't have enough money to buy anything, and decided to smile at me anyway. It was a nice smile, and it went all the way up past her eyes.

"Beautiful work," I told her, and I mostly meant it.

"Thanks!" she said, and immediately went into details of technique that made about as much sense to me as particle physics. I nodded and uh-huhed at all the right places, and when she wound down, I asked her how much the painting with the blue girl in it was.

"That one?" she said. "Sorry, not for sale. Personal collection, you know. Best thing I've done so far."

"It's good," I agreed. "Though everything you've got here seems to be part of, I don't know, a bigger world? Different pieces of a bigger painting?"

She smiled again. "You noticed? Yeah, it's this place I sort of invented in my head, and I love painting it. Sharing it with someone, you know? Cause otherwise it just stays locked in my head."

"Some folks, the stuff they've got locked in their heads ought to say there," I said, thinking of things I'd seen and things I'd had to put down, and she looked worried and a little shocked. "No, no, not this. This is something else entirely."

That got half the smile back, and I decided to push my luck. "So the woman in the blue dress, is she part of this imaginary world? Or did you use a model."

"A model," she said hesitantly. "She sort of blew in here and turned everything upside down. Invited herself into the picture, if you know what I mean, and suddenly it didn't make sense without her. So I had to paint her in. And then that was it. No more. She was gone."

I'd heard the same note in many of the others 'stories, that little coda at the end that had loss and longing and maybe a little bit of love in it, too. She'd left her mark, Michelle had.

"One last question," I said. "You miss her?

And Miss Lee's face brightened up all over again, and she pointed at the painting. "How could I miss her? I could see her any time I want."

I nodded, and I thanked her, and I went out the door into the relative quiet of the hallway.

No one else in the building had seen Michelle or a model like her. The same went for a building across the way. She'd just gone out of that world and hadn't been seen again.

Later that night, I went back to the office. The remorse was sitting on my desk, still wrapped up, right where I'd left it. Carefully, I undid the packaging and let myself have a little taste. Not much, as the real stuff will knock a psychopomp like me on his ass for a week if you just slam it straight. Just a hint, enough to get the flavor and the texture of his feeling, and to maybe get a sense of what he was remorseful for.

It was there. Bitter, oily, like almonds dunked in spoiled cream. I pulled back, pushed the package away from me.

It was remorse, all right. Rare. Powerful. Genuine.

And I knew why his daughter had finally run, and how far she'd go to get away from him.

Carson was digging a hole in his yard when I drove up, a funny thing for a man to be doing at three in the morning.

"Evening," he said as I got out of my car. Like he'd been expecting me.

"Evening," I said in return, and walked over to where he

stood. He took that as a sign to stop moving dirt, and leaned up on the shovel instead. "You're not Blood, are you? But your wife was."

He nodded slow, and took a drag off a wreck of a cigarette that dangled from his lip. "Right in one. Her momma was what you'd call a wild talent. Could do damn near anything if she concentrated on it. Told me all about the Blood; was convinced I had it even if it never showed. I," he paused there to take a deep breath. "I didn't ever argue with her on that. You didn't argue with her."

"What happened to her, Carson? Where'd she really go?"

He gestured out at the farm, a vague wave that took it all in. "She's still here. In all of that. Put herself into it, she could. She could feel the whole farm at once, everything living in it and growing. That was the big one of her Gifts, is what she told me. But every time she used it, she went a little further out. Was a little harder for her to come back."

I stepped up onto the porch. "Until one day she didn't come back at all?"

He nodded, looking miserable. "She was out there, and she stayed out there. Couldn't come back. Wouldn't come back. To our daughter. To me. I took care of her, but her body just...stopped. No breath. No life. So I did the only thing I could."

"You buried her out in the field?"

"That I did. Thinking maybe if she was in the field, and her body was in the field, then maybe she'd find a way into it, rise up and come home. Stupid idea, but it was all I had. And it wasn't til I was done that I realized I had someone watching me the whole time."

"Michelle?"

"Michelle. She thought I killed her momma. Finally accused me of it in that last fight we had. I tried to tell her … I tried, but…"

"But she saw you put her momma in the ground, and probably thought you might do the same to her before she could get away. So she ran." I folded my arms, staring down at Carson and daring him to deny anything.

"Close enough to the truth." He coughed, deep and ugly. "That's why I'm digging this hole now. Gonna be for me soon enough. Gonna put myself in it, maybe she'll take me in."

I stared at him for a moment, thinking hard about what I'd seen. What I'd learned from that hit of remorse. He stared back, daring me to challenge him.

So I did. "It's a good story. Has the ring of truth on it. But it's not the sort of thing a man feels remorse over, not the real stuff. And I've held what you felt in my hand, and let it run through my veins. You put her in the ground when she was still breathing, didn't you?"

Carson went rigid, his knuckles white. "That's a lie. That's a damned lie."

"I don't think so, Jubal. I think she went away into the farm, and you got jealous. Got mad, maybe. Easy enough to tell yourself she wasn't coming back, especially when there was enough dirt over her that you couldn't hear any screams. But you knew better, and every time you looked at your little girl, you knew she knew, too. So I've got to ask - is that hole for you, or for your daughter when I bring her home?"

"It's for you!" he snarled instead, and brought the spade up in a wild swing. I ducked underneath it and drove a shoulder into his gut. All the air went out of him with a "whoof" and he went over backwards, but somehow he held onto the shovel and jammed the top of the handle into my kidney. Reflexively, I dropped my arm to protect my side, and he used that as a chance to wiggle out from under me. He rolled to his feet, the blade of the shovel out, and took a stab at me. I twisted, letting it slide past me, then grabbed the shaft just below the join. He snarled at me and pulled on it while I held on, a tug of war from hell under a three-quarter moon. Then he gave a yell like a kicked dog and yanked on that shovel with all he had.

And me, I let it go.

Without any resistance, the spade flew free. The strength of his effort drove him back, staggering, a half dozen steps.

Which was where the pit he'd dug was waiting.

I could see his eyes get big as he went over, his mouth open in a scream he never had time to make. There were a couple of wet thuds and a low rumble, and then there was silence.

"Carson?" I called out. "You all right down there?" There was no answer, so I took myself over to the edge of the pit to see if he was unconscious or worse.

Except there wasn't a pit anymore. Just fresh-turned earth, smooth as a baby's ass and smelling like fresh cut hay. If Carson was in there, he was buried deep, and there was no way I was getting him out.

Just for an experiment, I knelt down and lifted a handful of dirt from the fresh patch. It filled itself back in immediately, which was exactly what I'd thought it'd do. When Carson had said his wife was still out there in the farm, he was more right than he knew.

With Carson dead, that left me without a client and no way to pay the bills on this one. I had the remorse, but that's not the anything you can buy groceries with, and my expenses weren't going to get covered any longer.

Which left me with the question of what to do with the painting I'd bought. I thought about stopping payment on the card, but a move like that buys you bad karma, and mixing that sort of thing with Blood's an invitation to trouble. Besides, I thought I should have something for my work on this one.

So I waited until afternoon, then drove myself over to Hernan's little studio to pick up my property. He saw me coming and rushed to the door. "Hey, hey," he said. "Painting's ready if you want it. Or, if you want to let it stay on display here..." He let his voice trail off hopefully.

"Sorry, I'm taking it home. Just wrap it up to travel."

"All right," but his body language told me it was anything but. He pulled the piece off the wall and wrapped it up in butcher paper. Did it slow, too, so there was plenty of time to talk, which I did.

"You never did tell me how you met the model," I said. "Everyone else in the building said she wandered in and demanded to pose."

"Not everyone," he snorted and carefully measured some twine to wrap the package in.

"Oh?"

"Yeah. Johnette introduced us. Said they were friends."

"Uh-huh," I said, as the last piece fell into place. "You hang on to that for me. I'll be back in a bit."

"Make up your mind," he said plaintively, but I was already gone.

I was waiting in Lee's studio when she got there. She was smart - didn't scream, didn't ask how I'd gotten in. Just stayed by the door, ready to run if she needed to.

I held up my hands. Empty. She didn't seem too impressed, taking out a cell phone and holding it up.

"You," she said. "I don't know what you're doing here, but I'm going to call the cops right now, you understand?"

"You made one mistake," I said quietly.

"What are you talking about."

"I said, you made one mistake when you were lying to hide Michelle. You pointed to that picture when you talked about her," and I nodded in the direction of the painting of the girl in the blue dress. She didn't wave at me. "But your eyes, they were focused over there. On that picture, the one with the mountain in the distance. Which is where I'm guessing where Michelle was that night."

"Shelly," Lee said softly. "She likes to be called "Shelly".

"She's still here, isn't she?" I asked. "Her mom could go into places. I'm guessing she could do the same with pictures."

Lee nodded, once. "She showed me. Told me that my paintings where the place that she wanted to be. Stepped into one, then stepped back out. It was our secret..."

"She doesn't have to be afraid of her father anymore," I said. "He's gone."

"But she's still here. And she always will be." Lee smiled. "And maybe someday, I'll join her. Until then, she's happy inside. I'm happy making her world. And if her father's gone, well, the world's a little happier, too."

And then I saw it, out of the corner of my eye - a flutter of movement. A flash of blue here, a hint there - Shelly was watching us. I made a big show of looking away.

"If she ever wants to go back home," I started, but Lee was already shaking her head.

"She is home," she said. "and she always will be."

I got up after that, paid my respects and went out the door. Picked up the painting I'd bought and hung it in my office, a reminder that solving the case and the good guys winning and justice are sometimes three different things. And I could see why she didn't want to stay in that vision; she'd grown up in a place too much like it, and if the expression was true that didn't make it any better. But every so often, I get the sense that maybe she's stopped by for a visit, or a reminder.

And maybe someday, I'll figure out why.

A FINGER'S
WORTH
OF
COAL

It was in Bratislava where they put the fireman off the train, with the help of two burly passengers and a larger contingent from the local gendarmerie. The incident caused no small amount of scandal among the passengers, at least those who were aware of the disturbance, as it isn't often that a screaming, thrashing man covered in coal dust and blood is hauled bodily from his station by officers of the law. In an odd reversal of fortune, those impecunious enough to have purchased berths in the cars closest to the locomotive had the best view of the proceedings, which made them suddenly and briefly sought after by the curious among the wealthier travelers. Later, over drinks in one of the dining cars, more than one witness suggested that they'd seen the man, a thick-legged Magyar who'd come on board with the lumbering Hungarian 4-8-0 engine they'd acquired in Vienna, contorting in inhuman fashion and heard him screaming in a language that none of them could either translate or identify. This odd fact was later confirmed by those same two burly gentlemen, who after some delay had returned to the train and were now being feted like conquering heroes.

Graciously, the two--one a lawyer named Higdon with a

London legal firm on his way to Istanbul on business, the other, Walters, the stolid personal assistant to a certain professor of natural sciences *en route* to a series of speaking engagements in Sofia--allowed the other passengers to purchase refreshing beverages for them in exchange for further details of their adventures.

It seemed, said the professor's assistant, that the fireman had suddenly begun acting as if he were *possessed.* When pressed for details as to what this meant, he rose briefly and demonstrated flailing his limbs, commenting that it was if the man had suddenly become unacquainted with the proper use of his limbs. In addition, he said, the man had been seen swinging a coal shovel about, and generally screeching in what could be understood as no human tongue. His assistant had tried to restrain him and had gotten a vicious blow from the shovel in return. He, too, had been taken off the train, albeit on a stretcher, and it was doubtful as to whether he'd survive the night.

"Curious thing," interjected Higdon, clearly tired of having Walters relate the lion's share of the tale, "was that after they took the man to the police station, he just collapsed. No more screaming, no more of that damned animal talk. No, sir, out like a candle in a stiff breeze, that one was. Couldn't wake him up or get a word out of him, either." A bevy of young ladies traveling together heard this pronouncement and cooed in the lawyer's direction, fluttered eyelashes telling him how impressed they were with this new tidbit. He flushed, and smiled, and wriggled up a bit straighter in his seat.

Walters coughed slightly, and all eyes turned to him. "Actually," he said, "there was one thing the man muttered after he stopped struggling. Under his breath, though, so I'm not surprised you missed it." The lawyer stopped flushing and started glaring, but Walters ignored him magnificently.

"What was the word, dear boy?" asked the professor himself, a balding yet thoroughly mustachioed man named Madison. "You must share."

Walters nodded. "He said--well, whispered really--one thing. One word before he slipped away."

"Yes?" Even the lawyer was leaning forward now, and if the young ladies had been dewy-eyed before, now they were positively limpid.

"He said something that sounded like '*szen.*'"

"Ah," Professor Madison said and sat back in his chair. "Of course he would."

"It's nonsense," blustered the lawyer.

"No," Madison countered. "It's Magyar."

"What does it mean?" twittered one of the young ladies. "Something dark and mysterious?"

"It means," Madison said, "coal."

"I suppose it wasn't entirely necessary to embarrass Higdon like that, was it?" asked Walters as he and his employer picked their way back toward one of the restaurant cars for their evening meal. Ordinarily, Madison had confided in his man, he would have disembarked for his evening repast, as he had quite been looking forward to a meal at *Traja Muskieteri*, and perhaps finishing his evening with a *pajgle* or two. The incident of the fireman, however, had put a pall on the day, to the extent that very few of the passengers had disembarked even with the announcement that there would be an extended stay while the police examined the scene for evidence. That they had found none in no way reflected on their thoroughness, nor on their enthusiasm (which was much remarked upon by the passengers). Indeed, they had taken so much time that it was now well past six, the train's departure having been delayed nearly half a day by the police investigation.

Now, however, it seemed that whatever conclusions there were to be drawn had been drawn, and the Orient Express had been released to seek its destiny farther down the line. At the front of the train, the lumbering 4-8-0 bellowed its discontent with the state of affairs. Clearly, someone had been found to feed it the coal it desired, and the engine was stoked and ready to travel.

Madison stopped to regard his protege as the train lurched slowly into motion, jerking unsteadily forward as it restarted its long journey to Istanbul. "Embarrass Higdon? I supposed we did, at that. Not that he didn't deserve it, mind you - the man's a bully and a fool, only interested in making himself look more dashing to a gaggle of silly young things. Such habits are unbecoming and should be discouraged wherever possible."

Walters, whose thoughts had briefly drifted to the young ladies in question, shook his head. The train had started moving, the *click-click* of the wheels coming faster and faster until they blended into a satisfying hum. And for an instant, the hum became something more, a buzzing that filled his brain; all around him was not the luxury of the finest passenger rail Europe had to offer, but rather a vista ancient and green and poisonously alive. Then it was gone, and all that was left was the train, the professor, and a vague sense of unease.

"Is something wrong?" Madison asked, but Walters shook his head. "Nothing, I'm sure," he muttered.

"Dinner, then," said the professor, "and then I'll need to

prepare for those talks a bit. You might want to spend the evening reading about the geology we're passing through. Fascinating stuff, really." It was not, Walters knew, a suggestion.

"Of course, Professor," he said. "To the dining car?"

"To the dining car."

Walters read until late into the night, long after Professor Madison had himself turned in. The minutiae of the fossiliferous coal swamps that dotted the region were less than enthralling, and yet he pressed onward, lest he fail to acquire the breadth of knowledge Madison required in his assistant. After all, the professor was a man of many and varied interests, some of them esoteric, and to apprentice under him was to need to know a veritable cornucopia of disconnected facts and call them forth at a moment's notice.

Twice more, as the train adjusted its speed for some curve or bridge, he had those faint, unsettling visions, but they vanished quickly. No doubt brought on by thoughts of the ancient landscapes he'd been reading about, he told himself and eventually folded himself up for bed. The book he'd been attacking lay discarded on the floor, its impressive color plates of ancient insects and lumbering amphibians temporarily forgotten.

And it was only as consciousness faded that he remembered, dimly, that the buzzing and the first vision had come well before he'd read the first page.

"Ahem."

Walters looked up; Professor Madison did not, instead choosing to concentrate on the *pfannkuchen* that comprised the largest part of his breakfast. Standing ostentatiously by the table was the lawyer, Higdon, whose piggy gaze was focused on the professor with an expression of triumphant contempt.

"Can I help you?" asked Madison.

Higdon's gaze swiveled over to where Walters sat, the demolished remains of his breakfast spread out before him. "Oh, I don't think you can. You certainly can't help that poor fellow back in Bratislava?"

"The fireman?" Walters asked. "Is there a new development?"

"More like a final one," Higdon puffed. "He's dead, you see."

"Dead?" the professor interjected, putting down his paper and looking up from his apple pancakes.

"Oh, quite so." Higdon stopped for a moment, looking around as if to ensure the whole car could hear him dispensing a little tidbit of knowledge the so-wise professor did not possess. "Word just came over the telegraph. Flung himself out a window in the hospital once he understood that the train had left without him. Shouting "Szen, szen, szen" the whole time, too. Loved his work a little too much, I guess, eh?" The last was accompanied by a buffoonish chortle, and then the lawyer turned to go. Walters rose to go after him, but Madison put a restraining hand on his arm.

"Let him go," the professor advised, but Walters pulled away. "He's damned rude."

"As you noted, we did embarrass him. Only natural of him to try to get back."

"Yes, but to use a man's death to do so? Despicable!" He glared at the other passengers who'd been watching the drama, who had the common decency to flush and look away.

Madison raised a solitary eyebrow. "You're not going to get us thrown off the train, are you? The last time you thrashed a man in a dining car, it cost us two days 'layover in Cincinnati."

"He swung at me first, as you may recall," Walters retorted. "And no, I merely intend to express my dismay at his rudeness and perhaps to call him a blackguard, a rake, and a cad."

"If you must." Madison sighed and hoisted himself to his feet. "As for me, I'm more interested in what Higdon said than in why he said it. *Szen* indeed."

But Walters was already gone, headed for the rapidly closing door at the end of the dining car. He passed through it and across the swaying gap into the next car, where he fully expected to see Higdon forcing his unpleasant company on some passenger or other.

Instead, there was nothing. Travelers sat here and there at tables, sipping drinks and playing cards or reading novels, but of the brusque solicitor, there was no sign. Nor did the door at the far end of the car appear to be in any state of activation.

"You," he said and wheeled to face a porter. "A man came through here just now. What happened to him?"

The man shook his head in confusion. "No man came through, sir. I'm sorry, sir, but you must be mistaken."

"But I saw him," Walters protested, to no avail. The porter was firmly polite but certain no one had passed him. In fact, the door hadn't even been opened until the young gentleman came through. If he wanted to ask the other passengers...

"Very well," Walters said, perplexed, slipping the man a crumpled banknote by way of an apology. He thought about heading back to breakfast, but his irritation with Higdon's bad behavior had settled in his stomach like a knot, with no chance now to exorcise it. Better, he thought, to return to the compartment, retrieve the book, and return to his studies whilst the train chugged onward. His course decided, he nodded to the porter and made his way through the car.

But still, Higdon's disappearance nagged at him. Where could the man have gone? Surely he hadn't jumped from the train between cars, and yet, he'd evaporated as surely as water left on a hot stove. The whole thing felt unreal, the train and everything on it suddenly taking on the cast of ephemeral phantoms as solid as smoke.

The steady thrum of the train's wheels sang counterpoint to his internal debate as he passed out of the car and on to the next one, a buzzy hum that made stringing together complex thoughts impossible.

The new car was mostly empty, at least--the side route through Bratislava was not the most popular, he knew--and the absence of fellow travelers was a relief. Even the porter of this car had abandoned his station, no doubt for one of the innumerable cigarette breaks that were as much a part of Eastern Europe as crumbling signs of Turkish occupation.

A couple of old men drowsed at a table by a window, neither of them conscious of the scholar's passing. He gave them a nod as he trudged forward, bracing himself as the train threw itself around a curve and into a long, level straightaway.

As it did, the humming grew stronger, a low, insectile sound that persisted underneath the normal clank and bustle of the rolling stock. Walters could *feel* the sound now as well as hear it, could sense it climbing up from the carpet and through the soles of his shoes. Shaking his head, he took another step forward and immediately regretted it. His left foot felt leaden, his right tingled uncontrollably to the point where it went numb, and he lost his balance. Pitching forward, he caught himself with a splayed hand against the doorframe, which proved to be a mistake.

Instantly, his palm felt as if he were grasping a handful of angry hornets. Sting upon sting upon sting bit into his flesh in rapid succession. The sensation crawled up his arm, climbing nerve to nerve until everything below the shoulder was a nest of agony. The force of it was enough to drop him to his knees, driving the breath out of him in a singular grunt. He held there for a moment, unable to make the muscles of his arm work well enough to pull his agonized fingers away before the torment crept up his legs as well. Marching forward like jungle ants, the feeling crawled along every limb, meeting and twisting together in the space around his heart. Slowly he sank to the floor, his vision blurring as the buzzing grew louder and the pain crept up his spine to electrify the very base of his brain, and then ...

... then suddenly, he wasn't on the train at all. With no wall to brace against, he toppled down into thick, oozing mud. The painful tingling in his arms and legs had stopped, however, and after a moment of wondering exactly what had happened, he pulled himself up out of the muck.

Kneeling--he didn't quite trust himself to stand--he wiped mud from his face with his good hand, marveling at the clingy qualities of the thick, black stuff. It was not the mud that truly startled him, though; it was what was growing out of it.

He saw now that he knelt on a small island or tumulus in the middle of a vast swamp, one that positively thrummed with life. Gleaming insects in iridescent green and blue and gold swooped and swarmed, dragonflies cutting the thick, steamy air with doubled wings and a steely sense of purpose. Everywhere, plants rose up out of the discolored water, an explosion of greenery reaching upward to a thick canopy that nearly shut out the sky. These were not trees, though; instead, they could only be titanic ferns or cycads, whose golden trunks speared up from black water to disappear in the canopy overhead. Some, he guessed, were over two hundred feet tall.

Which implied that the creatures swooping among them were huge as well, surely too huge to fly. And yet there they were, larger than birds, wings beating the thick, rich air.

Now that the visual shock was done, the sounds of his surroundings had a chance to assault his ears. And what sounds they were: the buzzing of those titanic insect wings, the thick sounds of muddy water flowing, the croaking of frogs, and in the distance, the wet bellows of massive beasts yet unseen. But just as disturbing were the sounds that he did *not* hear. There was no birdsong, no scuttling of squirrels in the "trees," or mice in the ferny undergrowth.

And, of course, no sounds of men. No thunderous engine, no clack of wheels over well-laid tracks, no voices calling or axes cutting into ancient, unfeeling wood. The entire scene sounded unfinished, absent so much of what Walters realized he took for granted. All evidence of mankind was absent, and he was utterly alone.

Or nearly so. He looked around at the island he stood on, a hummock a few hundred feet across rising up out of the muck and yet made largely of muck itself. Too many steps in any direction would lead him off its edge into the turgid waters, and his imagination quickly conjured the sorts of creatures that might dwell under the surface in a place like this.

And yet, in the mud he saw footprints, shod ones. They circled his position, he saw, then led away toward the water's edge. Treading carefully, he followed.

The prints were deep, deeper than his own, which implied a heavier man had made them.

Higdon had been larger than he, Walters recalled. And his shoes might have made tracks very much like these.

Six feet from the water, the tracks stopped.

More accurately, they vanished, wiped out by a greater disturbance. The ground had been torn up here, obliterating any record of the man's passage. Instead, there were great sharp gouges dug into the earth, ones that looked suspiciously like the work of massive claws. And there was a familiar scent here, too, coppery but faint. He started to kneel down for a closer look, but some primal sense of danger stopped him, some unsuspected clue that told him he was in terrible danger.

The insects, it seemed, had found him.

He turned as a gleaming battalion of dragonflies plunged toward him, gleaming mandibles clacking with hunger. Questions of where he was became academic as he threw himself down to the ground, just under the first wing of swooping predators. They buzzed past as he rolled to his knees, wheeling about in obscene formation to come around for another pass.

Then they were upon him, diving for his face and the tender softness of his eyes. Crouching down, he swung wildly at them, hoping to drive them away. One fist connected with a shocking *thwock*, the sound of wood on wood, and a monstrous bug spiraled down into the mud. Quickly, he smashed down with his fist and was rewarded with a satisfying crunch of chitin and a spray of foul-smelling innards. But that was just one of hundreds, and even as it twitched its last more swarmed to the attack.

One fastened on his forearm, its mandibles plunging down through the fabric of his shirt to pierce the meat underneath. He flung it away, but there was fresh blood in the air now, and more and more insects converged on him. Swinging, flailing, he was blinded by the cloud until, inevitably, he lost his balance, falling back into the warm, wet mud. He tried to escape, but the sucking, gooey muck held him tightly. The insects, sensing their prey was helpless, dove in for the kill. Hetherington shuddered as the ravenous jewels descended upon him.

And then, from somewhere close, a monstrous, bubbling roar split the air.

The dragonflies reacted instantly. They froze, holding position like a deadly curtain of the aurora while the roar sounded again. Then there was a sudden, sharp crack, and one of the dragonflies disappeared in a cloud of foetid vapor. A second sound, and another one burst, and then they were flying in all directions, a frantic explosion of vanishing color.

Desperately, Walters pulled free from the muck, and scrambled to his feet to face the new danger. What he saw defied rational description. Rising up out of the water was a creature, green-skinned and rubbery, with a rough slash for a mouth that extended halfway around its bulbous head. Its front two feet rested on the island itself and they were heavy and clawed, barely supporting the beast's pendulous belly. It chewed, its lower jaw cycling in an odd, circling motion as what was undoubtedly one of the dragonflies crunched between its teeth. From nose to tail, Walters estimated, it was at least twelve feet long.

The real monster sat on its back.

It was huge, a wet gray cone that rose up to a series of four odd points. What only could be described as tentacles drooped from these, and Walters could not fail to note that the two extended in his direction ended in lurid claws clutching odd silvery objects. A third blossomed into a cluster of bright red mushrooms, while the fourth was festooned with bulging, inhuman eyes. They stared at him for a moment, during which time Walters got the shuddering sensation that the thing was studying him as he himself had studied amphibious specimens staked out in dissecting trays, pondering where to make the first incision.

The creature's mount opened its obscene mouth and roared, the sound echoing out of its fleshy gullet. Then, step by ponderous step, it lurched forward. Its claws reached for him amidst a storm of excited clicking noises. He threw himself back as best he could as the horror plunged closer until ...

... he found himself on the floor of the compartment he shared with Professor Madison, who was staring down at him with raised eyebrow.

"Good heavens, Walters, you're filthy," the professor said. Walters tried to answer and found himself gasping for air, but Madison waved him off. "Go wash up and change, for God's sake. I think you've got a story to tell me."

An hour, one shower and several brandies later, Walters found himself seated across from the professor, who gazed at him with keen interest. He'd been through the story of what he'd seen, or at least most of it: the swamp, the insects, the titanic cycads. The rest, though, he kept to himself. It was a vision too far - monstrous insects were one thing, actual monsters were another, and there was only so much a man of science like the Professor could be expected to accept.

"You're hiding something," Madison finally said, "But it'll be out in due time. Now this vision of yours--what do you think you saw?"

"I didn't see it, Professor, I lived it," Walters protested. "The mud, the blood--"

"The bites and the ichor all over your clothes, quite convincing, yes. So what did all that say to you?"

"It said to get home in a hurry," Walters replied, and took another swig of brandy. "That it was no place for men."

Madison nodded. "If pressed, I'd say it sounded like a swamp of the Carboniferous Era. Which, coincidentally, is some of what I'm having you study. Are you certain this isn't some charade to get me to assign you more reading on the late Cretaceous?"

"Professor!" Walters was ready to rise out of his seat in protest until he saw that Madison was chuckling.

"Easy there, young friend. I have no reason to doubt your story. The evidence-"and he pointed to the muddy footprints that now dominated the compartment - "is most compelling. Besides, even if you'd faked the other bits, your materialization on the carpet was most impressive. But it adds another mystery to the ones we were already investigating."

"Other mysteries?"

Madison ticked them off on his fingers. "The fireman who went mad. The disappearing Mr. Higdon, Esq. And now your sojourn. I find it worrisome in the extreme."

"So you think they're connected?"

The professor nodded. "It seems likely. Speaking of which, what do *you* think really happened to the poor Magyar?"

Walters rubbed his aching head. "The conventional wisdom is that he went mad, yes?"

"You saw him. We're long past the conventional. But why mad now, and why on this train? He'd done the run, with that same fellow that he attacked, dozens of times before. And don't forget, he said something about the coal."

"I'm afraid you've lost me."

Madison smiled thinly. "Never mind. I think it may be time I made some inquiries. And it's definitely time you lay down and got some rest."

"But I can help."

"Rest," said Madison. "There'll be plenty of time to help later, I'm sure." He ushered Walters into his bunk, pulled down the shades and then left. His footsteps echoed down the corridor as the young man sank back into his pillow, gradually merging with the relentless thrum of the train's progress.

Muzzily, Walters closed his eyes, counting in a dreamy four-four time as the wheels below rolled and clicked, eventually dissolving into a comforting, buzzing hum.

There was something about the hum, he realized. Something that he should recognize.

It was getting louder now, and he forced himself to open his eyes. All around him he could see the berth in the dimming light, the now-familiar brass fixtures gleaming with sunset glints. But there was another world there as well, a green haze settling over everything. Beyond the walls, he could see vast trees and vaster differences, could almost hear distant bellowing, and in his fingers and toes he felt a familiar tingling.

The shock of it jolted him to full consciousness. Professor!" he shouted, and threw himself out of bed. The impact with the floor dimmed the vision for a second, but as he rose to his feet it returned with a vengeance. Half-guessing where the compartment door was, he staggered after Madison. Every step yielded the wet squelching sound of ancient mud. Ever blink overwhelmed the ornate decor of the train with lush walls of primal green. "Professor!" he shouted again as he stumbled forward.

Dimly, he could see other passengers diving into the compartments, alarmed at the madman who now lurched down the passageway toward the end of the car. A figure stood there, perhaps Professor Madison. But the professor had never had claws, had never stretched forth welcoming tentacles, had never wished to ...

"Here, my boy, take this!"

A hand reached out for him, or perhaps a snaking tentacle, and then something cold and metallic was pressed into his fingers. *Pocket watch*, he thought dimly as he clutched it. He could feel the wheels and gears within, the steady tick of the hands advancing cutting through the haze, and then suddenly, the green vision vanished.

"Professor," he said, and pitched forward.

Madison caught him as he fell. "Easy there. You'll want to Keep that with you. It's the only thing that'll anchor you, at least as long as we're on this train."

"Anchor me?"

"To this era." Madison regarded him gravely. "I think it is time we put all our cards on the table."

Weakly, Walters nodded, then pushed himself upright. "There *is* something I didn't tell you." The professor, he saw, was headed towards the front of the car, and he followed. "When I was gone, I saw a...creature. Riding some form of amphibious beast. And I saw it again just now. It was reaching out for me."

"Hmm." They got to the end of the car, and a porter opened the door with a brisk salute and a surreptitious sign of the Cross. Madison stepped through, followed by his protege, and they passed into another carriage. "Would this creature have been roughly the height of a man, possessed of four asymmetrical appendages?" He went on to describe the monster of Walters's vision so precisely the man's jaw dropped.

"Yes. That's it. That's it exactly. How did you know?"

"Not all of my research is approved of by the Royal Museum," he said grimly. "There are certain books in my possession that my more rational peers frown on. Accounts of pre- and post-human civilizations, vast beasts from the gaps between the stars, ancient demon cults - not the typething that plays well on Great Russell Street. And there are mentions of the creature you saw, vague hints at horrors out of time."

"What do they say?" They passed through another car, moving steadily toward the front of the train. "What do those things want?"

Madison laughed, a bitter sound. "What they want is to remain hidden. So anyone who has knowledge of them, or who might acquire it, such a man would attract their attention." He stopped and turned. "A man like you, now."

"Or the dead man?"

Madison nodded. "Quite possibly. Or perhaps he was merely an instrument, used to dispose of evidence."

"Evidence?"

"Think, Walters. You were drawn back to their time somehow. To the Carboniferous, when the vast beds of coal all around our route were laid down. What does this train run on? What did the man *do*!"

"Of course! It's something in the coal!" Walters sprang forward, and now it was Madison who hurried to keep up. "We've got to find it before they try again!"

"And you've got to be careful, my boy," Madison puffed. "You've drawn their eye. They'll stop at nothing to silence you.

Hold onto the watch. It's the only thing anchoring you to the now." Passengers and benches sped by as they ran headlong for the front of the train. "My best guess is that the vibrations of the train, mixed with some strange susceptibility of your own, is what flung you into the past."

"Higdon! He and I carried the poor man, and then he disappeared!"

"You did, too. Good God! It's the only thing that makes sense!"

And then, without warning, they were through the last car and into the cramped compartment at the back of the train's engine, the air thick with smoke and coal dust as two shirtless men shoveled away for all they were worth.

"You there!" Madison shouted. "You've got to stop. There's something in the coal, something terrible."

The two men straightened and looked at each other. One strode over to Madison, while the other shrugged and returned to his work. "Am sorry, sir. No passengers are allowed here."

"You don't understand. There's something wrong." Madison's earnest pleading was almost drowned out. The roar of the flames added hellish counterpoint to the chug of the wheels; the light from the furnace reflected luridly off the stokers 'half-naked forms.

"What is wrong is that you are here," the man explained, less patient than before. "We are already behind schedule. The other passengers, they complain. If we stop shoveling coal, the train, it stops. It stops, they complain more. So you will go back to your seats, and we will keep the train moving, yes?"

"No," said Madison. "Look, if you'll just let me in the coal bin, I can - oh God, what's that?"

He pointed, eyes wide with horror. Walters and the stoker

turned. The other man paused, the blade of his shovel half-buried in the mound of fuel.

And plainly visible hard by it was something in the gleaming, unmistakable shape of a gun, gripped in the blackened fossilized bones of a human hand.

"There!" shouted Madison. "Do you not see?" And indeed they saw, gaping as the one man dropped his shovel. Disregarding the effect of the coal dust on his trousers, the professor dropped to his knees and gently extricated the find, Walters standing right behind him.

"Is not possible," said one of the stokers. "The bones--"

"The bones indeed! And what else, *Szen, szen*, of course it was buried in the coal! This is what they were hiding, Walters, what they didn't want seen! Incontrovertible proof of their meddling in Earth's past!"

Walters stared. "The gun wouldn't burn. Even in the furnace, it would be found, and there would be questions! They possessed that poor fireman so that he'd destroy it."

Madison's voice was strained, but jubilant. "But they failed, and now we've found it, my boy! Oh, we'll blow their secret history wide open, we will!"

"There's more there," Walters said, and pointed. "The rest of the bones." And indeed there were, a radius and an ulna, both remarkably well preserved, leading back into the depths of the pile.

"Well done, Walters. There might be more artifacts back there, too! Hold this, will you?" Madison passed the hand and what it held, up to his assistant, then leaned forward to dig at the distended arm.

Walters took the bundle without comment, and gave it a once-over. The gun, if gun it was, seemed poorly designed for the human hand. The grip seemed more suited for a claw than for fingers, and the hand that was wrapped around it, still held in place by bits of coal, was positioned awkwardly. Frowning, he held it up. Something about the sight lines seemed off, and he rotated it until something about the shape clicked.

He'd seen it before. Seen it held in that inhuman pincer reaching out for him. Seen what it could do.

"Professor," he said, leaning forward as his mentor burrowed busily into the coal.

"One moment," Madison replied.

Trembling, he stretched his hand around the stony knucklebones.

"Professor, I really think ..."

"I said not now!" Walters had never seen Madison like this, face pale, almost pleading. Sweat stood out on his forehead, no doubt a product of the coal chamber's intense heat. His eyes gleamed with excitement as his hands scrabbled in the detritus of the ancient strata. "We're finding ... we're going to find ..."

Walters closed his grip. The fossilized bones and his were a perfect match.

"Professor!"

And Madison turned, and Walters immediately wished he hadn't.

For the Professor, it seemed, was suffering a seizure. Hunched over in agony, he screamed wordlessly. His fingers had twisted into claws, curled so tightly on themselves he could hear bones snap and ligaments pop. As for his face, it was a mask of horror. Eyes bulging, lips suddenly bloody where he chewed on them in frantic spasms.

"*Szen!*" the Madison-thing hissed, and then launched itself at his assistant with outstretched hands. Walters barely had time to raise his arms in defense before Madison was upon him. Fingers crooked into claws raked his flesh, desperately clutching at the alien device. With a shout, Walters flung him away across the width of the car, sending his employer sprawling into the coal pile.

"You cannot fight in here," said one of the stokers. Madison turned to look at him, snarled, and then flung a fistful of coal dust into the man's face. He screamed and stumbled back, clutching his eyes, even as the other stoker fled the car.

"Professor! What are you doing?" It was a vain hope to think that any trace of his mentor remained in the creature that hurled itself at him, body contorting unnaturally. Its fingers found the punctures the insects had made in his arm and dug in, causing him to gasp in pain. Involuntarily, his grip loosened and the alien device tumbled to the floor. Coal and fossil bone splintered free as it hit, and the gun spun away.

"No!" Walters flung himself after it, arms outstretched. The possessed Madison followed, a split-second later and a half meter behind. The train took a curve, wheels roaring, and the device slid crazily toward the side of the car. Walters tumbled after it, blocking it from tumbling off the edge to the track below. A tug on his leg told him that his sudden opponent had grabbed ahold of him, and without a second thought he kicked. There was a gruesome crunch as his boot connected with the professor's shoulder, and then he could hear fabric tear as the Madison-shaped thing fell away.

Wheels screeching, the train pulled out of the curve and started accelerating. As it did so, the gun slid away once more, now toward the center of the car. Stumbling, Walters lunged for it. For an instant he thought it was too late, and then his fingers closed on it. He tightened his grip and turned, half-expecting to see Professor Madison lunging at him once again.

Instead, the Professor stood there, blood streaming down his face. In his hand was the pocket watch.

"*Szen*," he said, and then the rising hum took Walters away.

He'd lost them some time ago. Of that, Walters was sure. Now he hid, carefully concealed amongst the roots of a cycad that would have dwarfed any redwood of the modern Earth. Mud caked his hair and skin, the better to protect him from the ravenous appetites of the swarming insects. Across the steaming swamp he could hear the heavy-legged beasts the monstrosities hunting him rode, each calling to each in a chorus of grim hunger.

He could outrun them, he'd discovered. They were surefooted but they were slow, and the beings riding them could or would not descend off their backs to pursue the hunt. So he ran from them and he hid, using the dense forest and the cool mud to hide.

There was no way back that he knew. It had been too long. Across the aeons, the train would have moved on, the peculiar vibrations of its wheels humming too far away to draw him back.

Or perhaps he'd been the one to go too far in his flight from star-headed hunters. He no longer knew where he'd first come back into this world, or where the train tracks would someday run. There was no return to the future for him now, just black water and greenery and sucking mud.

But, Walters resolved, he would not go down meekly. Let the monsters pursue him. He would make a home of the jungle, and pick them off one by one when he could. The ancient weapon he'd brought back in time with him he'd long since abandoned. Why not, after all, when he was sure he'd soon find a way to retrieve a much younger, more functional version of it.

They would never catch him, that he already knew. When his time came, he would be taken by the thick waters, his bones sinking down with the rotting leaves and broken branches. And over the millennia he'd become one with them, as time and heat and pressure did their work, until someday, some poor train stoker's shovel would strike too close to where his remains lay, at the bottom of a pile of coal.

"Are there any questions?" Professor Madison asked. The lecture hall was full of the usual first year students, equal parts terrified and bored. Ten years on from the incident on the Bratislava train, seven years since he'd been released from the sanitarium and still they flocked to the classes of the "mad professor".

For such blessings, he was occasionally grateful.

He looked back and forth across the room. Only one student raised a timid hand, a reedy, thin young man with too much hair and not enough chin. One was good enough to start with, he supposed, and pointed. "Yes?"

"Professor." He hoisted himself to his feet and assumed a declamatory pose. "Today you told us about fossils forming in different strata according to the time period in which they evolved. But what do you have to say to anomalous fossils, like human footprints next to dinosaur ones, or the human skeleton workers supposedly discovered in a coal car on a train? What about those?"

Rather than respond, Madison reached down into his pocket, and pulled out a watch. It had seen hard use, as the marks of careful repair from some devastating accident were evident. Carefully, he popped it open, feeling the reassuring whir of gears and wheels in the palm of his hand, the steady progression of time.

"I'm afraid we don't have time for questions after all," he said, and turned and walked away.

THE BEAST
OF
SICA HOLLOW

"They say he wears a hat."

"Bull. Shit." Sam Reeves spat the words out, then spat into the campfire for emphasis. It continued to burn, oblivious to his donation.

The man sitting across the fire from Sam shrugged. "Believe it or not, that's what the stories say. That he wears a stovepipe hat. Sometimes a coat, sometimes not." Leon Hayes was tall and lean and used to Sam's outbursts. He'd been party to them for the better part of five years, the duration of their business partnership, and he generally just let them pass.

Sam leaned forward, closer to the fire. "Taku-He's supposed to be a wild man. All the stories we've heard, all the places we've gone, we've never heard tell of a wild man who wore a goddamn stovepipe hat. Next thing you're gonna tell me is that he can talk."

Leon poked at the fire with a stick. One of the larger branches in the flames collapsed, sending up a shower of sparks and nearly singeing Sam's beard. He scrambled back, sputtering, while Leon continued his ministrations to the fire. Finally, satisfied, he tossed his stick onto the fire and reached for the flask in his pocket. He took a long swig, then offered it to Sam. "Hooch?" he said.

"No, I don't want a sip of hooch," Sam said angrily. "What I want is to know where you got those crazy stories. We're looking for work, dammit, not tall tales from settlers who are scared of their shadows."

"Suit yourself," Leon said and took another sip before putting the flask away. "But this is rough territory. The locals are tough. They have to be, and that means they go easy on the crap. If they say they saw a wild man wearing a hat, I'll at least reserve judgement until I see the thing for myself. Hat or no hat."

"You want to see it? Is that it?" Sam had a gleam in his eye now that Leon didn't like. That gleam had gotten them into trouble many times before. It was one of the reasons they were currently enjoying the scenic Dakota Territory, as they were no longer welcome in Kansas or other points south.

"I didn't say that," Leon offered cautiously. "I'm just telling you what I heard when I was getting supplies. The locals were fair buzzing over it. Couldn't get them to stop talking long enough to take my business."

"Hmm." Sam looked thoughtful for a moment, "If these locals really are talking about this thing, hat or no hat, I'd bet they'd pay good money for its carcass"

Leon shook his head. "Jesus, Sam, no. If the stories are true, I don't want any part of it, and if the stories aren't, then you'll have us on a wild goose chase. Neither of those two sounds good to me."

"There's no work here. We want to make some money, we either hold up a bank, or we find a way to make some scratch on our own."

"No more banks. After Kansas, you promised." Leon was

firm. "And there will be work. We have to keep looking, that's all."

"There wasn't none in any of the two-bit towns we've been through." Sam was on his feet now, agitated and pacing back and forth within the circle of firelight.

Leon watched him with growing concern. "There'll be work, I'm sure. We don't have to go hunting no wild man. There isn't even a bounty on him, for Christ's sake."

Sam stopped and turned. "You started the conversation. I'm just trying to take it someplace useful. The money from Kansas won't last forever. So tell me about this wild man, and we'll see what we do next."

"Fine, fine." Leon waved him off. "If I tell you all I heard, will you lose this foolishness and go to sleep?"

"Can't promise nothing, but I'll listen. Now start talking."

Leon shrugged. "All right. Taku-He's the local version of the wild man. They say you can see him sometimes on the plains, dragging his prey behind him."

"Prey?" Sam interrupted. "He eats meat?"

"Apparently. There's stories of him attacking livestock. Gouging their eyes out, ripping out their tongues, tearing the balls off bulls, and drinking the blood."

"Do tell." Sam was all ears. Behind him, the flickering fire cast a long, wavering shadow. Sam himself was short and compact, and in the firelight he looked a little like a wild man himself.

"I'm telling you what the locals said," Leon replied. "A couple of them claimed Taku-He would eat human flesh if he could get it, but the rest of them shouted that down. Mostly they say he takes deer. Runs them down and snaps their legs, then snaps their necks."

Sam blinked. "Runs them down? I never heard of a wild man that fast."

"I'm just telling you what I heard. The storekeeper told me one more thing, that Taku-He lives in Sica Hollow."

"Where's that?" Sam asked.

"Four days 'ride from here. Eastern part of the Territory, by the border." Leon gave an exaggerated yawn. "Enough of this foolishness. Bank the fire. I'm turning in."

"Why do I always have to bank the fire?" Sam complained.

"Because you're shit at starting them. Now take care of it, and go to sleep."

The morning brought with it a cold wind out of the west and low clouds scudding along under gray skies. Leon got up and tidied his bedroll, then went to see to the fire for morning coffee. Sam woke with a start at the smell of coffee and came over to where Leon was sitting on his haunches.

"So we can probably make the next settlement by nightfall," Leon said without looking up, his hands busy.

"I told you last night," Sam replied. "We're heading for Sica Hollow."

Leon turned, his face a mask of incredulity. "I thought you'd give up on that foolishness. Why the hell do you want to go there? It's a bad place. Local Indians say it's cursed, that the name means evil. And you want to go chasing a legend up in there?"

Sam waited for Leon to wind down. "Leon, we've been up and down this part of the territory, and there's no work unless we want to pick up a plow. I say the hell with going hat in hand to these sodbusters for permission to round up their sheep for a pittance. If we bring in the pelt of the Taku-He, someone's going to pay a pretty penny. Or we could have it stuffed and show it, and make money that way. Hell, I'd even let you keep the damn thing's hat."

"Haven't you been listening? This thing, if it's real, is supposed to be eight feet tall. It can run fast as a horse and snap a deer's neck with its bare hands. That ain't something I want to mess with. If it's real, which I'm not saying it is, any trip to Sica Hollow's probably going to be a disaster."

Sam stretched, grinning. "Make up your mind. Is it nothing, or is it a monster? And if it's a monster, do you think it's bulletproof? Cause we got a couple of rifles that will put a hole in anything, eight feet tall or not."

Leon sighed. "You're not listening to me. Either it's just a story, in which case we waste a week of provisions chasing it, or it's real, in which case...don't you think there's a reason the locals have left it alone?"

"The locals are chickenshit," Sam said dismissively. "They hunker down at night afraid of anything that makes a noise in the dark. You and me, though, we ain't afraid. We can bring this thing down, and if it has been tearing up the livestock like you say, they'll pay us well for doing so."

"Coffee's gonna get cold," Leon observed and poured out two tin cups 'worth. He passed one to Sam and took the other for himself, holding it in cupped hands to warm them.

"We kill this thing, we can actually buy some good coffee for a change, instead of the ground up dirt you keep on buying." Sam took a sip and grimaced at the taste, daring Leon to contradict him.

Leon didn't. Instead, he drank all his coffee in one long swallow, then put the cup down before responding. "All right," he said. "We'll go to Sica Hollow. Likely as not we find nothing, but like you said, it beats begging farmers for work. Let's give it a shot."

"I knew you'd come round," Sam crowed. "And I'll give it a shot, right between the eyes."

The first day passed quietly. Leon took lead while Sam rode behind and led the pack horse with their supplies. Neither of them spoke much, as there wasn't much to say. As evening came on, they made camp and tethered the horses. Sam turned in early, leaving Leon to watch the dark for hours before finally fading himself. There was nothing out there that he could see, but something felt plain wrong, like they were being watched, judged, and found not worthy.

The second day's travel, they picked up the pace by unspoken agreement. The wind was cold again, and neither of them wanted to be caught in an early season snowstorm.

As night came in, they tied up the horses and made camp.

"Two more days," Leon said noncommittally.

"Yup." Sam was preoccupied with setting up his bedroll, and practically grunted his response.

"I'm just saying it's not too late to turn back." Leon looked at Sam expectantly.

Sam looked up. "Are you nuts? We're halfway there, with nothing to show for it yet. Don't tell me you're getting cold feet."

"Not exactly." Leon shuffled his feet. "Just got a bad feeling, that's all."

"You always have a bad feeling," Sam told him.

"And I'm usually right," Leon replied hotly. "Or did you forget Kansas?"

"Would you leave it be about Kansas? We got away. That's what matters."

Leon turned away to face the prairie. "We're running out of places they ain't heard our names."

"And that's why we have to do this. We bring in that monster's pelt, we'll be heroes."

Shaking his head, Leon sighed. "If you say so."

"I do," Sam said. "I really do."

Around midnight, the horses kicked up a ruckus. Sam was first up, gun in his hand. Leon followed a second later. "Bear?" he asked.

"Could be," Sam said and stopped. The horses were rearing up, whinnying in fear and pulling at their tethers with desperate intensity.

"What the hell's gotten into them?" Leon said. "They've never gone this crazy before." A flailing hoof narrowly missed connecting with his head, and he took a step back. "Easy, boys, easy."

"Jesus!" The roan pack horse was giving Sam all he could handle. Then abruptly, its tether snapped, and it bolted off into the darkness.

Sam took a couple of steps after it, then stopped and stomped the ground in frustration. "Goddammit! What are we going to do now?" He paused for a minute, then said "And what the hell is that smell?"

Leon moved to calm his gray, rubbing its heaving flanks and murmuring calming words. Then the smell hit him, too, and he had to take a step back. It was pungent, a cross between wet dog and rotting vegetation, and it made Leon's guts churn. The horses didn't seem to like it either, and they redoubled their snorting and rearing. "Help me!" Leon yelled, and Sam belatedly rushed to assist. Together they calmed the horses, but it wasn't until the scent wafted away that the horses truly settled down.

"What the hell was that all about?" Sam demanded of the night. The night didn't answer, but Leon did. "Don't know, don't want to find out. I've never seen horses go that crazy before. Not from bear, not from anything."

"It had to be a bear," Sam insisted as he paced back and forth, nervous energy animating him. "Pack of wolves, we would have heard them. So, bear." Leon shook his head. "That didn't smell like any bear I've ever seen."

"How many bears you smelled up close and personal?" Sam asked.

"Not a lot," Leon confessed, "but the ones I did get too close to didn't smell like that."

Sam snorted. "Well, now you know they do." He looked around at the dark and sighed. "I guess this means we're keeping watch in case the bear comes back?"

"Or the horse." Leon agreed. "You want first?"

"Might as well." Sam stopped pacing and suddenly turned to Leon. "You don't think it was...."

"Taku-He?" Leon answered. "I sure as shit hope not. See you in a couple of hours."

"Yeah," Sam said. "Couple hours." He took a deep breath and

turned to face the night.

They found the pack horse in the morning, or what was left of it. Its neck had been snapped, dropping the horse where it had stood, and then something had gone to work on its belly. Entrails were strewn across the dry grass, and the corpse was a bloody disaster.

"Well, shit," said Sam, and Leon nodded along with him before dismounting to get a closer look. "Well, look at that," he said and squatted down. "Look at what?" Sam asked, doing his best to keep his skittish horse in line. "The guts. They weren't just pulled out. Something went through them, looking for something. And the liver's missing."

"Huh," Sam said. "Smart bear. Got peculiar tastes."

"That's not all," Leon added. "Where's all the blood?"

"Huh?"

"A kill like this, there ought to be blood everywhere. But there's not much here. Something...I don't know, drank it?"

"That's crazy talk," Sam said and backed his horse up a few steps. "It soaked into the ground or something. There's got to be blood."

Leon rubbed a finger on the ground. It came away dusty and dry. "I'm telling you, there's no blood." He stood and walked over to the animal's head. "And look at that. Neck's broken. Never seen a bear do that."

"Alright, cougar, then. They snap necks." Sam's annoyance was clear.

"Where's the bite marks? I'm telling you, nothing natural did this." Leon kicked at the dirt. "I don't like it. I don't like it at all."

"What are you getting at, Leon? That Taku-He did this?" Sam's voice was low and dangerous.

"Maybe." Leon knelt down by the dead horse's head and examined it. "Tongue's gone. Pulled out, it looks like."

Sam's horse chose that moment to rear, and he swore, sawing at the reins until he got it under control. "God damn, Leon. You're not just spooking me, you're spooking my horse!"

"Sorry," Leon said, not sounding at all sorry. "So, do we turn back?"

"Turn back?" Sam was incredulous. "Who's going to pay for this here horse if we turn back now?"

"I'm thinking about cutting our losses."

"And I'm thinking about gaining something," Sam replied. "Saddle up. No sense hanging around here anymore." Without looking back, he rode off.

Leon cursed, but scrambled back onto his horse and followed.

Sam and Leon scarcely spoke that day. They made good time, not seeing another soul as they rode. Sam kept pressing on until it was nearly dark, and Leon insisted on making a halt. They set up their camp in awkward silence, and Leon cooked supper while Sam looked nervously out at the darkening horizon. Finally, he spoke. "We should keep watch tonight. In case that mountain lion..."

"Or whatever it was."

Sam cleared his throat in annoyance. "That mountain lion

comes back. We can't afford to lose another horse, not out here."

Leon nodded. "You want first watch?"

Sam looked away. "Fine by me."

"Right. Wake me when it's time."

Time came too soon for Leon. He felt like he'd barely closed his eyes when Sam was shaking him awake. "C'mon, your turn."

"Give me a minute." Leon yawned and crawled out of his bedroll. "See anything?"

"Not a blessed thing," Sam grunted. "You ready?"

Leon stood, stretching. "I guess I am. Get some sleep."

"I intend to." Sam was already crawling under his blankets. "I hope you don't see shit."

"Me, too."

Leon waited until Sam was sawing logs loudly before stooping to rebuild the fire. Sam let it dwindle during his watch, but Leon had a feeling he'd want the light and warmth before the night was over.

The first hour passed without incident, as did the second and third. But as the fourth hour dawned, Leon caught a faint whiff of a familiar, foul stench. The horses had apparently caught it as well, as they started stamping and snorting. Cautiously, Leon picked up a rifle and stalked out to the edge of the firelight. Raising the rifle, he let his eyes get accustomed to the darkness and scanned the night.

A second wave of stink hit him then, stronger than before. Wet dog and shit and rotting meat, all mixed together, rolled in and set him to coughing. The horses were wilder now, their eyes wide with fear.

"Jesus," Leon muttered to himself and took another couple of steps out into the dark. How Sam was sleeping through this, he didn't know, but he didn't dare go back to the campfire to wake him. Something was out there. Something was close, and Leon had a feeling that if he turned his back on what was lurking in the darkness, it might be his last mistake. Instead, he cocked the rifle and offered soothing words to the horses, who didn't seem inclined to listen.

A third wave of odor assaulted him, this one so strong it nearly made his knees buckle. Taking shallow breaths in through his mouth, he brought up the rifle and sighted down the barrel. If the thing was close enough to smell this bad, he reasoned, it had to be close enough to see. Anxiously, he scanned the dark, praying silently that it was, in fact, a bear out there. A bear would be difficult to bring down, even with a rifle, but it would be something natural, something he was familiar with.

A cold chill up his spine told him that wasn't what he was dealing with.

Scanning the darkness, at first he saw nothing. Then, slowly, as his eyes adjusted, something came into view.

Red eyes in the dark. Damn near eight feet off the ground.

His first instinct was to fire, but his gut told him that if he missed, he wouldn't have the time to get off a second round. Besides, the eyes weren't moving. They were just staring back at him, daring him to do something.

Leon held the rifle steady and backed up toward the fire. "Sam," he said urgently. "Wake up! Wake up, damn you!"

"Huh?" Sam struggled awake. He took a deep breath and choked on it. "Jesus fuck, what is that?"

"It's out there! Look!"

Sam shrugged himself out of his blanket and stood. "Where?"

But it was too late. The eyes blinked once and then faded into the shadows.

"Shit." Leon held the rifle up for a moment longer, then let it drop. "It's gone now." And with that, a chill breeze whipped the stench away. In a moment, it was as if nothing had happened.

"What's gone?" Sam demanded.

"Taku-He," Leon answered. "I saw him. Well, I smelled him, and then I saw him."

"What the hell are you talking about?"

"I'm telling you, he was out here. I saw his eyes," Leon protested.

"The hell you did. Getting me up for nothing but bear stink." Sam spat for emphasis. "You're seeing things. Can't have you on watch if you're seeing things. Get some sleep. I'll take over." "I am not seeing things," Leon protested. "I saw its eyes. It was staring at me."

"Sure it was." Sam shook his head. "Good night, Leon."

Defeated, Leon handed Sam the rifle. "Good night, Sam," he said and headed for his bedroll near the fire. But he didn't sleep 'cause every time he tried, he saw red eyes glaring in the dark.

The next day's travel brought them to the edge of Sica Hollow. They paused there and tied their horses up to trees at the edge of the wood. "Last chance for us to turn around," Leon said as he pulled his rifle down and checked it.

"I told you, we ain't turning around. We're here, ain't we?" Sam's voice was low and grim. He cocked his rifle and started forward.

"They say Sica means "cursed" or "evil" or something like that," said Leon as they passed under the shadow of the trees.

"Who says?" asked Sam.

"Folks," Leon answered vaguely. "Same folks what told me about Taku-He."

"Well, then it don't mean shit." Sam shook his head. "Nothing evil about this place. Just a bunch of trees."

"Then where's the birds?" Leon asked.

"What are you talking about?"

"Listen." Leon stopped, forcing Sam to do the same. There was a long moment of silence, then Sam broke it with a curse.

"Shit. I don't hear any birds."

"That's what I'm trying to tell you. There's no birds. There's no nothing. It's too quiet. Woods ain't never this quiet." Leon turned to face Sam. "I'm telling you, I don't like it. We should get out of here before something happens."

Sam glared at Leon. "Nothing's going to happen except we're gonna bag us a..."

And Taku-He took him.

An arm reached out from the shadows as a wave of stink rolled over the both of them. Neither had time to react before Taku-He fastened its hand on Sam's head and squeezed. With a sound like cracking walnuts, Sam's head crumpled under the pressure. Blood and brains spattered everywhere as Sam collapsed in the creature's grip.

Leon gasped, getting a mouthful of gore. He spit it out, tasting brains and bright copper, then dropped his rifle and ran.

Taku-He stepped out from behind a tree and watched him go, fleeing deeper into the woods. Then it let go of Sam, who collapsed to the ground, legs kicking and scrabbling in the dirt. The creature watched Sam for a moment, then knelt down and snapped his neck. Sam gave one final kick and died. Leon had long since faded into distance, but his desperate footsteps still echoed in the forest's silence. Grabbing Sam's corpse by the ankle, Taku-He loped after the fleeing man, leaving a bloody trail in the leaves behind him as he went.

Leon ran. He ran without direction, without plan. He ran in blind panic, terrified that, any minute now, something would reach out from the dark of the woods and seize him the way Sam had been seized and taken down. He stumbled over a tree root and went down hard, lay there for a second and then got back up and kept running. All the while he kept looking over his shoulder to see if he could spot anything following him, but all he saw was trees and shadows in the dark of the silent woods.

Eventually, he stumbled into a small clearing and slowed to a walk. The sun shone down through the gap in the trees, illuminating what seemed to be a profusion of sticks on the ground. He took another step forward, and something cracked under his feet. He looked down and saw that he'd stepped on one of the sticks, which wasn't a stick after all.

It was bone. A deer rib, from the size of it.

Leon froze and looked around. Everywhere he looked in the clearing, grey and white bone poked through the grass and greenery. Across the way was a hollow tree with bones spilling out of it.

Something had feasted here, and feasted well, and Leon knew what it was. "Taku-He," he whispered to himself. Almost unwillingly, he stepped gingerly across the clearing to where the bone tree stood. As he made his way, more bones snapped under his feet. Most were old and weathered, but a few looked fresh, still gleaming white in the sunlight. None had meat on them.

Finally, he found himself in front of the tree. The stench of spoiled meat filled the air, as he approached what could only be Taku-He's larder. He looked around nervously, then examined the bones spilling out. There were deer bones there, sure enough, and ones from smaller animals, rabbits and squirrels and God alone knew what else.

And then there were other bones, ones he instinctively knew were human. Some of those still had meat on them. Others had marks where they'd been gnawed on.

"Lord Jesus, help me. I'm sorry for that bank guard we killed in Kansas. Just get me out of here, and I swear I'll make amends" Leon whispered and sank to his knees, shaking uncontrollably. He stayed that way for a long minute, tears pooling in the corners of his eyes, until he finally got a hold of himself. On unsteady feet he stood and took a deep breath.

By then it was too late.

A wave of fresh stench rolled through the clearing, announcing Taku-He's arrival. As it stepped out from under the trees, still dragging Sam's corpse behind it, Leon got a good look at it for the first time, and he wished he hadn't.

Taku-He stood fully eight and a half feet tall. It was covered in dark brown hair, matted and unkempt and clumped in places from dried blood or shit. But it was the creature's face that struck fear into Leon, because the face was all too human. Red eyes glowered from beneath heavy brows.

It stared at Leon for a minute and growled.

"Oh God," Leon said, and staggered backwards until his back hit the tree, and his feet got tangled in the pile of bones. He went down in a heap, and Taku-He let out a sound that could only be laughter. Leon let out a moan of fear and tried to get up, but that caused a cascade of more bones to come pouring out, keeping him off his feet.

Taku-He stared at Leon for a moment, then hauled Sam's ragged carcass into the clearing. It dropped Sam's feet onto the bone-strewn ground and sat cross-legged next to it.

Leon took a deep breath and threw himself forward, trying to claw to his feet so he could run, but as he did so, the creature looked over at him and growled in warning. Leon froze, and Taku-He grunted approval. Then it turned its attention to the corpse, grabbing Sam's right arm at the wrist and planting the other hand on his rib cage and pulling. The arm came away from Sam's body in a shower of gore, blood spattering Taku-He's face and front. The creature licked his lips and wiped the blood away, then flipped the corpse over and repeated the process. Then it dropped the arms next to the body and went to work on Sam's guts, ripping his belly open and spilling intestines everywhere. More blood gushed out, and Taku-He bent down to lap it up like a cat licking cream from a bowl. Then, its thirst sated, it stuck its hands in the ruin of Sam's belly and upward, emerging a minute later with a bloody liver in its hands. It took a bite, then gave a howl of triumph that froze Leon's blood. He stared in horror as Taku-He gobbled it down, hunks of flesh flying everywhere. Finally, he could stand no more.

"What are you?" he whispered.

Taku-He looked up from its feast. It reached down into the weeds and pulled out a battered black stovepipe hat, which it jammed onto its head with authority.

"Hungry," it said and smiled.

ON SEAS
OF
BLOOD
AND SALT

This is what Reb Palache does when he finds a ship crewed by the dead.

He does not know it is crewed by the dead, not at first. He is in his cabin, discoursing with the nameless angel who speaks in the silences of his mind. They are speaking of the Pirkei Avot and debating the words of Rabbi Chanina ben Dosa, who held that a man who was pleasing to others was pleasing to HaShem, but that a man who was displeasing to others was, in turn, displeasing to the Lord, when a great shout comes down from the crow's nest.

A ship, the lookout said. Dead ahead and low in the water!

And these words that rain down were caught and carried by the men on deck, passed along and repeated until one pounds on Palache's door in his excitement.

It is ill tidings, the angel says. But they are ones that cannot go unheard.

"And if these tidings are pleasing to the men, are they not also pleasing to HaShem?" the rebbe jokes gently as he rises from where he sits cross-legged on the floor.

I asked Reb ben Dosa a question as he sat in his study, the angel replied. What of the man who is displeasing to his fellow men because he is pleasing to the Lord? And for that, he had no answer.

Reb Palache does not reply; there is no time for him to do so. For again the sailor is pounding on the door, and now he is shouting, Rebbe, Reb Palache, there is a ship!

It has been a while since they have taken a ship, Reb Palache knows. The oceans are vast, and even the greatest galleons are small adrift in it, and the men in his pay who work in the treasure-houses of his enemies have fallen silent of late.

It would be good to take a ship. The men would find it pleasing.

So says Reb Palache to himself and steps out onto the deck.

The sailor at his door is beside himself with excitement.

It is one of the younger men; the older ones would know better than to do so. The first growth of his beard has just come in, sparse black hairs curling over a weak chin, and his eyes are wide and blue. Joachim, his name is--Palache remembers him now, a dock rat from Zeebrugge who had demanded at rusty dagger point to be taken aboard. He is earnest, and he is eager, and he is too young to think that death will ever find him.

" Tell me of this ship," Palache says, and Joachim beams.

" There," he says, and leads his captain to the bow. "Can you see her?"

Indeed Palache can, though she is near the limits of her vision. It is a merchant vessel he sees, and it seems as if he has not been seen in return. But that is not possible; they are too close, with the rising sun framing them against the brilliant sea. There should be alarms ringing out across the water. There should be cries of defiance and orders given. There should be, above all, action on that lonely ship.

And yet, there is nothing as she sails on, serene and unconcerned.

He frowns and reaches for the spyglass. Someone puts it in his hand, and he raises it to his eye. Now the ship comes into sharp focus, and the reason she has not fled is clear. She is wounded, this one, wounded and barely afloat. One of her masts is cracked. It hangs over the rail, canvas dragging in the water behind it like a ragged seabird's wing. Only a few sails remain set, and they are rent by wind and storm. Ropes dangle and twist in the wind. Some are unbound, others have snapped and been left to hang. She flies no flag, this mystery ship, flies no nation or captain's colors.

By all rights, Palache thinks, she should be abandoned.

And yet, she is not. For he can see figures on her deck, and others in the tatters of her rigging. There are men on board, men who move slowly and patiently about their tasks. Men who, he thinks, might be glad of rescue, but have not hailed his ship.

There is still time to turn away, the angel says.

Palache frowns. Behind him, he can hear the men. They are anxious, and they see prey. The creak of leather armor, the rasp of weapons kissing sheaths, the muttered prayers of the men who are wolf-eager to put themselves in harm's way, they form a palpable cloud of longing. They are hungry for this ship, the men are, and they look to him to give the order to feast.

And yet, the slow, silent men, they give him pause.

" Close with them," he finally says. "Ready the guns, ready the men. But we make no effort to board, not until I am satisfied."

" Satisfied of what," asks Joachim, and the others draw a step or two away from him. Palache almost chuckles, that they think asking a question would incur wrath, but instead he just answers.

" I do not know," he says, and the men shudder. "But I will," he continues, and then like birds exploding from dead tree branches, they all move to make ready.

As for Palache, he tucks the spyglass in his belt and walks back toward his cabin. There are preparations to be made there, against he knows not what. Meanwhile, the men swirl around him, sparks in the blaze he has just stoked. The ropes hum as the ship comes about, turning toward the wounded vessel, and the heavy thud of the cannons being made ready is the drumbeat belowdecks that spurs all their labors.

The men will be ready. He hopes he will be as well.

It is an hour before they close with the other ship, an hour Palache puts to good use. Shaddai, the name of HaShem that wards against demons, this he inscribes in nine places along his ship. For each man he laid out a portion of salt and bread, known to drive away spirits, and he spat three times at the base of the wheel so as to protect it from unwelcome attentions. Only when this is done, when the 91st Psalm has been duly chanted and the proper benedictions recited, does he ready himself for battle.

The other ship is close now. He has instructed the helmsman to bring them up alongside the vessel so that he might see what sort of prey she might be and if it is right and proper to take her.

It also lets him see the crew and their quality. Something about those steady, slow men disturbs him, and the angel's warning has him on edge. Better to observe first, he thinks, than to commit to acts unrighteous or foolish.

And then a shout goes up for him as they close, and the men want him at the rail, among them. The other ship is perhaps a dozen yards off to starboard, and the gap is closing. Already the men are readying ropes and grappling hooks to tie her fast.

Already men are climbing into the rigging with muskets, prepared to make the enemy's deck a killing floor.

Already, they are here, and there can be no turning back.

He stares across the water. The ship is old. He can see that now. The wood of her hull is a weathered grey, and deep gouges up and down her length show where she had been scarred by sea and shore and battle. Here and there thick crusts of barnacles and mussels foul her beam like the marks of a pox on a diseased man's back. Pale crabs scuttle here and there, claws snapping. There are no gun ports, or if there are, they have been sealed shut by the relentless growths along her flanks.

Here and there, bits of her rail have been torn away, by gunfire or by storm. The broken mainmast shows no jagged edges; time and weather have conspired to smooth the break.

This is not a ship that has seen port, or the care of man, for a very long time. She is defenseless, and she is old, and she would not be worth manning with a prize crew and bringing back into port. The next storm she sees surely will sink her.

But it is not the ship that causes him to pause in giving the order to board. It is the men who sail her.

They are men, in form if not in spirit. Perhaps a dozen of them roam the deck, working slowly, laboriously at their tasks. Others cling to the tatters of the rigging. One stands at the wheel, staring straight ahead. None notice the ship alongside them; none turn their heads to see. Their footsteps drag, their hands are slow and clumsy. As he watches, a spar falls and smashes onto the deck. The men there do not notice and do not call out. Instead, they step over it, those who do not simply stumble.

" What are those things?" mutters a man at Palache's side. For it is easy to see now how their garments are rent, and their flesh is dry and shrunken. Their visages are like skulls, skin pulled tight to the bone, and their eyes show no light or life.

And then a wave comes up and sweeps over the ship. It is not a wave of water but rather one of stench. It smells of rotted meat and sickness and dead things left too long in the sun, of floating bodies washed up on beaches and old blood on a surgeon's table. It smells of death, and it smells of fear, and it chokes the air from Palache's men's lungs. Some call out. Some faint, overwhelmed. Most stumble back, coughing and puking.

" Ready the guns," Palache says. "We need no part of this one. Its cargo is death."

Belowdecks, the guns on their runners slam into place. The smell of black power burning threads its way into the corruption, a tickle of the nostrils to remind the men of who they are.

" Sink her," says Palache, and the guns roar.

One after another, the shots slam into the rotted, aged hull of the ship. Splinters fly, and shell fragments explode. Smoke blooms in deadly flowers, trailing down to the waterline.

" Again," Palache orders, and again his cannon vomit fire and iron. Again the dead men's ship shudders like a wounded thing.

And then the smoke clears, and she is whole. Fresh scars line her, yes, but even as Palache watches they fade to the dull grey of age, another forgotten line in the ship's ancient story.

And on the deck, heads turn. He has been seen, Palache knows. Seen, and judged, and found wanting. The empty dead eyes are not empty now. They burn with hate, and they burn with hunger.

Slowly, the withered hands on the ship's wheel turn, and she responds, groaning.

" She's coming for us!" Joachim shouts, and it is true. The prey has become the hunter, and it is closing.

" Hard starboard! All speed! And keep firing! Sweep the decks!" Palache is in motion even as he gives the orders. Behind him, the men aim their guns at the grim figures on the deck of the other ship. Canvas flaps open and bellies with wind. Small thunderclaps dot the deck as Palache's ship turns, turns away and runs. And from the other ship, the creak and moan of ancient wood under duress, and the flat wet smack of lead hitting flesh.

Just like their ship, the men do not fall. Indeed, it seems as if they move about their tasks with renewed vigor.

A grappling hook sails out, somehow, from the dead men's vessel. It snags the railing and pulls taut, but then Palache is there and he cuts the rope. It falls away into the sea, even as other clang and bounce off the sides of his ship. "More sail!" he bellows, and the men leap to respond.

But he was incautious, and he let them get too close, and where the wind hits the stench of death, it dies.

" They're not falling," Joachim cries, standing at Palache's elbow. He turns and gives the sailor his knife.

" Cut the lines," he says. "Do not let them close." And then he is running back to his cabin, to the hidden chest he keeps therein.

It is carved of mahogany and bound in brass, and it sits cunningly hidden against one of the walls. No man on board has seen it opened; few know it even exists. Inside, Palache keeps rare and dangerous things; the finger bone of a man possessed by demons, a vial of tears cried by one of the Lilim, a stone from the wreckage of the first Temple.

Buried among them are two small terra cotta jugs, unmarked and tightly corked. It is these that Palache takes, for within them dwells fire.

The other ship is close now, too close. No more ropes fly out from her deck. Rather, it is the splintered wreck of her figurehead that ruins, a serpent hacked in half long ago and edged like daggers. Gunfire still blasts across her decks, smacking into wood and flesh, but it does no good.

" Salt purifies and protects. Fire cleanses," he says and launches the first jug. It spins through the air and then crashes to the deck of the other ship. There it shatters, spilling pale white liquid in a vast arc. One of the dead men, the first to turn, sees this. He raises one bony hand to point at the rebbe, and he shrieks. The others take it up, a chorus of the damned that drowns out the guns and the wind and the waves. It is the voice of the cold wind that blows at funerals, the early frost that freezes the harvest, and it drops Joachim to his knees. One man falls from the rigging, screaming. He hits the deck with a wet cracking sound, bone and meat splitting open in a single instant.

Palache turns and sees that he can do nothing for the man. On the deck, Joachim whimpers. He has dropped the second jug, and it is rolling away. The rebbe seizes it and throws. It follows the arc of its brother, up and over the gap between ships before plunging down.

The men watch it. The dead men watch it. The world seems frozen in that instant, all save Palache, who draws his pistol and fires.

And the world explodes into flame.

The screaming stops, replaced by a single howl of surprise.

Flames erupt all along the deck of the dead ship. They climb the rope of the rigging and leap into the sails. They dance from bow to stern, and they run down to the waterline. The dead men stagger about. Some are caught in the conflagration and burn themselves, others are merely trapped. Palache's ship, Palache's men - these are forgotten.

" Now!" he commands, and his men drop their blades and their guns. It is time to flee. They will leave the burning hulk to its fate, let it and whatever cargo it held sink beneath the waves.

A hot wind blows from the dead men's ship. It fills the sails, filling them fat, and Palache's ship leaps forward. As the fiery wreck recedes in the distance, the true wind picks up. The ship flies over the waves, and the flames are left far behind. In an hour, they are barely visible; in two, they are gone. The men celebrate their escape, and Palache does a divination that suggests their luck will be changing soon. There is cheering, and there is drinking, and there is joy, the joy of men who know they are lucky to be alive.

It is six days later.

Palache is on deck as the sun sets, having said the evening prayers. There are fewer men with him than there were a week ago. Two days prior, they took a merchant ship out of Santander, and he had manned it with a prize crew. If all went well, they would see each other again in Haarlem in a month's time. Until then, they would cruise and seek targets of opportunity, and take what the sea gave them.

A whistle from above catches his attention. It is an early warning of bad weather on the horizon, one he has heard a thousand times before. The men do not need him to give them orders. They know their work, and they set to it with a will.

Instead, he takes out his spyglass and observes. The wall of cloud the lookout spotted is plainly visible, dark grey and shot through with orange lighting. There is no chance to run before this storm; it is coming too fast. Better, he thinks, to reef the sails and ride it out than be caught unprepared and driven by the wind. Some of the younger crew have not seen rough weather, and it will be good for them to learn. Already, the wind is picking up, and the spray of the waves is crashing onto the deck.

Smiling, he raises his spyglass. And then he sees her.

From the storm, she emerges, still dragging her tattered canvas across the waves. She burns, oh, how she burns. From stem to stern, she is alight with flame. Even the sodden canvas of her shattered sail burns, sending steam hissing up into a vast cloud.

She is impossible. She is burning.

She is closing on them, and closing fast.

The men see it too, now. Some stop to point, others to pray. One lunges for the rail, to throw himself overboard, and is only restrained at the last. The tide of panic rises.

" Men!" Palache bellows. They stop. They turn. They look at him. He must be careful now. If he fails to convince them, they are all lost. There will be but one more encounter with this dead ship, one they must win. And panicked men win no battles.

And he calms them. He soothes them. He tells them to see to the ship, that he will deal with their pursuer. The older men trust him, the younger ones follow their lead. They return to their labors, double-quick now. As for Palache, he takes something from his cabin, and he looks across the waters. The burning ship is drawing near, closing the gap with vengeful speed. He can feel its heat, and he looks up.

He climbs the rigging, as agile as the men half his age. There is no other way. He cannot allow the dead ship to ram his; the flames cannot be permitted to leap from sail to sail. So he climbs, and he says invocations to Shaddai under his breath, and he does not look down.

And when he reaches the top, he leaps.

For a second, he thinks he has misjudged, that he has jumped too soon. The burning sails look terribly far away, and he knows he will not reach them. Then, suddenly, he is lifted, and borne up, and he slams into a nest of smoldering ropes with thunderous force.

You, he asks the angel silently.

Salt purifies and protects, the angel replies. Fire cleanses. Go down, and see what you find.

There are already dead men coming towards him, their bodies wreathed in flame. They burn and are not consumed, unholy in their endurance, and their knives and swords blaze, too. The first to reach him thrusts with a broken dagger. Palache twists, the blade rushing past, then shoves the dead man back and away. It loses its grip on the rigging and falls, one ankle snagged in the ropes holding it dangling above the inferno of the deck.

Two more surge past it, attacking in unison. Palache parries one and kicks the other in the face. It does not fall. Instead, it rears back for another swing, and when it does so, he drops down upon it. It cannot get its sword up in time and Palache crashes into it, fingers scrabbling for the ropes. Its sword goes crashing down as it tries to rid itself of its unwelcome passenger, and then its partner swings and Palache lets go and the one dead man hacks the head from the shoulders of the other. It pauses for a moment, perhaps understanding what it has done, and Palache seizes it by the leg. It turns toward him but it is too late, he has already pulled it away from the ropes and it is falling.

So it goes until Palache reaches the deck, wreathed in fire. Through the flames, he can see the outline of his ship so very close. A half-dozen flames have jumped the gap; men are pouring buckets of seawater over them. Time, he knows, is running out.

More dead men come at him. He swings, he parries, he dodges, and he dances. There is no winning any of these fights, trapped between the walking dead and the conflagration that will not die. There is only escaping to take another step, another breath, and hope he can find what he seeks before too late.

Then, abruptly, there it is: the stairs leading belowdecks. A corpse rises up in front of him; he smashes it in the forehead with the pommel of his sword, and it goes over backward, arms spinning. Palache leaps after it, down into the dark.

When he lands, the breath is squeezed out of him. Not by the impact, though the dry crunch of deadstick bones underneath his feet tells him he has landed on his late adversary. No, this is the place where that cold wind of death and rot originated, and this is where it dwells.

The flames have not reached here, but dim light from their work above shines through. And what it illuminates is a horror beyond comprehension. There are men here, or pieces of them, and children and women as well. All are bound. All have been cut by the butcher's knife, flayed and vivisected and brutally hacked. This one's legs are gone; that one is missing her tongue and eyes. Still others are laid open, the skin lovingly pinned back so that Palache can see where this organ or that one has been harvested as a delicacy.

And all are still alive.

They do not speak. They cannot speak. They have been here too long and have been subjected to too much pain. Some manage wordless howls. Others merely whimper. But all plead wordlessly for release.

It is all he can do not to cry out, to demand an explanation for how such a thing can exist. Instead, he takes his sword and slashes the throat of the nearest victim, a man whose face has been cut away until his visage is naught but bone.

The blood gushes. Palache stands back to observe his work.

And the chained man, the man hoisted high on a metal hook through the flesh of his back, a man whose eyes rest in a ruin of dried blood and broken bone, he raises his one remaining hand in supplication.

As above, so, below. As the deathless sailors cannot die, neither can their prey.

This is the heart of things, the angel says. Where it begins and ends.

There is a rumbling crash, and Palache is thrown from his feet. He can hear wood splinter and flames crackle, and men shouting in alarm and rage. There is no more time. He must find a way to kill the deathless, before his men are taken by them.

Before his men wind up down here.

He stands and spits three times, as is proper when seeking to banish evil from a place. Blood sloshes around his ankles.

The undying around him moan.

The ship shudders again. He can hear gunfire now, and the clash of steel. There are shouts of alarm, and a smell of thick smoke. Bits of burning canvas drift down through the hatch, illuminating the hellish scene before him.

Fire cleanses, he thinks. But this place has not been cleansed. It is unholy. It resists.

It must be made ready to burn.

With that, he sheathes his sword. Footsteps clatter on the stairs and he sees dead men coming for him. There is no room to maneuver here, no way to defeat them.

The first one sets foot in the rolling foulness. It turns, sword ready, and favors Palache with a grin. It is the one who first met his eyes, the one who first knew him.

Palache does not draw his sword. Instead, he reaches into

the pouch at his belt, digs deep and brings out both hands filled with gleaming white.

Salt purifies. Salt protects.

The dead man shrieks and charges.

Palache opens his hands and flings the salt in all directions. It strikes the bound victims and they sag against their bonds. One grain, one single grain is enough. It frees them.

Where the salt touches the dead men, they burn. The flames on deck snake down below to embrace them, stripping them of their unnatural vitality and leaving them burned husks. The last collapses at Palache's feet, sword arm outstretched, the pooled blood hissing and steaming around its blackened corpse.

And where the salt, the pure and blessed salt touches the ship itself, there the ship burns too. The unclean thing that dwelt here, that animated muscle and sinew, beam and spar beyond death is gone, driven out. There is a final gust of the foul-smelling wind and then Reb Palache is alone, in the hull of a burning ship, with the peaceful dead all around him. The aged wood burns quickly, he sees, the years catching up to it in an instant. Surely, he thinks, his men will be pulling away. He has taught them that much, that they are to save the ship and themselves.

He prays they remember.

With a sharp crack, a section of the hull gives way. Dark water pours in. The only question is, will the ship burn to the waterline before it sinks. Reb Palache does not know. Another plank gives way, and then another. To stay here is certain death. The stairs leading up from this stinking den of torment are gone, devoured by flame. More planks are breaking, as the ship comes apart.

Choose, the angel says.

He does, and he leaps, and then all goes black.

It is Joachim who pulls him from the water, who lifts him into the jolly boat from the waves. "Thank you," he says, as he is brought on board and a blanket is wrapped around him.

There is a canteen of water for him, and a skin of wine, and bread as well.

"Are they gone," Joachim asks after what must be a suitably respectful wait. "The ship, I mean."

Palache nods. "We will not be troubled by them again." He pauses, and waits for the angel to say something, but his invisible companion is silent. Perhaps he agrees. Perhaps this knowledge is not for Palache, not yet.

" Good," Joachim says, and pauses. The other men in the boat bend to their oars. The steady chop of the water is soothing. The storm is gone, having crumbled as the ship it shepherded burned. The waves are small and gentle.

In the distance, the ship, Palache's ship waits, and so do the rest of his men. All is well. He closes his eyes, then, trusting no further adventure will befall them over the last hundred yards of open water, and drifts toward sleep.

And as he does so, he hears Joachim say softly, "I think when we put in at Zeebruggen again, I'll be going home."

Paul Cory Photography
http://paulcory.com

Richard Dansky is a twenty-plus year veteran of the video game industry. He has written for acclaimed franchises such as The Division, Splinter Cell, Rainbow Six and many more. He has published eight novels, most recently GHOST OF A MARRIAGE. In addition, he was a key contributor to White Wolf's original *World of Darkness* setting. Richard lives in North Carolina with his cats, his books, and his collection of single malt scotches.

Printed in Great Britain
by Amazon